MY CHOICE, MY CHANCE

MEN OF CROOKED BEND BOOK 2

TAYLOR RYLAN

MORTIMER PRESS, LLC

Copyright © 2017 by Taylor Rylan

Published in the United States by Taylor Rylan

All rights reserved. No part of this book may be reproduced, copied, scanned, or transmitted in any format or by any means without the prior written permission from the author, Taylor Rylan. Unauthorized reproduction or distribution of this work is illegal. Criminal copyright infringement, including infringement without monetary gain, is investigated by the FBI and is punishable by up to 5 years in federal prison and a fine of $250,000.
This book is a work of fiction. Names, characters, places, and events are a product of the author's imagination. Any similarities to actual persons, living or dead, is pure coincidence. As are any similarities to any businesses, events or locations.

All products and brand names mentioned are registered trademarks of their respective holder and or company. I do not own the rights to these, nor do I claim to.

ACKNOWLEDGMENTS

Cover Design and artwork by Jay Aheer
Proofreading by Judy Zweifel

1

JASPER

December

*I*t was cold in Wyoming in December. Stupid cold. Freeze-your-balls-off cold if you were unprepared for the weather. I learned my lesson back in the fall and always made sure I dressed in layers. Especially during December.

I lost my breath momentarily when I got out of my truck to make my sprint toward Simon's parents' cabin. We were all meeting there for dinner since it was so close to Christmas. I'd already dropped my stuff off at Simon and Sean's cabin. I let them talk me into staying on the ranch with them. In actuality, it made sense. Everything would be happening out there anyway so instead of driving between Wild Creek and Crooked Bend every day, I just bunked with Sean.

When I arrived at Sam and Cammie's, Sean let me know immediately that Rhett was on his way and would be there shortly. I was surprised, the last I'd heard, he was staying in Seattle because he had to work. What was even more surprising was that he brought someone with him. I didn't know that my little brother was seeing anyone. First Sean, then Rhett. It appeared I was destined to be the only single Welsh brother left. I was okay with that.

Surprise number two awaited me; Dad and Papa were already there. I thought they were arriving later in the week. Apparently they'd become fast friends with Simon's parents and decided to arrive early. That probably wasn't a bad thing considering the surprise Simon planned for Sean on Christmas Eve.

Before I knew it, Rhett's Hypergreen Wrangler pulled into the driveway. Sean quickly rushed out to greet our little brother. I was anxious to see him, but I was willing to wait until after he got inside to say hello. I'd hug him soon enough.

When Rhett made his way inside, I did my utmost to not cringe or stare but I saw red. I never understood that saying until that moment. I wanted to hurt whoever harmed the guy Rhett brought here with him. Under the floppy blond hair and baggy clothing, he walked stiffly and I'd not have been surprised if he didn't have bruises we couldn't see. I couldn't imagine causing such pain. Certainly not to the degree that had been inflicted upon that poor boy. I'd never hurt anyone, especially not the way he'd been hurt.

From what I could tell by looking at the one eye that wasn't almost swollen shut, he had some of the brightest blue eyes I'd ever seen. He had a very slim build and was definitely what I would consider a twink. He was a couple inches shorter than Rhett, so he'd only be around five and a half feet tall. Unfortunately, I realized that my little brother's boyfriend was exactly my type, I liked smaller, slim, blond men.

When Papa approached Rhett, he stepped back, the look

on his face showed his discomfort at Papa coming toward him and Rhett. Papa was an intimidating man. At six feet, six inches, he was formidable. His broad shoulders and dominant stance were frightening under the best of circumstances. There was nothing small about Papa, though he was one of the kindest men I knew and would never hurt another person unless it was seriously warranted.

When I looked over at Dad I noticed he had a concerned look on his face as he walked toward Rhett and Papa. Dad had to pry Rhett out of Papa's arms to give him a hug. I saw Dad flinch when Rhett whispered something into his ear. He quickly relaxed when he pulled away from Rhett. No one else seemed to notice. I only noticed because I'd been watching the two closely.

Once everyone had hugged everyone else, Rhett reached back for his friend, introducing Liam to us all. Of course the little imp's name was Liam. He looked like a Liam. We were told that they were best friends and they met at the bakery Rhett worked at in Seattle while Liam was in there working on his laptop. Not that I didn't wish my little brother happiness, but I was thrilled to know that the two weren't dating. We also discovered that Rhett no longer worked at the bakery. So many surprises! I understood that Rhett loved that job and wouldn't willingly leave so I knew something serious had to have happened.

Dinner was hectic, as one would expect considering the number of people in one room. I felt like a creepy stalker, though I tried to hide it, as I watched how Rhett and Liam interacted with the rest of the people in the room. It was clear that they were both exhausted and on edge. It wasn't surprising to see them gladly accept Sean's suggestion to leave shortly after dinner. I chose to stay behind for just a little while longer. There was so much I needed to talk to

Dad and Papa about. I wanted to know what Rhett told them. After Sean had taken Simon, Rhett, and Liam to their cabin, I followed my dads into the office. I was hell-bent on finding out what was going on.

After talking to my dads, I wasn't just seeing red, I was seeing flames shooting up from the base of that red, searing into my brain. I knew Liam had been beaten, but to find out it was by someone who was supposed to care for him? To find out it was his boyfriend who'd done that to him? I was beside myself with rage. Not only was the dick his boyfriend, but he was a cop! A trained fighter! Someone who should fucking know better! I was in such a state that I had to leave that room before my head exploded.

After spending a few minutes outside in the freezing cold, Dad came out to check on me. "Are you okay?"

I couldn't give him an answer. I didn't know how I felt—or why, for that matter. I'd only just met Liam. For some reason, I still wanted to protect him, to keep him safe. I couldn't believe that a person who was supposed to love him had beat him so badly; a person who was sworn to protect others had done that to him. The level of abuse made my stomach churn.

This new knowledge gave me better understanding why Liam would shy away from Papa. I knew Papa was a kind and sweet man. Liam didn't, and it was understandable that he was fearful around large, alpha males.

Knowing how Liam responded to Papa and why didn't explain Rhett's behavior when Fiona tried to play matchmaker for him with Logan. He'd turned absolutely pale, all the color draining from his cheeks. I couldn't imagine what Rhett and Liam had gone through for them to have such a negative reaction to Logan or any other man for that matter.

I understood with Liam, but what had Rhett been through to cause such fear?

"I called Stealth Securities about Liam's abuser." Dad looked at me to assure me he was trying to help Liam. "It seems Mike, the ex, is on the run. He left after Liam was found unconscious and taken to the hospital. Liam was in bad shape. He was raped and beaten within an inch of his life. They wouldn't even release him unless he had a safe place to go, for his own protection."

That was where Rhett came in. Not only had Rhett spent Liam's entire hospital stay with him, he also gave him his safe place to stay, with us.

"Liam filed charges against Mike. When the papers were taken to his place, the police found Mike had left. Nobody knows where he went. When they searched his place, they found that his service revolver wasn't there. It seems there's a dangerous, well-armed, well-trained police officer on the loose, running from the law," Dad informed me.

I shuddered when I considered the ramifications of Liam being with us. I could never turn him away. Neither would anyone else in my family.

My head was spinning and my body was humming from stress. I told Dad and Papa goodnight and drove to Sean and Simon's cabin.

I had mixed feelings about staying at their cabin. On one hand I was elated. I'd get to spend time with both Rhett and Liam. On the other hand, I promised Dad and Papa that I'd update Sean and Simon on what I'd found out regarding Liam's ex-boyfriend. I wondered how they would react to the possible danger of the little man being in their cabin. I'd no idea how much Rhett and Liam had already told the others.

The drive was short and my truck didn't even warm up

before I was pulling into their driveway. Jesus! It was cold outside! I ran from my truck to the cabin, my teeth chattering so harshly that I thought they'd crack and break off. I couldn't believe I'd gone outside without my coat! Then add the freezing cold truck, a heater that didn't warm up in time to relieve my discomfort, and the frigid winter night, I'd not made many good choices. Yes, I was freezing.

A roaring fire, a warm seat, and a fresh beer were all welcome. I looked thankfully to Simon, my brother's otherhalf. "Dad told me more about Liam and what happened to him. His jerk-ass ex-boyfriend beat the hell out of him and raped him. So bad he put him in the hospital." Right then, there wasn't much that any of us could do except watch out and care for Liam and Rhett.

"Jesus, Jasper. Why would someone want to hurt that little guy? He's so sweet." Sean shook his head, worried about Liam.

I didn't have a good answer for that, so I just continued telling the tale. "It seems the man's missing, too. The cops don't know where he is. And..." I hesitated, "he has a gun. Liam's ex-boyfriend is a cop."

We talked a little longer, and after another beer, I trudged my way up to the guest room that'd be mine for the next week. When I passed an open door, I realized that Rhett and Liam were likely sharing a room. I understood that. I really did. For some reason, at that moment, I was incredibly jealous of my little brother. It surprised me to feel such a strong emotion over a stranger. I didn't know why. It made sense that Liam would be uncomfortable in a strange place so it made sense that Liam and Rhett share a room. That didn't mean that my thoughts would resolve that knowledge sensibly.

After getting ready for bed I crawled between the sheets;

eventually they warmed up. My mind raced and I couldn't help but think about why someone like Liam was better off without someone like me.

First and foremost, the last thing he'd want was another relationship, and he didn't seem to be the hook-up type. There was a reason why I jumped from one hook-up to the next, never staying with the same guy for more than a few times. I never commit. The one time I tried a commitment, look where that got me. Alone, heartbroken, and too afraid to risk my heart again. Yeah, Rupert really did a number on me.

No matter what, my mind would not stop thinking about that lost love. I thought about all of the time we'd spent together. As I dozed off that night I did something I promised myself I wouldn't ever do again; I thought about Rupert and what he'd meant to me.

Lying in bed after an intense scene, I looked up adoringly at Rupert, at my Dom. He was my entire world. Not even my twin knew about my relationship with our architecture professor. No one knew. That was Rupert's stipulation to our relationship.

I'd hoped that he'd be willing to remove that stipulation after we'd been together for so long. He told me, numerous times, that I was the perfect sub. I was always eager to please and always willing to do anything that Rupert asked of me. It was under his strict guidance that I was able to consciously think about the way I spoke. I learned to use contractions and speak with less formality, much to my twin's dismay. It was under his domination that I was able to fully understand just how enjoyable sex could be when you put your partner's pleasure first. Because of the love I had for my Dom, I decided to take a chance.

"Sir, may I speak?"

"You know you may Jasper. What's on your mind?"

"Well Sir, I was just wondering if we would ever make our relationship more permanent?"

As soon as the question passed through my lips, I felt Rupert stiffen at my side. That couldn't possibly be a good thing. The next thing I knew, Rupert started shaking. It took me a moment to realize that he was laughing. That became painfully clear when he next spoke.

"You don't truly believe that we're in an actual relationship do you? You are an amazing sub and a good fuck, but that's it. That's all you are and that's all you'll ever be to me. You, and the five or six other boys I have here during their scheduled nights. You didn't think you were the only one I'm fucking, did you? Besides, there's absolutely no way I'd ever leave my wife for a man. Did you think of the scandal it would cause? No, never going to happen. Especially not with someone like you." I saw a sneer cross his mouth. He was disgusted with me.

My mind went completely blank. I couldn't believe that I knew so little about the man I felt I loved. It was all I could do to not throw up right there in the bed Rupert and I'd just fucked in. I couldn't believe that he was married. How'd I not know that? Sure, I was technically his sub but he wanted me to top him on multiple occasions over the past year. I thought that meant he wanted more from me.

I pulled back to look him in the face. "You're married?"

"My marital status is really none of your concern. Now, be a good boy and suck me off before you leave."

My mind was still blank and all I could think about was getting out of there. I got up from the bed and quickly grabbed my clothes and headed to the door. I didn't make it far before Rupert grabbed me and spun me around.

"Just where do you think you're going?" he said through clenched teeth.

"I'm finished. Our arrangement is over. I'm ending it."

"Our arrangement is only over when I say it's over. Do you understand me, boy?" Rupert growled.

I never saw the punch coming. It landed square on my left temple completely throwing me off balance.

It was the punch in my dream that jerked me awake. When I awakened, I realized I was still in bed in one of Sean's spare rooms, trembling from the perceived impact.

What. The. Fuck.

2

LIAM

One of the best things I ever did was decide to walk into Get Baked in Seattle. It was there that I met my best friend. Without Rhett, I know that I'd be dead because there was no way that Mike wasn't going to kill me.

At first Mike was the perfect boyfriend. He was attentive and loving and always took care of me. I constantly felt the need to pinch my arm or something to give myself a reality check because I thought there was no way that someone like Mike would ever be interested in someone like me. We were as different as night and day. I was only five and a half feet tall, while he stood six-two. He had almost a hundred pounds on me. He was quite athletic, I wasn't.

None of that seemed to matter to Mike. What mattered was that he seemed interested, he wanted me, and he was nice to me. We had a really wonderful relationship for nearly a year.

One day I stumbled upon a cute, new coffee shop/bakery named Get Baked. It was there that I met Rhett. I absolutely fell in love with the scones they served there. When I asked about them, I was told their sole baker, Everhett, had made them. When we first spoke, I was quickly corrected and asked to call him Rhett.

I learned a lot about Rhett as we talked and got to know each other. For instance, he told me he'd only been at Get Baked for six months, having recently graduated from CIA. I giggled when he told me that, but was quickly told that it wasn't what I thought. Rhett had gone to The Culinary Institute of America and earned his degree in baking and pastry arts management.

I confessed that I didn't know there was such a place nor such a degree. I knew I'd be using my new knowledge in a future book though. I just loved being an author and getting inspiration from life made my stories interesting.

I got Rhett's attention when I told him I wrote murder mysteries. When I disclosed my pen name, he became excited. He told me that he'd read all my books and was anxiously awaiting the next in my series. Officer Swanson and Detective Holloway definitely had a fan-base.

That was how I met my best friend; the man who currently slept at my side. I was happy that he could doze off and rest comfortably, even though I couldn't myself. I just lay there, my fear of the next nightmare keeping me awake.

Rhett was an absolute godsend. He was the one who found me after Mike had beaten me unconscious and then raped me. I was lucky that he and I had made plans to go to the movies. We were going to meet at the theater. When I didn't answer my phone or show up, he got concerned and came to my place to look for me. I get chills every time I think about how I must have looked when he first saw me on the floor. I'm grateful that Mike didn't bother to lock the door when he left. If he had, Rhett wouldn't have been able to get in.

Rhett found me unconscious, bruised, bloody, and

barely breathing. If not for him, I probably wouldn't have made it through the night. I feel blessed that I did. When I finally came to, he was there. Luckily I escaped without any broken bones or internal bleeding. Everything was superficial and would heal with time. Well, my body would heal. My mind would take longer. There was no way I wasn't going to press charges, so I did.

To say that Mike's fellow officers were surprised would be an understatement. I told them about Rhett and how Mike became jealous of our friendship. As our friendship grew, he'd become increasingly controlling, restricting when and where I was allowed to go. As expected, most of the officers didn't believe me when I told them Mike had been my assailant. Thankfully, the doctors had DNA proof to back up my accusation. I wasn't surprised when the police went to Mike's apartment to bring him in for questioning they found him gone. When he didn't show up for work or respond to phone calls, they put out an APB for him.

While I was in the hospital, Rhett talked me into going to Wyoming with him for Christmas. I felt I didn't have much of a choice. After all, who knew where Mike was or what he might be planning to do? I figured if nothing else, there was certainly safety in numbers.

On the drive to Wyoming, Rhett told me about his family and where we were going to be staying. He told me how his twin brothers, Sean and Jasper, had decided to move to Wyoming a few years ago in order to open an architectural firm. It was there, in Wyoming, that his brother Sean met his boyfriend, Simon. This year would be the first Christmas they would spend together and Simon's family had invited Sean's entire family for Christmas.

I'd never been to Wyoming and was looking forward to

it. Well, until we arrived. You would think that having just gotten out of the hospital after my ex-boyfriend beat me unconscious, I shouldn't be attracted to any man, however when Rhett introduced me to his brothers I couldn't stop staring at them. Holy shit they were *hot*!

To my dismay, or delight, hot brothers wasn't enough for this family. Once I pulled my tongue back into my mouth, a massive man, a sexy fox if there ever was one, came forward. He wasn't the only one, either. My God! They were massive; each one was well over six feet tall! Of course, that wasn't all; adding to their impressive height, every one of them was incredibly well built. All had broad shoulders and large hands.

My happy perusal was halted without warning; my brain began to associate large hands with large fists, and large fists were something that I knew I wanted to stay away from.

When Rhett's dad, who I later learned went by *Papa*, approached us, I unconsciously shrunk back and curled into myself a little. On some level I knew that I was okay, that he wouldn't hurt me, but right then my brain wasn't exactly working at one hundred percent. After the initial shock at first meeting Rhett's family of giants, I made it through dinner, though it was difficult.

I was relieved when Sean and Simon offered to take us immediately to their cabin to get some rest. I was both physically and mentally exhausted. Being surrounded by so many massive men had frazzled what was left of my sanity for the evening. We got to their cabin soon enough as it was a short drive. Sean quickly showed us to the spare bedrooms and Rhett told his brother that we were going to share a room so we would only need just one. I quickly showered while Rhett went downstairs to talk to his brother and

Simon. By the time he came back upstairs, I was already in the massive bed, trying desperately to fall asleep. I hurt, everywhere.

Frustrated, I took another oxycodone. I didn't like taking them because they made me loopy. I knew that I had to go to sleep. My body and mind needed to rest. I did my best to only take the strong pain medicine at night if at all possible. I was relieved that ibuprofen worked well during the day.

Feeling loopy wasn't the only side effect from taking oxycodone. One I really didn't appreciate was the very vivid dreams I experienced when I was under the influence of the drug. To be more descriptive, in my case, not dreams—nightmares. Horrible night terrors that I couldn't escape. The last thing I wanted to do was relive Mike's attack over and over, but I did. On some level, I'm thankful that I was unconscious for some of the assault. Mike made sure he made me suffer intense pain before he beat me unconscious.

Unfortunately, the parts I remembered were the worst parts of the beating. Those were the parts that were most painful for me afterwards. I fought to stay awake because I knew where my mind was going to take me, I lost the fight and succumbed to the sleep that my pain meds enforced upon me.

I was back in my apartment in Seattle getting ready to go out to the movies with Rhett. We both wanted to see the same movie and decided we would go together. That wasn't anything new for us. We'd gone to the movies many times while Mike was working evenings or nights.

I was nearly ready to go when I heard pounding coming from the front of the apartment. I knew it couldn't be Rhett. We'd agreed to meet at the theater; not to mention he'd never beat on my door like that. I walked to the entrance and peeked through the peephole. I wasn't surprised to see Mike on the other side. When he shouted for me to open the door, my neighbors also knew who was there.

My first mistake was to unlock the deadbolt, because when I unlocked it Mike forced his way into the apartment. I wasn't fast enough to dodge the door before it smacked into my face, making me momentarily dizzy. That gave Mike immediate advantage, not that he needed it. He was so much larger than me that he had no problem throwing me around and manhandling me.

"I thought I told you that you weren't allowed to go out with anyone but me!" I felt spittle on my face as he shouted at me.

Still dizzy, I had problems deciphering what he was shouting. When my brain finally caught up, I looked up at Mike only to get backhanded across the cheek. He hit me with enough force to send me to the floor though the impact didn't knock me unconscious.

He leaned forward until we were nose-to-nose, his hand fisted in the front of my shirt, popping two buttons. I could feel his hot breath on my face. "You know that I don't want you hanging around him. I told you that you couldn't be friends with him anymore. You wouldn't listen, though, would you? You'll pay for not listening."

When he finished spitting out his threats, he picked me up and hit me again, this time on the other side of my face. When I fell to the floor, I instinctively curled into a ball to try to protect myself. It didn't work. He was now in prime position to start kicking me instead.

I remember getting kicked at least three times before Mike yanked me up from the floor. I weighed next to nothing compared to him and he threw me around like a ragdoll. I don't know if I passed out from the pain or if I finally took one too many hits to the head. Either way I was relieved to no longer feel anything.

Unfortunately for me, that's not where my nightmare ended that night. For whatever reason, my mind pulled Rhett into my nightmare. In my dream, he arrived at the apartment earlier than he had in real life. Mike attacked him when he came through the door. I was heartbroken and terrified as I lay on the floor of my apartment and watched Mike beat Rhett and throw him around like he'd done to me.

No matter what I did, the me of my dream couldn't scream, couldn't move, couldn't do anything except watch. The moment I watched Mike drive a knife into my best friend, Rhett woke me up. Unfortunately he didn't wake me up soon enough. There was more of the dream that refused to fade immediately. I didn't know while dreaming, but what I'd dreamed was prophetic and would happen to Rhett, becoming a living nightmare for us both.

"Hey, Liam, wake up!" Rhett shook my shoulder hard enough to finally bring me back to consciousness. Still groggy, I did my best to reply to him. It must have been sufficient because he reclined beside me.

"Are you okay? Do you want to talk about it? Do you need to write it down? Remember, the doctor said if you had nightmares you should write them down that way you won't forget them."

I felt annoyed by the reminder. "It's not a dream that I'll forget anytime soon, Rhett. It's always the same. Mike attacks me in my apartment before I lose consciousness. Really, I'll be okay. Try to go back to sleep. Sorry I woke you." Even though I knew I was lying to my best friend, there was absolutely no way I'd tell him everything I dreamt about. I'd never wish that on anyone, especially him.

"You sure?"

"Yeah, I'm sure. Go back to sleep. I'm tired. I hope I can fall back asleep as well. Good night."

"Good night, Liam," Rhett replied as he rolled over to get comfortable. It wasn't long before I fell back under the pain meds' spell. Fortunately for me, this time I was able to get rest without dreaming at all.

3
JASPER

I definitely didn't know what had come over me. I hadn't thought about Rupert in almost a decade. I left that night completely and totally crushed and when I made it back to my room, I didn't have a choice. I had to tell Sean what happened and what had been going on. Rupert gifted me with a nasty bruise on my temple and there was no way Sean would let that slide.

Sean was more angry than shocked. He wanted to immediately retaliate against Rupert. I managed to talk him out of it. Even though he'd known about my relationship with our professor, I hadn't gone into specific details. There were just some things that even your twin didn't need to know.

Not knowing exactly what triggered the dream, I got out of bed feeling tired and sluggish. I had an idea about the cause though it was only a guess. Seeing a battered and bruised Liam the day before was likely the trigger that caused me to recall that night, the one and only time I had been bruised.

Never again did I let a man close enough to affect my

heart. Never again would I ever be submissive to another man. I'd never allow another to top me. I'd stay in control. After the situation with Rupert, I only engaged in casual, non-committed hook-ups. I developed a fondness for twinks and never had a problem finding a willing partner for a night.

In order to arouse my sluggish brain and to try my best to completely erase any and all thoughts of Rupert out of my mind, I got up and went to the bathroom, resolved to take a shower to cleanse my body and my thoughts. I figured that a relaxing shower might clear my head and allow me to get started with my day.

I was thrilled that I'd get to catch up with my little brother. He was so much younger than Sean and me; he was still a little boy when we both left for university. We'd seen him several times a year when we went home on break but it wasn't the same. I felt that we missed so much of him growing up and I found myself longing to spend as much time with him as possible this Christmas.

When I left my room, my nose was assaulted with heavenly aromas coming from downstairs. Rhett was obviously already awake and in the kitchen. At least I knew that we'd be well fed while he was here. Breakfast turned out to be bacon and eggs and the wonderful smell was French toast bake and scones. Yes, we would definitely be eating well as long as Rhett was baking in the kitchen.

I finally got Liam to open up a little bit in a completely neutral and friendly way. It took subtle, clearly obvious movements for him to relax around us. Even then, he never truly seemed calm.

It was understandable that he was in a lot of pain. You could tell just from looking at the visible discoloration of blue, black, and deep purple skin. The attack happened over a week ago. That gave the bruises plenty of time to darken and change hue. Liam's fair complexion only made the injuries appear worse than they were, and they were bad enough.

We found out that he was an author and that he wrote murder mysteries. Apparently, Rhett was a fan even before he'd met Liam. Personally, I wasn't a reader, but I made a mental note to look up Liam on Amazon and read one of his books.

When Sean told Rhett about an abandoned bakery in town and suggested Rhett consider opening a bakery here, I got right on board and tried to encourage him to think about it. I'd see my little brother more often. More importantly, though, it meant that Liam might visit sometimes. After all, his job was very mobile. All he needed was an Internet connection and somewhere to place his laptop, and we had those!

I'm pretty sure I managed to keep from seeming too creepy regarding my attraction to Liam. I knew the last thing he needed right now was for me to make advances toward him. I did my best to be what I believed he needed most, a friend. Even though my attraction to him, in spite of his bruises, was definitely there.

Rhett and I told Liam about the surprise that Simon planned for Sean. When we were in California for Thanksgiving, Simon asked Dad and Papa if he could ask Sean to marry him. If I didn't think Liam was adorable before, I definitely did after he squealed with excitement when we told him about Simon's surprise proposal. It was quite obvious from his reaction that even in his current state, he still believed in love.

I got to learn more about Liam when we went into Jackson later that day to help Rhett and Liam finish their Christmas shopping. I took multiple breaks and stayed in a more central area with Liam because, with his injuries, he couldn't shop for extended periods of time. That didn't stop him from finishing his shopping, though. Since he was the first to admit that he was complete and utter shit at wrapping gifts, he utilized the gift wrapping services in each of the shops. Rhett did as well, just so he didn't have to wrap. Lazy shit!

During one of our multiple breaks, I found out that Liam was an only child and that when he turned eighteen and went off to university in Vancouver, his parents disowned him because they disapproved of his attraction to men. They'd known for years that Liam was gay. I guess they must have loved him a little bit. After all, they were decent enough to not kick him out when he was still a teenager. He seemed to be okay with the situation and said he didn't mind not having any contact with his parents.

Liam seemed to smoothly fit in with our family. He started opening up more with Simon, Sean, and me, and even seemed comfortable with Dad and Papa. There was still some hesitation when it came to Papa, though Liam was beginning to warm up to the big teddy bear. That was understandable; the man stood tall and intimidating. When Liam and Rhett arrived, one of the regulars, Logan, wasn't there. He was another story altogether. At the same height as Papa, he was formidable. I knew, when Liam met him, he'd be apprehensive. Logan's face seemed to be in a permanent scowl. Completely not endearing. Not in the least.

Liam was as excited for Simon's proposal as the rest of us. When it came out, he cried right along with the rest of the family. As the week progressed, I managed to talk to him more and more. As his bruises faded, his personality started to emerge. Rhett told me that Liam was quite spunky and full of sass. Some of that sass appeared when we discussed the New Year's Eve party.

He wanted to go because he loved to dance, though he told me that he didn't want to dance with a bunch of strangers. He figured nobody would want to dance with him, anyway, with all those bruises in sight. He was noticeably upset, knowing he didn't have a date. He didn't know many people in Crooked Bend. Rhett smirked at me and asked Liam why he didn't just go with me, I wanted to both kiss my little brother and ask him what the hell he was thinking.

Liam looked to me with a hopeful expression. Fuck! I knew I was trapped. I was a goner. My attraction to Liam grew over the past week, but that look clinched it. I was definitely attracted to Liam. Not in the I-just-want-to-fuck-him way, either. After almost a decade, I felt something for someone. That scared the shit out of me.

"Sure, I'll be your date for the New Year's Eve party, Liam. I don't mind dancing with you and keeping others away if they make you uncomfortable," I said while looking toward Liam.

The smile he gave me in response made my discomfort worth it. The last thing I wanted to do was spend a lot of committed time in close proximity to Liam. I was sure that if I spent too much time with him he'd either think I was a complete creep for lusting after him when he was so obviously battered by his ex, or he'd realize I had a thing for him and somehow use that to his advantage.

I didn't recognize myself. That wasn't me. I didn't have *things* for men. I had hook-ups. I fucked and either left or kicked them out. I didn't do feelings. Well, damn! It seemed I was developing feelings for the blond-haired imp. There was nothing I could do about it, either.

When Liam and Rhett went upstairs to get ready, Sean turned toward me and gave me a look. I knew that look.

"What? What was I supposed to do? Tell him he's on his own and make him even more uncomfortable because he's going to be around so many new people?"

"Did I say anything? I was just thinking that I haven't seen you acting like this in quite a long time. As in, not since we were in university."

"Please can we not go there right now? I'm confused enough as it is. The last thing I want to do is bring our university years back up."

"Is something wrong?" Sean asked.

"No, nothing's wrong. Well, a little. The other night I had an odd dream about that night back during junior year. Now I have all these *feelings* and I'm just a mess. You know this is not me. This isn't who I am, Sean."

"I know, Jasper. Maybe it's time for you to think about settling down. Maybe find someone to spend more than just a night with."

"Look at you using a contraction!" I teased. I knew that Simon had made it a point to corrupt Sean in an attempt to make sure he wasn't quite as formal when he talked. Thanks to one British father, we'd both had a very formal education during our early years. When our Papa Taylor came into the picture, and later, Rhett, things were much more lenient and lax, but the early education and influence was still there. I'd long ago learned to use contractions, my motivation much like Sean's, to impress a man. Though I still tended to speak formally at times. We'd both started making a concerted effort to loosen up a bit. We both enjoyed teasing each other if we sounded too *academic*. It was all in fun. It was working though; Sean was using contractions more and more.

"You are changing the subject."

I smirked at Sean. "No, not really. I've started thinking about things lately. Even before Rhett and Liam showed up for the holiday. That was one of the reasons why I moved to Crooked Bend last month. To tell the truth, I'm getting a little tired of the club scene. That doesn't mean that I've stopped hooking up. You know me. I did think about what you said last summer and decided it was time to focus on other things…sometimes."

When Sean chuckled and said to me, "Never change," I knew he understood. At the moment, I had a New Year's Eve party to get ready for. I definitely didn't want Liam to feel like I didn't put effort into my appearance. I went upstairs to shower and get ready for my date. The first date I ever had in my entire thirty years of living. I was nervous for sure.

4

LIAM

I couldn't believe my luck. I just *knew* there was no way Rhett's brother would've ever asked me out on a real date. I took what was handed to me and ran with it. Jasper was definitely my type. If only I was in a proper emotional and mental state to let him know I was interested. I obviously just got out of a horrible relationship—the hard way. After what I'd been through, there was no way Jasper would want me anyway. I was content with being friends.

When Rhett and I went upstairs to get ready for the party, he used the bathroom in the empty bedroom while I used the one in the room we were sharing. There wasn't a whole lot either of us needed to do to prepare. We didn't bring much with us and it was insanely cold in Wyoming in the middle of winter. Since we planned on dancing, we both chose long-sleeve button-downs instead of sweaters. I'd bought some concealer and foundation when we were out shopping for Christmas presents. With Rhett's help, the remainder of my bruises were almost invisible. I hoped with bad lighting, they wouldn't show. After messing with our hair and adding kohl, we were both ready.

Rhett told me he intended to dance with anyone that asked him. Anyone except Logan that was. I learned this past week that Logan ran hot and cold where Rhett was concerned. I guess Rhett was tired of it. I'd never really known Rhett to be one to play games anyway. From what I observed, that was what Logan seemed to be doing.

After Rhett and I finished getting ready, we went downstairs. We were surprised to see everyone else waiting for us. We left as a group as soon as Rhett and I reached the kitchen.

Because of the number of vehicles we had, the drive to town took about a half hour. When we arrived, I was pleasantly surprised with the size of the party. I didn't expect a small town to have such a large New Year's Eve party. They turned the town's community center into a beautifully decorated dance hall. There were balloons and streamers everywhere. There was a DJ who took requests. Even though there was a full bar, I stuck to water because of the pain meds I was still on. That didn't really bother me though. I was finally able to stop taking the oxycodone but I was still on other strong meds for swelling, thanks to the bruising on my ribs, stomach, and back.

That night I wasn't going to let a little bruising stop me. I needed to prove that I could and would go on and live my life. I was going to do it by getting my groove on with Jasper. After we ditched our coats, I grabbed his hand and dragged him to the center of the dancefloor. I heard Rhett laughing as we walked away. From our trips to the clubs in Seattle, he knew I loved to dance and also knew I'd been looking forward to the party from the moment I'd first heard about it.

I'll admit, after growing up in the Seattle area and going to college in Vancouver, country music wasn't exactly my first choice for dancing. I made it work, though. Jasper didn't seem to mind when I had my back to him and started grinding myself against him. No, Jasper seemed to like it. A lot. At least his dick did, because it was hard as steel and poking me in the small of my back. Sometimes I really hated being short. This was one of those times; I wanted his dick to be grinding against my ass and not my back.

Jasper and I danced for hours. True to his word, anytime someone else asked if either of us wanted to dance, Jasper told them we were both taken for the night. It was an amazing feeling to hear him say those words. If only they were true. For a few hours, I was able to forget about my problems. I liked seductively dancing against Jasper during the upbeat songs but I completely loved it when slower songs came on and Jasper would wrap his warm arms around me and hold me close, both of us swaying to the music. I was elated to find that he was such a good dancer. We didn't just shuffle back and forth, either. Jasper could really dance!

I swore a few times I felt his lips ghost over my temple. It was sweet.

Before we knew it, it was close to midnight and we got situated for the countdown. Jasper made sure that I was in his arms to ring in the new year. I had no idea what he planned, but whatever it was, I was sure I'd have no problems with it.

"Five! Four! Three! Two! One! Happy New Year!"

Before I could even get the word *year* out, Jasper had his palms on my cheeks and neck, tilting my face up to his. All I could think about as his mouth descended toward mine was how I wished that it was real. Jasper's kiss was soft yet firm and I'd never been kissed quite like that before. When his tongue swiped across my bottom lip, I gasped in surprise and Jasper took full advantage and plunged his tongue into my mouth. He tasted like cinnamon gum.

He continued to gently explore my mouth with his tongue. On some level it was almost as if he was scared and hesitant to kiss me. I knew there was no way that he meant anything by the kiss. I knew he was only kissing me because it was New Year's. I sure could dream, though, and dream, I did.

We finally parted when neither of us could go without taking in a huge gasp of air. When Jasper gently said my name and kissed me again, with more passion, I began to wonder and had just a little bit of hope that he felt something for me.

Jasper pulled gently away from my lips a second time and trailed kisses down the right side of my jaw toward my ear. He gave my earlobe a little tug with his teeth and quickly moved to the hollow just below my ear and gently sucked. If it wasn't for Jasper's arms wrapped tightly around me, I'd have fallen to the floor. He'd found one of my biggest erogenous zones. Jasper was sucking, nibbling, and licking it like he meant it.

He jerked away suddenly. He looked shocked. "Fuck, Liam. I'm sorry, I know you..." Jasper was interrupted by Rhett joining us to tell us Happy New Year and give us each a big hug. I was so happy to see Rhett having a good time. Damn, did he have the worst timing, though! After Rhett moseyed off toward the next person, Jasper and I were subjected to a constant stream of well-wishers. Oh well. By then, the moment was over anyway. I really wanted to know what Jasper almost said to me.

Simon and Sean found us a while later when looking for Rhett. We told them we hadn't seen him since right after midnight when he wished us Happy New Year. We were tired of the crowd on the dance floor and decided to join them in looking for him. After a search of the entire community center with no sign of Rhett, we tried his cell phone. The call went straight to voicemail, which didn't help us locate him. Nor did it set anyone's mind at ease.

We all knew that my ex was on the loose; everyone's mind went straight to fearing that Mike was in the area and may have done something to Rhett. I was certain I'd never forgive myself if that had happened. I knew first hand just how brutal and evil Mike was.

When we made our way outside, we found Rhett's phone in the parking lot. Taylor used his scarf to carefully pick it up and immediately used his own phone to call someone. It was so hard to watch the range of emotions that played out on his face. I'd gotten to know the blond giant a little over the past week and I knew that he adored all of his sons. He was such a softie when it came to Rhett. The look of absolute torment on his face as he hung up the phone did not give any of us hope that he had good news.

Sheriff McCoy had taken Rhett's phone from Taylor to dust it for prints. He let us know it wasn't likely that they'd find any. It had been found in the snow in the parking lot. The sheriff was good friends with the Redfeather family. He took all the information he needed to file a missing person report right away, instead of waiting the requisite twenty-four hours. He was more than willing to help locate Rhett, which was a relief.

We tried once more to search the general area of the community center then made the trek to Wild Creek. No one said a word during the drive back to the ranch. It was all I could do to not completely fall apart. I just knew that Mike was behind Rhett's disappearance. He was making me pay. He warned me what would happen if I didn't end my friendship with Rhett. I'd already paid, but it wasn't enough for Mike. He was punishing me more by taking Rhett.

I'd already told Taylor everything I could about Mike when Rhett and I first arrived in Wyoming. Now, I felt it wasn't enough. He still found me and had gotten to Rhett. Taylor knew the details of Mike's assault, so he knew what he was capable of. I knew in my gut that Mike found me and took my best friend. I prayed my gut was wrong.

Because of the nightmares I'd been having since Mike almost killed me, I'd been rooming with Rhett at his brother's cabin. Now I was faced with sleeping alone in the room we'd been sharing. Looking around the room, I couldn't contain the downpour of tears that I'd been holding back. All of Rhett's things were mingled with mine. I knew there was no way I'd get any rest in that room. I couldn't sleep in there knowing that Rhett was missing and probably in danger.

I left the room I'd been sharing with Rhett with the intention of going to the den and curling up on the couch in front of the fireplace. Instead, I found my body poised, knocking softly on Jasper's door. I wanted to make sure he was okay. When he opened the door, it just about shattered me.

5

JASPER

My mind was racing. I didn't know what to think about the situation with Rhett. Why couldn't we find him? Returning to Wild Creek was difficult. My only thoughts revolved around Rhett's safety. I was definitely worried. There was no way that I would be able to fall asleep. Instead, I paced back-and-forth in the room and pulled at my hair, just like I did every time I was stressed. Rhett was my little brother and there wasn't anything I wouldn't do for him.

Lost in my own thoughts, I didn't initially hear the soft knock on my door. When I realized someone was knocking, I stepped to the door and yanked it open. Standing there was an emotionally distraught Liam. I could only imagine what I must have looked like to him, because his already large eyes grew even bigger when I swung the door open.

Reaching for him, I asked, "Liam, are you okay?"

He just stood there, tears silently rolling down his cheeks. He kept opening and closing his mouth like a fish out of water.

"Come here." I reached for his shoulders. When I pulled him into my arms, he broke down completely.

"It's all my fault. If I'd listened to Mike and ended my friendship with Rhett, none of this would've happened," he sobbed piteously.

"What are you talking about?" I guided him toward the bed so we could sit down. Once we got settled, I wrapped my arms around Liam and pulled him into my chest. He felt so right in my arms.

I don't do this. I don't cuddle. I don't hold anyone. This was different. There was absolutely nothing sexual about the way I was holding Liam. This was protection, not intimacy.

"When Mike found out about my friendship with Rhett, he got so jealous. He told me to end my friendship with Rhett or I'd regret it. I didn't listen to him and that's why he attacked me. I just know that he has Rhett."

"Shh." I leaned back and pulled him half on top of me. It took a moment for him to realize what I was doing, but he settled with his head on my chest. Despite everything going on, it felt so perfect, so right to have him in my arms. This little imp was going to be the death of me, I just knew it.

"We'll find Rhett. This isn't your fault and I'm telling you to stop thinking it is. Papa and Dad have already called their guys and they're on it. They won't stop until they find him, I promise." It was all I could do to reassure Liam. He was understandably distraught; he felt responsible. If Mike did indeed have Rhett, then the only person responsible was Mike. He picked the wrong family to fuck with.

We both finally dozed off and got a few hours of sleep, if you could even call it that. Neither one of us woke well-rested. Knowing that Liam had a nightmare shortly after we both fell asleep didn't help.

Waking up next to someone that I had held all night was completely new for me. I'd never spent an intimate night with someone before. Sure, I had hookups I needed to kick out the next morning, but that was because we had fucked each other all night. But holding Liam in my arms all night was different. Even though Liam and I were simply sharing a bed in order to help each other cope, I couldn't regret the night I spent with his slight body draped over mine. Under different circumstances, I could definitely see wanting more nights with him.

Our innocent night came reluctantly to an end and we had to face the day. Sadly, we were reminded of Rhett's absence by the lack of aromas coming from Rhett baking in the kitchen. He hadn't miraculously shown up during the night. Instead, we awoke to more devastating news.

Dad and Papa were in the kitchen with Simon and Sean. They told us that Mike had been spotted in the area. He was caught on a local ski resort's video surveillance footage from the day before. Who knew where he was now? Papa believed that he was definitely involved in Rhett's disappearance. He had three of his security guys en route and they would be there soon. Shit just got real.

We called him Papa because we already had a Dad. We called James Dad from the moment we could talk. When Taylor joined our family, he became protective of me and Sean. Even though he was Rhett's biological father, he treated us all as though he was our father, too. It was just who he was. He loved us equally, unconditionally. Right now, though, he was barely keeping it together. One of his cubs was missing. That wasn't acceptable.

When it was agreed that we would go to Sean's parents'

cabin for the day, it felt like a relief. Anything we could do to distract us from the situation was welcome. While we were idle, just sitting around, our minds wandered. That sure as hell wasn't a good thing. Liam was calm until he saw the men from Stealth Securities. Jonathan and Travis didn't seem to intimidate him though. The Thompson brother's didn't seem to pose a threat to Liam. The threat came when their cousin Daniel got out of the back of the large black SUV. I'd met Daniel before and the guy was just a solid mass of muscle. He was a nice guy even though he was extremely quiet. Intimidating. Knowing him, I didn't want to piss him off.

Dad, Papa, and the guys locked themselves in Samuel's office. They had a lot to talk about and we weren't going to be in on it. At least not yet. The story of our lives, really. The locked door was nothing new to me or Sean, but still, it did bother us. We both agreed that we had a right to know what was going on. It was our little brother who was missing. It was more than just a client. This time it was personal.

Of course, until they knew anything, they wouldn't have any information to share. We waited. Drank coffee. Lots of coffee. Cammie was amazing, keeping the coffee pot brewed and full. Then again, we were on a working cattle ranch so coffee was a staple.

It took a few days, before Liam finally accepted that none of us blamed him for Rhett's disappearance. It'd been several days—nothing. We were still waiting to hear any news pertaining to Rhett and his whereabouts. All we knew was that Mike could've taken him anywhere.

Liam seemed content to remain as close to me as I'd

allow. I wasn't about to push him away, either. Not only was he upset, so was I. I needed his comfort as much as he needed mine. When you spend so much time near someone, you get to know them well. I'd already learned a few things about Liam. I got to find out a lot more over those few days. I discovered that he loved caramel. Like absolutely crazy about it, so I made sure there were caramels available for him.

I also discovered that he fidgeted, a lot. Not just when he was awake either. Sleeping next to the man was an adventure. Each night he started with his head on my chest, though he didn't stay there long. Liam was always on the move. Even when he was asleep. I discovered that his constant motion was a nervous habit. If I could redirect his thoughts, he calmed right down. A calm Liam was so much less headache inducing.

It took five days before we finally caught a break. Brian called Papa with some news, then Papa quickly called Jonathan to see if the lead panned out. We waited some more; there was nothing else we could do. We'd already waited five days. How much longer would we have to wait? Within minutes, Jonathan called again. We learned that Mike checked into a motel about forty minutes away from us. Jonathan and Travis were waiting for the rest of their crew to arrive before they called back with a plan of action.

Everyone was anxious. Waiting kept us all on pins and needles. Papa and Dad locked themselves in the office after talking to one of the crew again, and we were left to wait it out, once more. Those ten or so minutes of staring at the outside of the office door were agonizing. We heard sobbing from inside the office. That made us all even more anxious to find out what had happened. Was Rhett okay? Was he dead?

The door opened and I saw Dad holding a sobbing Papa in his arms. I squeezed Liam tight because I didn't know what else to do. Dad wasn't in much better shape than Papa. Both of them looking completely wrecked. For the first time in five days, I felt completely devastated, fearing the worse. That was until Dad looked at us and spoke.

"They've got him." He said it so quietly that even Sean must not have heard because he asked Dad what he'd said.

"Rhett. They found Rhett. He was in the motel room where Mike was holed up. He's alive—barely." We let our held breath go, just to suck it in again when he finished. "Mike didn't just kidnap Rhett; he beat and raped him repeatedly. He also stabbed him multiple times. He's lost a lot of blood, has several broken bones, and shows signs of internal bleeding. They'll call again later when they know which hospital he's taken to," Dad recounted in between his own sobs. Papa was beside himself with grief and relief at the same time. He was openly crying and unable to speak at all.

We all started crying when Dad told us that Rhett had been rescued. There wasn't a dry eye in the cabin. It was wonderful that so many people were concerned about Rhett's wellbeing, though I wasn't surprised. Most of Simon's family only met Rhett a couple weeks ago, but it was easy to love Rhett. Everyone was praying for Rhett to recover from what Mike did to him. It didn't matter if they knew him his whole life or only a short time.

Finally, we got a call telling us where Rhett was transported. We were out the door in no time, heading toward Rhett. After we arrived, we were told that Rhett had been taken in for emergency surgery.

Of course, that meant more waiting, but at least we had Rhett back and he was being cared for. It wasn't until Sean grabbed my hand and pulled me out of Liam's grasp that I realized that our dads weren't waiting with the rest of us. We found them at the end of the hallway, talking to Jonathan, Travis, and Daniel. Upon our approach, Dad and Papa each wrapped their arms around us. It was a familiar gesture for sure.

We felt more stress knowing that Mike hadn't been captured. He was still on the loose. The last thing I wanted to think about was that he was out there somewhere while Rhett was fighting for his life.

Papa assured us they would find him. When they did, he'd sure as hell pay for what he'd done to Rhett. In the meantime, we would wait and hope for the best for Rhett.

6
LIAM

When Jasper and Sean returned to the waiting room, you could tell they didn't have good news. We were really hoping for *some* good news, but didn't expect any. It was a little comforting having Rhett back. He was in surgery and who knew what would happen. I knew his family didn't blame me. I couldn't help blaming myself. If it wasn't for me, Rhett wouldn't have been kidnapped because he never would've known Mike. He wouldn't have been on Mike's radar.

"I can see those wheels turning in your head, and I'll tell you once more, stop it." Jasper surprised me when he came back into the waiting room. "This wasn't your fault. This wasn't your doing. This is completely on Mike. Got it?" I'd been so caught up in my own thoughts that I didn't even notice when he, his brother, and dads returned.

I frowned and shook my head at Jasper. "How do..."

He put his hand up to halt my thought. "No, stop right now, Liam. I mean it. This was *not* your fault!" Jasper had been saying the same thing for days. I still felt responsible.

Would they change their minds and look for someone to blame if Rhett didn't make it?

While I was trying to convince myself that I was not to blame, a team of doctors came into the waiting room. They didn't mince words when they told us the extent of Rhett's injuries, Sean turned away from Simon. He threw up what little was in his stomach. I can tell you that I felt like joining him. There was no way I'd ever forgive myself for what Rhett was put through.

Rhett would be in ICU for several days in a medically-induced coma that would give his body time to heal. We waited for Jasper and Sean to peek at their brother in ICU before we retreated to the cabin. Daniel came with us. I guess he was to be our shadow. It helped me feel a little more secure, considering Mike was still somewhere out there. Would he come after me again? Would he finish what he started back in Seattle? What about everyone else who was sheltering me?

It was unnerving to say the least. I was jumpy. Every little noise freaked me out. I couldn't help wondering if the source was Mike and if he'd found me at the ranch. I felt so bad for Jasper and Sean. Their brother was in the hospital. I needed to get my shit together so I could offer them even a little support. It was the least I could do since I knew I was at least partially responsible, even though everyone involved repeatedly told me otherwise. Try telling that to my brain, though.

I made my way toward Jasper's room. I just took it for granted that he'd welcome me into his room again. Maybe I shouldn't have. In thinking that, I stopped, hesitating in the doorway. I must have made a noise because Jasper turned and gave me a funny look.

"Are you okay?" Jasper turned toward me.

"I think maybe I should be asking you that. Are you okay, Jasper?"

"I've been better. Aren't you coming in? I figured we should try to get some sleep." I looked at my fingertips. "Though I doubt either of us will be able to."

"I wasn't sure that you would want me to share your room or if you wanted me to go back to the other room now that we know where Rhett is."

"What the hell are you talking about? Get in here!" Jasper grabbed my arm and pulled me into the room. I guess that settled that; I was sleeping in his room. I sure wasn't going to complain about that. I was still concerned about Rhett, I hoped that since he'd been returned to us, albeit in terrible shape, we could both manage a few hours of uninterrupted sleep.

"I just didn't know if you still wanted me in here or not is all," I replied to him meekly. What was it about Jasper that made me feel so off center? There was definitely something going on, but I couldn't put my finger on it. I'm not normally so unsure. I did have to consider that it'd been one hell of a month.

"Of course I want you in here, Liam. Why wouldn't I? It has been very comforting to have you beside me these past several days. Why would I want that to end?"

I didn't really know. Nor did I really care too much at that point. Really, I wanted some normalcy. A shower and curling up next to Jasper once again sounded wonderful. Who knew when he'd insist on me returning to the bedroom across the hall? If he wanted me with him for now, that's where I would be.

"Okay, if you don't mind, I'll just grab a quick shower?" I managed to stammer out while walking slowly toward the ensuite bathroom.

"Sure, not a problem for me. I'll be out here when you're finished," Jasper replied while sitting down to take off his boots. The last thing I wanted to do right then was go into that bathroom and shower, but that's what I'd said I was going to do so that's what I did.

When my quick wash and dash in the shower was complete, I brushed my teeth and made my way out into the room. I was so thankful for the thick log walls in Simon's cabin. Despite the snow on the ground as well as the below freezing temperatures, it was still nice and cozy in the rooms, which was a good thing because I was always cold.

When I made it back into the room, it looked like Jasper fell asleep until I approached the bed.

"All finished?" he asked while sitting up.

"Yeah, I'm finished. You know I could've showered across the hall and then you wouldn't have had to wait for me," I replied while grabbing a pair of warm flannel pajama pants and a long-sleeve T-shirt.

"Yeah, but it's really no big deal to wait. I'll only be a few minutes. Go ahead and get into bed so you don't get cold. I'll be quick."

He didn't have to tell me twice. After the week we endured, I was exhausted. It caught up with me all at once. I curled up on my side in the bed that Jasper and I shared for the past week, I immediately felt myself start to drift off. At the edges of my consciousness, I sensed Jasper crawl in behind me and wrap his arms around me. If I hadn't been more asleep than awake, I'd have reacted to him kissing the back of my neck before he let out a deep breath and drifted off to sleep.

We pretty much awoke in the same position we fell asleep in; Jasper spooned behind me. Unlike other mornings, this morning Jasper's hard cock gently pressed against my backside. When Jasper moaned quietly in his sleep, I felt myself instantly grow hard.

There was no way he'd be thrusting his dick into my ass like he was if he'd been awake. The two of us slept next to each other for a full week and never once had he given me any indication that he was interested in me, well not in a sexual way, anyway.

I tried to pull away before I embarrassed myself by moaning in pleasure. That attempt was halted by a sudden tightening of Jasper's arms around me. He was certainly no longer asleep.

When his hips gave one last thrust, I couldn't help the squeak that escaped from my throat. Now he was awake and rolling away from me quickly. I immediately missed his warm, hard body behind mine.

"Shit, sorry, Liam. I didn't realize. I was asleep. I wasn't thinking. I'm so sorry."

His apology told me that he hadn't been dreaming of me. He didn't desire me. His apology, his guilt, that was what I wanted to avoid. I felt a twinge of sadness because I wanted him to desire me. I wanted that more than anything. He was sorry for what happened while he was sleeping; that sure didn't scream *Liam, I want you*.

I pretended like it wasn't a big deal, like I understood how accidents happen. To me, though, it had been everything. "Don't worry about it Jasper. I know you didn't mean anything by it. You were probably dreaming about some hot, sexy guy next to you," I replied before I rolled out of bed and went toward the door. I needed to escape before I made a complete fool of myself.

I reached and entered the bedroom and its adjoining bathroom across the hall before Jasper caught up with me. In my distress, I'd forgotten to lock the bedroom door so I could throw my pity party in solitude. I was simply too focused on reaching the bathroom.

Obviously, Jasper had other ideas. He grabbed my arm and spun me around to face him. When I looked up, I was face-to-face with a very pissed off Jasper.

"Why would I mean nothing by it, Liam?"

My mouth opened and shut, no sound coming out. It was quite an impressive impersonation of a fish out of water. That seemed to jolt Jasper. His anger quickly changed into something different. Something devious. Jasper picked me up and plopped me down on the bathroom counter. Damn it all if I didn't squeak again! I really needed to do more than squeak when I was close to the man.

He pulled me to the edge of the counter and ground his still hard cock against me. My squeak turned into a gasp. When he moved forward and nibbled my neck, the gasp turned into a moan. I didn't even think about holding back.

"Tell me something, Liam. Does this feel like I don't want you?" Kiss. "Does this feel like I mean nothing by it?" Nibble. "I want you, and I do mean it." Lick "Someday soon, I'll have you." His words sounded like a threat but there was no heat behind them. Well, not dangerous heat, anyway.

I was done for, completely turned on. Jasper could've done absolutely anything that he wanted. With his last words, he ground his hips against mine one last time. The delicious friction of his cock pressed against mine. He pulled away after placing one last gentle kiss against my neck. I got one last lust-filled smile before he gave his steel-hard cock a tug through his pants. He turned around and walked awkwardly out of the bathroom.

I couldn't do anything except sit there on the counter and pant. Jasper made one of my most desired fantasies come true. He wanted me. That sexy man wanted *me*. He left me with a throbbing, leaking cock. I knew I had two choices, I could either jerk myself off in the shower, or hope and pray it went down on its own. I knew there was no way in hell it was going away without help so I opted for choice number one. I stripped out of my pajama pants and T-shirt and climbed into the steamy shower to jack-off to fantasies of Jasper plowing into me.

When I came on the shower tiles a few minutes later, I just about fell to my knees. The intensity of my orgasm roared through my body. It was so strong, my legs shook. I'd never had such a reaction to any man before. If the thought of Jasper did that, would the real thing be even more intense? Jesus, I sure hoped so. I imagined us lying on a bed, him pumping into me and my body limp as a wet noodle, satisfied and trembling with passion.

7
JASPER

Holy shit! I couldn't get out of the bathroom fast enough. I knew if I stayed I'd do something that I'd regret. I could have scared him off. The last thing I wanted to do was come on too strong, but I almost did. Maybe I *did*.

I had to remind myself that he had been put in a hospital by his boyfriend, beaten and raped, less than a month ago. He was still healing. How could I even tempt him? Why would I think he'd want to go a round or two with me between the sheets, or against the wall, or in the shower, or on the counter? My imagination was in overdrive; the possibilities with Liam were endless. He was so much smaller than me. I could easily handle his slight frame in any number of positions.

Even though I clearly turned Liam on and he wanted me, what exactly did that mean? Since Rupert, I have become extremely dominant in the bedroom and could be quite forceful. The way I wanted him in that moment, there was no way I could have altered my primal behavior. Not even for him. I knew I had to take a step back and get my need for him under control. There was absolutely no way that I wanted to hurt him, ever.

I did the only thing I could do, I tugged my leaking cock and walked away from him. I didn't stop until I was locked in the bathroom attached to the room Liam and I shared the past week. I didn't even bother turning on the shower. I knew I wouldn't be able to last long enough for the water to warm up. Instead, I stood in front of the sink. It was similar to the one I'd just set Liam on. I closed my eyes and thought about the blond-haired, blue-eyed man of my dreams. It took only a few pulls before I was painting the granite countertop with stripes of cum. Oh hell. I was in so much trouble.

After catching my breath, I decided to be my devious self and took a picture of my cum painting the bathroom sink and sent it to Liam with the attached message.

Me: *Does it really look like I'm not interested? Because this is what happens when I think about fucking you against the bathroom sink.*

When I didn't get a reply back, I decided to clean up my mess and go about getting dressed. I wanted to go to the hospital and see if there was any change with Rhett. Before I could do that, I had to locate a little imp.

I found him hiding in the bedroom across the hallway. I tried the doorknob and was thankful that he still hadn't locked the door. There was a towel wrapped around his small frame. He wasn't wearing anything else. I couldn't help but notice the tented towel he was sporting, which led me to believe he was pretty much in the same state as I was, completely turned on and needy.

If he was surprised to see me barge into the room again, he didn't show it. He simply stood there and stared at me, his mouth opening and closing, like a fish out of water. That made me chuckle.

"Are we back to that again?" I asked while advancing toward him.

"Huh? Back to what?"

I didn't bother replying, I simply took what little bit of him I knew I'd be able to handle. I attacked his mouth with everything I had. When I didn't get the response I wanted, I reached down, grabbed his ass cheeks, and picked him up. His tight little ass felt so amazing. When he wrapped his legs around my waist and started grinding his dick against my stomach, I knew I had him.

I pulled back just enough that he chased my mouth with his lips. I loved the little whimper that escaped his throat. I moved toward his chin with my lips and started kissing my way toward his ear. I was pleased to discover, on New Year's Eve, that the hollow below Liam's ear was a hot spot for him. I remembered correctly because once I reached his ear, he moaned loudly and thrust his hips against mine even harder. Working my way down his neck, I reached where his neck met his shoulder and give it a little nibble. When Liam quietly muttered the word "please," I latched on and sucked hard.

I knew I was going to leave a mark. I didn't care. I wanted to mark him, to tell everyone that he was *mine*. When his entire body jerked, I pulled away and looked at his face to make sure I hadn't gone too far. The look on his face wasn't one of fright, though. It was of someone in the midst of an orgasm. Standing there in the middle of the bedroom holding a shuddering Liam, I realized that I'd made him cum from nothing more than kissing and sucking on his neck. Oh hell, I was completely and royally fucked.

I made my way to the bed to sit before I fell. The gift that he'd just given me was one that I'd treasure forever, even if he didn't know what he'd done.

It only took a few minutes for Liam to come down from his orgasmic high. When he did, he turned a pretty shade of pink and tried to hide his face in my neck. I didn't want him to be ashamed for what he'd done. It was beautiful. I wanted another look at just how sweet his pink cheeks were because my mind was working overtime thinking about another part of his body I'd love to see pink, from my hand. Gently grabbing his chin, I pulled his face out of my neck.

"None of that," I told him. "Tell me, Liam, should I be upset with you for cumming without me? Have you always achieved orgasms without direct stimulation?"

The pink turned into a darker shade of red at my questions. When he realized he couldn't pull his chin out of my grasp, he started to squirm, turning his eyes away from mine. Dropping my voice an octave I continued.

"Sit still and look at me, Liam."

Liam responded beautifully and immediately when he heard my firm expectation. He calmed and looked at me briefly before lowering his eyes in submission.

On a shallow breath, I muttered, "Oh fuck." I just couldn't believe I'd been gifted with a submissive lover that didn't completely irritate the living hell out of me. Looking at Liam, I began to wonder about the possibilities. Was he naturally submissive or was it something his ex-boyfriend ingrained into him?

I realized so many things that had crossed my mind the past several weeks. They finally made so much sense. When Liam finally raised his eyes back to mine, I completely lost my heart to the younger man right then.

"Yes, Sir?" With those two little words, I came in my jeans.

"Fuck!"

I couldn't mask the moan that escaped as my orgasm pulsed through me. The look of complete shock on Liam's face made the mess and humiliation worth it. As soon as I was able to speak again, I begged, "Please tell me you aren't playing, Liam."

"Please tell me you want me, Jasper," was his reply.

"Oh, sweetheart, I most definitely want you. I don't want to play either, I want to keep you."

"I don't want to just play either, Jasper. I want to be yours."

Drawing him toward me, I placed a gentle kiss on his throat in the same spot I'd marked him. He shuddered a little and I made a note to remember that and how sensitive his throat was.

Pulling away from him was harder than I thought it would be. I didn't want to let him go but we both needed to get cleaned up and ready to face the day. He certainly wasn't ready for all of me. Not yet, but he would be.

"We'll be talking more about this soon. Right now, we both need to get cleaned up and head downstairs."

"Yes, Sir," Liam replied.

I shook my head. "Jasper, Liam. Just, Jasper. I only want to be Jasper, I'm not really a Dom, nor do I want to be, but I'm a *huge* control-freak in the bedroom. I know I can be controlling and dominant in the bedroom, but I'm not what I would consider an actual Dom. I don't want that type of lifestyle. Understand?" I paused and looked at Liam. He looked guilty for having called me *Sir*. "Is that acceptable?"

The smile he gave me was almost too much. I knew then, he was my one singular choice.

"Yes, Jasper."

"Good. But, Liam. We *will* talk about this. Soon, I promise."

I was left with no other choice. We had to go. It took everything I had to remove Liam from my lap. We both needed to get cleaned up before we could join the others.

"Get cleaned up and dressed, and then come downstairs. We need to see when everyone wants to head to the hospital," I told Liam on my way out the door.

When Liam finally made it downstairs, I already had his coffee ready for him. We planned to meet at Sam and Cammie's for breakfast. From there we'd go to the hospital and check-in on Rhett. I already decided that I'd be having a long discussion with Liam tonight.

There wasn't anything new to report or learn at the hospital. Rhett was still almost unrecognizable and was still in a coma. There were so many wires and tubes on him that it was both scary and intimidating at the same time. Each of us was careful to only spend our allotted time with him. We each held his hand and talked to him. All we could do was wait. We'd spent the past six days waiting for Rhett to heal enough to be brought out of the coma. We would have to continue doing so, as we weren't given a choice. Rhett needed time to heal physically as well as mentally and emotionally.

When everyone had taken their turn with Rhett, we returned to the cabin. I knew my conversation with Liam was forthcoming and I hadn't been able to think of what to say. With Mike still out there somewhere, the two of us couldn't act like a normal couple and get to know each other on a date. We'd need to wait until we could retire to our room for the night. I was getting really damn good at waiting.

Fuck! It occurred to me, just now, that he lived in another state. How could we have a long-term relationship while living a thousand miles apart? Anything that we wanted to do, we could. We could work it out somehow. Of course, I didn't want to only see him a few times a year. I wanted Liam permanently and full time.

How could I convince Liam to move to Crooked Bend? I'd have to do it, though, or I'd need the resolve to forget about him. I couldn't imagine not having Liam, and I sure as hell couldn't figure out how I'd forget him, so I had no choice. I had to figure out a way to convince him that he needed to move here to Crooked Bend.

8

LIAM

I didn't know if I should be ecstatic or should run back to Seattle and never look back. I'd never been in the type of relationship that Jasper hinted at. Being a self-respecting gay man and an author, I definitely read more than a few books that involved the type of relationship Jasper had hinted at. After all, how else was I going to figure out what type of books I wanted to write? Some of them were just so damn sexy. When Jasper used that sexy-as-fuck voice on me, my mind and body completely relaxed and I found myself calling him, *Sir*. It seemed like the right thing at the time. I also had to think about how my mind would respond to it long-term. I was still suffering from the psychological effects of Mike beating me half to death. Could I even *do* it?

How was I to know that by simply saying *yes, Sir*, he'd cum in his pants? It was such an erotic thing to see. I definitely wanted to see Jasper cum again and again. I wanted to be the reason why he came. I wanted to watch his face while he came buried deep in me.

Shit! I was hard again. You'd think that with the two

breath-stealing orgasms I already experienced this morning that I wouldn't be horny, but I was. It was all because of one sexy architect. I definitely had it bad for him.

I really put some thought into this potential relationship. Maybe what Jasper hinted at was exactly what I needed. Maybe that was why none of my previous relationships ever worked out. It was obvious why my relationship with Mike didn't work, but what about the few before him? They were always just *meh*, and left me feeling so restless and empty. Hell, Jasper hadn't even fucked me yet and already I could say it was the best sex of my life.

Wasn't that just something? Did that mean he'd render me completely useless once we finally got around to actually having sex? So far, we had managed to give each other an orgasm without even touching each other's dicks. When could we get to the main event? I was ready, now. I didn't want to wait.

I secluded myself in our room for an hour. When Jasper entered the room, all I could do was stop and stare at him. I didn't realize that I'd been pacing back and forth until he entered.

"Are you okay?" Jasper asked me after he closed the door.

Was I okay? I couldn't say for sure. I knew that Jasper was there and that somehow he'd make it okay. I really needed to kiss him again because I hadn't kissed him all day and it seemed that I couldn't live without another.

I marched over to him and climbed him like a tree, attaching my mouth to his. What can I say? At only five and a half feet tall, he was eight inches taller than me and it really made a difference when trying to kiss. Jasper didn't seem to mind. He merely grabbed my ass to hold me in place and kissed me back.

With my legs wrapped around his middle, Jasper effortlessly walked us to the bed and climbed on. I found myself on my back with Jasper on top of me. I felt none of the tension that I had in the past. With Jasper, I felt safe. I whined when, all too quickly, he pulled away.

"As much as I want to be buried deep inside you, we can't. Not yet, Liam. I promise you I'm not rejecting you nor am I saying no. I'm simply saying not yet. Alright?"

With a nod of my head, Jasper seemed to relax a little. When he did I realized that he was nervous, just like I was.

"I said we would talk, and we really need to, Liam. We need to discuss what's going on between us and talk about where we see this going."

"Okay. Do you want to go first or should I?"

Jasper looked at me and chuckled. It seemed to relieve tension. This was a serious discussion and we needed to talk about it rationally.

"You're going to be complete trouble, aren't you?" he asked me.

"Do I look like I'm trouble?" I replied to Jasper as he smiled at me. "On second thought, don't answer that. I promise to be good. Or at least try. Will that work?" I asked while lifting my hip and pressing my hard cock up into his. He let out a quiet moan before giving me a stern look. He controlled further interruption by lowering a little more weight onto my body, efficiently holding me in place..

"Hold still. Behave. We really need to have this discussion, Liam. I mean it."

When my eyes met his, I realized that he was in serious mode and there would be no sexy times right then. I gave in and let him know that I understood. "I understand. I promise, I'll behave."

"Good"

"The biggest obstacle to us being a couple is that you live in Seattle and I live in Crooked Bend. That's what, a twelve hour drive?"

"A little over thirteen. It's much quicker if you fly. Only a couple of hours." The only reason I could answer his question was because Rhett and I just made that drive. We discussed flying and I admitted that I was uncomfortable with the idea of flying. I didn't want anyone to see my bruises so I would be more comfortable driving than flying. To appease my reservations to being in such close-quarters and under scrutiny, we drove.

"Okay, but that's still several hours apart. Are you looking for a hookup or something long-term?" Jasper asked me.

"Honestly, I wasn't looking for anything when I met you. I never came here thinking I'd meet you and be instantly attracted to you."

The smirk Jasper gave me made me stop and think about what I'd just said. When I realized what had just left my lips, I could feel my face start to turn red.

"You were attracted to me immediately, huh?" he asked me.

"Maybe. That's not really the point, though. You asked what I was looking for and to be honest, I don't know. I haven't been too successful with past relationships. Rhett is my best friend, so the last thing I want to do is cause tension if things between you and me don't work."

"Don't worry about Rhett. There will be no issues or tension between us. I promise you that. When he's ready, I'll talk to him. So, you're looking for a relationship then?" I could see stress lines fading on his forehead.

"If you're willing to give it a try, then yes. I'd like to be in a relationship with you. I agree, though, there is a huge problem with distance."

He furrowed his brow again. Jasper looked like he was contemplating whether to ask me the next question. I could see when he'd made up his mind. He looked me right in the eye and asked, "Do you think that you would consider moving closer if things go well? I can come and visit you every once in a while, but my job is here. I really can't leave it very often."

I realized what he was talking about. Of *course* he couldn't just pick up and come to me. He was an architect here in Wyoming. He had responsibilities here. He couldn't just up and go somewhere else like I could. Ah! *Like I could.* My job required me to have a table, chair, and Internet connection. I could work from anywhere. "I realize you can't just up and come and visit me, but I can visit you."

The sun hid in shame when I was hit with Jasper's smile. I knew I wanted to see *that* again.

"Okay. We'll see how it goes with us so far apart. If things work out, we'll discuss you moving here to Crooked Bend. Sound good?"

"Yeah. It does."

"Great. Now, how about we discuss the other elephant in the room?" Jasper sat and pulled me upright with him.

Did I want to discuss it? I guess I didn't really have much of a choice in the matter, did I?

"Okay, what about it?" I was unable to make direct eye contact with Jasper.

"Well, for starters, have you ever done anything like that before? Have you been in a relationship where one partner was completely dominant over the other sexually?"

"No, have you?"

With a grin on his face, Jasper replied, "I've played

around a little. Although, I haven't had that type of relationship since I was in my early twenties. Even then, it was completely different than what I want with you. Then, I was the one being dominated, and that's not what I want with you. I want to be the one in control. I can't let someone have that kind of control over me again. I know it seems hypocritical of me since that's exactly what I'm asking of you, but that's the way it needs to be."

At his admission, I became a little jealous. Why I was jealous of someone Jasper was in a relationship with a decade ago I couldn't say.

I nodded to let him know I was listening. "What exactly are you looking for? Like are you looking for the whole Dom/sub thing? Earlier you said you weren't a Dom."

"I only want one thing, Liam. I ask for your complete trust in the bedroom. That's it. I tend to be dominant in the bedroom." He shrugged then continued. "I like sex and have a very high sex drive so I'm going to want it a lot. Is that something that appeals to you? Can you handle that? I want you to think about what I've told you. Don't answer yet." He looked at me for a moment then added a little more. "I'm more than willing to have a regular relationship with you, and try my best to tone it down in the bedroom, Liam, if you don't think you can do it. I'll take you however you will allow."

My mind was reeling after Jasper's revelation. There was so much to think about that I didn't reply right away. My emotions must have shown on my face because Jasper smiled sweetly at me, I guess to allay my concerns. If he kept doing shit like that, he was definitely going to be the death of me.

I shook my head. "I want to try this. Like I said, I've never done anything like it before, but I gotta say when your personality got dominant, you turned me on."

"I couldn't tell," Jasper replied with a chuckle.

"Yeah. I mean, I want to try some dominance, well, submissiveness for me. I know we haven't even had sex yet, but I really want to. When you took over, I felt both peaceful and aroused."

"Like I said before, I don't classify myself as a Dom. I have learned that I like to be in control in the bedroom and I also like to play a little, some very light stuff. I'm just not into full-on Dom/sub role-playing, alright?"

"What do you mean by *a little*?"

"Remember, we don't ever have to do anything. I just want to be with you. There are a few things I would love to do with you though. What I'd like to do is tie you to my bed and worship every inch of your body with my lips and tongue. I want to bend you over and turn your ass rosy red with my hand before I pound you into the mattress. I want to bring us both immense amounts of pleasure. Is that something that sounds good to you? Is that something you would be interested in?"

I gasped. The things he described. Oh. My. God. I could feel a familiar twitch in my jeans. "Holy shit Jasper! I'm about to cum in my pants right now! When can we start? Yes, I'm interested. I'm *very* interested. When? When can we play?" I begged Jasper. My dick was so hard and leaking. I wanted nothing more than to get right to playing.

"Not any time soon, Liam. You're still healing. The last thing I want to do is jump into an intense sexual relationship with you before either of us is ready. We're going to take things slow and work up to 'playing' as you put it."

I felt disappointment, but I was also relieved. Jasper wasn't rejecting me. He wasn't forcing me to get in too deep too quickly, either. Still, I was a horny twenty-five-year-old man!

"Does that mean..."

Jasper cut me off by grabbing me and pulling me on top of him. "I said we weren't going to play. I said nothing about abstinence." He pulled my face toward his, pressing my mouth against his. The man could definitely kiss, that's for sure. Before we hardly started, he stopped. I was about to protest until I heard his command.

"Liam, you need to wait to cum this time, got it? Try and see if you can hold back longer instead of just letting go."

I was back to doing the fish out of water impersonation. All I could manage was a nod because it was taking everything in me to do as he asked because right then, I was just seconds away from cumming in my jeans like Jasper had done this morning. What was it about that man?

The praise I received from Jasper made it so much easier to follow his wishes.

"Good, that's exactly what I wanted to hear."

9

JASPER

Saying goodbye to my dads was always difficult. Saying goodbye to my brother was even more so. Several weeks passed since he was rescued and he was finally out of the medically-induced coma and healed enough to make the trip back to California. He'd be going with our dads to finish recuperating at home.

Good news, though. While Rhett was still in the coma, Stealth Securities caught up with Mike in Washington. It appeared he was heading to Canada. If not there, at least his old stomping grounds. Who really knew? He was no longer a threat to any of us as the Stealth team neutralized him. He wouldn't be hurting another person ever again.

That was only marginally reassuring though. Because leaving with Dad, Papa, and Rhett, was Liam. Liam and I'd gotten quite close since Rhett had been rescued. We were quietly giving a relationship a try, even though we still hadn't fucked each other. That was a first for me. I'd become the king of hook ups. With Liam I wanted more. I absolutely loved spending time with him. I'd grown quite fond of him. I was also really used to him sharing a bed with me. I understood he was leaving to be with Rhett while he continued to recover. I didn't like it, though. I wanted him to stay with me in Wyoming.

I wanted to continue to get to know him better. This was the first time in my life that I'd spent so much time with someone without having sex with them. It was new, it was different, and I liked it, and I liked him. Sure, we'd given each other multiple orgasms over the past few weeks, even if we never took it further than groping, touching, and kissing. Technically you could say we'd had sex even if his hand is the closest my dick has been in contact with him. It went both ways. We'd given each other more hand jobs than we could count.

I made sure I had all of Liam's contact info in my phone before he left and that all of mine was in his phone as well. There was no way I was going to let him go off without having a way to reach him. Even before he agreed to give a relationship a try, I'd decided that he was going to be mine and I was going to do whatever I needed to in order to make that a reality.

We talked on the phone every evening. Liam was going to help my dads care for Rhett in California. Rhett obviously needed Liam more than I did and I understood that. I missed him. When I realized how much I missed him, even with us talking every day, I started texting him.

I did my best to leave him alone, but I couldn't help myself. He became a hard habit to break, even if I'd wanted to, and I definitely didn't want to. Work didn't help though I tried to stay busy. When I wasn't insanely busy, all I did was think about Liam and his floppy blond hair and bright-blue eyes and his facial expression when he came in my arms.

Me: How are you doing?
Liam: I'm okay. You?

Me: Busy. Work is crazy already.

Liam: Yeah? How?

Me: For once people seem to be planning ahead and have already contacted us for jobs they want done this summer.

Liam: That sounds good. Busy is good, right?

Me: Yeah. It keeps me from going crazy.

Liam: How?

Me: It keeps me from missing you so much.

Liam: Dammit Jasper! I was okay until you went and mentioned missing me.

That was how the first exchange went. We ended up texting on and off throughout the day and always made sure we ended our night with a phone call to each other. FaceTime was our friend. Even with so much contact with Liam, I missed him. I physically ached for him.

I decided to see if I could get him to come to see me. It'd been a couple of weeks since Liam left and I really needed my Liam fix. I needed to kiss him. I needed to feel his body next to mine, on top of mine. I needed to suck on his neck and see if I could still make him cum without touching his cock. I simply needed Liam.

It was almost Valentine's Day. That was supposed to be all about romance, so why not?

Me: What are you doing this weekend?

Liam: Hang on...

When the text bubbles didn't progress, I started to worry. I gave up waiting and called him. Thankfully, he answered on the second ring.

"Hey, Jasper. Sorry, I'm at the airport on my way to Seattle."

"What do you mean you're on your way to Seattle? Why are you going to Seattle? Why didn't you mention it before?" When Liam didn't tell me he'd planned on going to Seattle, it freaked me out a little bit. After all, we were in near constant contact, and yet he'd failed to mention this really big thing.

"Jonathan and I are going up to Seattle to pack up some stuff and to bring it back down here."

My heart started thumping heavily in my chest. Had he moved on? Did I lose him? "What do you mean you and Jonathan?" Try as I may, I couldn't keep the panic out of my voice. "Why are you going to Seattle? You said to pack. What are you packing? Why?" The only Jonathan I knew worked for the security agency. Was *that* the Jonathan who was escorting Liam to Seattle?

Liam seemed oblivious to my building panic. "Sorry Jasper, I'm at the gate and I really don't have a lot of time to chat. I'm going to Seattle to pack up some stuff for Rhett and me. We need more stuff where we're staying."

He was going to hang up without answering my questions. Why didn't he tell me before he was getting on a plane? "Okay, but why is Jonathan with you?" I fought to keep my tone even.

I wasn't normally a jealous person. I'd never been jealous that I could recall, before Liam. Before he was sleeping in a bed with Rhett when I'd wanted him in mine. Right then, I felt like I wanted to hurt Jonathan. He was a good-looking guy. I was burning with jealousy. Liam was mine and he shouldn't be going to Seattle with Jonathan.

I realized too late that we never said we were going to be exclusive with each other and my mind started running a million different scenarios through my head at once. Was he with Jonathan, too? Were there others in Seattle?

"Jasper, you still there?" Liam called through the phone. I lost my ability to think clearly while I fantasized about ways I could eliminate Jonathan as a rival for Liam's love.

I shook my head to clear it before I spoke. "Yeah, I'm still here. What did you say?"

"I said Jonathan is with me because I need help getting stuff packed. He volunteered to help me get Rhett's stuff. We'll be driving my car back in a few days. Look, I'll call you when we land and get to my apartment, okay? I've got to go. We're boarding the plane, now."

"Yeah, sure. Liam, I..." I was pissed. So, Jonathan *volunteered* to help Liam. Why did he feel the need to volunteer? Why Jonathan? What did he want with Liam?

"Don't worry, Cupcake, I'll call you when we land. Talk to you soon."

After those parting words, he was gone. I blinked. Since when in the hell was I Cupcake? My little imp was going to pay for that when I saw him next. If I had my way, I'd definitely be seeing him soon. Why did he think I would accept being called Cupcake? Was he confusing me with someone else? I slapped myself in the forehead to stop that line of thoughts.

Since Liam was flying from Monterey to Seattle, I had a couple hours to kill. I tried my best to busy myself by going over plans and blueprints. It didn't really work. After I realized I was causing more harm than good, I gave up and decided it would be best to just head for home.

I sent Sean a quick text letting him know I was leaving the office before locking up and leaving. Although it was only a forty minute drive, I was realizing the appeal of Sean's suggestion of opening a satellite office in Crooked Bend. With me living in Crooked Bend now and Sean out at Wild Creek, it made sense. It would get us home sooner in the evenings and would be a shorter drive in the winter when the roads could be treacherous. I sent myself a quick email to remind myself to talk to Sean about it in more detail.

We'd need to contact the Realtor if we chose to open a second location.

We obviously wouldn't get nearly as much foot traffic in Crooked Bend as we did in Jackson, but being closer to home was really starting to appeal to me on so many levels. I knew that the closer Sean was to Simon, the happier he'd be, too.

By the time I reached my home in Crooked Bend and made myself a sandwich that I didn't want, I figured Liam should've had enough time to have landed in Seattle. When I called him, he didn't answer and his phone went straight to voicemail. My stomach roiled with nerves. I didn't bother leaving a message, I was feeling angry and afraid at the same time. I would keep calling him until he answered or until he called me back. I didn't have to wait long because he called me back just a few minutes later. I breathed a sigh of relief when I saw it was him.

"Hey, Jasper. Sorry about that. I was leaving Rhett's place and I didn't know if you wanted Jonathan to know that you were calling me so I didn't answer the phone."

Hearing Liam's voice was both calming and reassuring. But his words hurt my heart and brought out my need to claim him. His explanation hurt because it seemed like he didn't want anyone to know we were even talking, let alone in a relationship. Was he ashamed to be with me? I decided to approach the subject carefully.

"Why wouldn't I want Jonathan to know I was calling you?" I asked.

"I don't know. We never really mentioned anything about how open we were or weren't going to be with our relationship. Technically we just started seeing each other so I didn't know if you wanted to announce it to everyone or if you wanted to wait and see how things went."

At Liam's reply, my heart relaxed and I breathed a sigh of relief. It appeared he was just taking things slow. I could handle that. I could do slow. Now, all I had to do was find out when he could come to Wyoming for a long weekend.

"That makes sense, Liam." I took a deep breath. "I'm not hiding us, okay?" I swallowed before continuing. "How was your flight? Did you get what you needed?" I asked trying to work my way up to asking what I really wanted to know. When would he be back in Wyoming—with me?

"The flight was quick but necessary. I really want my car in California since we left Rhett's Jeep in Wyoming. I need different clothes, too. I'd only packed for a little over a week, for snowy Wyoming, and so did Rhett. We both need more appropriate clothes."

"I can see that. I guess I didn't really think about you two only packing for a couple of weeks in winter climate. I never thought about the weather in Monterey being different than in Crooked Bend."

"Yeah, it is. I wouldn't necessarily call it warm. I guess I should when comparing to your weather."

"How long are you planning on being in Seattle?"

"Just a day or two. Just long enough to get stuff and then return to California. Like I told you before, Jonathan volunteered to help."

I hadn't been in the loop, not being with everyone in Monterey. "I haven't talked to Rhett in a couple of days. Is he not planning on going back to Seattle?" I was still fighting to keep my tone of voice even. This last-minute trip to Seattle, alone, with a super-hot and sexy Jonathan was not sitting well in my mind.

"He hasn't really talked about that, yet. He has a long recovery ahead of him and he is so much more settled with your dads than he'd be here in Seattle. He's having nightmares, Jasper. They're really bad ones, too. I know he's a lot more comfortable with your dads."

I assumed Rhett would have nightmares; I wasn't surprised to hear that. When he was first released from the hospital, he'd had a bad one and only Logan was able to calm him. At first it was shocking how close those two seemed to become since Rhett's kidnapping. I reconsidered my surprise. Hell, look at me and Liam. We'd gotten quite close too, but Logan and Rhett had known each other for months with nothing.

"Yeah, it makes sense that he'd want to be near Dad and Papa. Do you know when you'll be able to get away again? Or are you going to stay with Rhett?"

"To tell the truth, Rhett doesn't really need me. He doesn't want to have much to do with me, either. Travis is the one that really comforts him at night and it's your dads that he seems to want during the day." I heard Liam sigh. "Jasper, is that your way of asking me when I'll be back in Wyoming?" Liam flirted. I decided to lay everything out.

"No, Liam. That was me letting you know that I need you. When are you coming back to *me*?"

After a long pause, Liam claimed the rest of me when he replied, "I'll be there just as soon as I get Rhett's stuff to him in California."

10

LIAM

When Jasper told me he needed me, it took everything in me to not drop what I was doing and immediately fly to Wyoming. Responsibility tapped me on my shoulder and reminded me I had to get Rhett's things to California first. All I wanted to do was go to Jasper and have him wrap his arms around me. I missed him so much! It was quite a change not seeing him daily. I hadn't slept for shit since I left Wyoming. It was almost as if he was my security blanket. He made me feel safe. Until Jasper, I hadn't felt safe in a long time.

Remembering what I needed to do and realizing I was going to Wyoming and not staying in California, I began packing as soon as I got back to my apartment. Luckily, Rhett and I only lived a few minutes apart. If I was going to spend any amount of time in Wyoming during the winter, I'd definitely need to go shopping for clothes to wear in the snow. I only had enough for a couple of weeks and then I'd be re-wearing them. Taking that into consideration, I went into my bedroom and started re-packing my suitcases. My car was on the small side so I needed to make sure everything I took counted.

I was so engrossed in packing that I just about shit myself when I turned around and saw Jonathan standing in the doorway. I'd been so caught up in Jasper and thoughts of what he promised he'd do to me that I completely forgot that he said he'd pick me up for dinner.

"Sorry, I didn't mean to scare you. I knocked. When you didn't answer I tried the knob and it was open." Jonathan put out both of his hands and gave me a shy smile. Seriously, if I wasn't already completely hung up on Jasper, I'd consider hooking up with Jonathan, but I didn't even know if he was gay. The man was gorgeous! Short dirty-blond hair, bright-blue eyes, and completely toned. Yeah, he was hot, but I had a thing for a certain architect in Wyoming. Totally a one-man guy.

"No big deal. I was just lost in thought. Are you ready for dinner? Did everything get settled at Rhett's apartment?" I asked in rapid fire succession. The sooner we could leave Washington, the sooner I could get to Wyoming.

"Yeah, the moving crew got everything packed for California. The rest will go into storage until Rhett decides what he wants to do. Otherwise, after dinner, we can hang out at the hotel and get on the road first thing in the morning."

"Dinner sounds good. Where did you want to go?" I asked.

"You're the local, you pick. I'm not picky and will eat just about anything."

I smirked at the double meaning behind his comment. "I know just the place! Let's go!"

I was excited to visit one of my favorite little hole-in-the-wall places. Mike never liked the place, but Rhett and I did. If Jonathan wasn't picky, we were going to Salvatore's, the best Italian food around. They were always busy because everything was delicious, not to mention the excellent service. All the locals knew about it which was why they were always busy. If you were a tourist, you probably wouldn't give it a second glance.

Once we were seated at Salvatore's it didn't take long to decide what we wanted. After, we sat and stared at each other. Yeah, it wasn't awkward at all. Thankfully, our waiter brought out bread and salads with our drinks and we weren't forced to talk much. I didn't really know what to say to Jonathan. For the most part, he was quiet, and a little intimidating. Come to think of it, he was *a lot* intimidating. Thankfully, he broke the silence and started a conversation.

"Have you and Rhett been friends long?"

"About five months or so. We've been friends since he first moved to Seattle. We've got a lot in common so I guess that's why we get along so well," I replied in between bites of the fresh garlic breadsticks. I could fill up on their breadsticks alone.

"Have you worked for Taylor long?" I asked.

"A few years. I like it. I get to travel a lot and I love knowing I get to help those who really need it but might not otherwise get it."

"What do you mean? You work in security, right?" I asked.

"Sure," Jonathan replied to me.

"What do you mean, 'sure'? I thought the company was Stealth Securities? Don't they provide security? Like bodyguards and stuff?"

"Is that what you think we do?"

"It's not?" I volleyed back at him.

"Maybe you should ask your boyfriend what it is that his

papa's company does," Jonathan told me with a devious smirk on his face.

"What? What are you talking about?"

"Jasper? Your boyfriend? It's his papa's company. Ask him what it is we do."

I wondered first why his tone was so strange. Why would I ask Jasper when I was sitting right there with him. The second thing I wondered was how he knew that Jasper and I were involved. "How did you…"

I was interrupted by the waiter bringing out our entrees. I ordered the chicken Alfredo. I was crazy about it. Jonathan opted for an enormous sampler plate with four different entrees. How he could eat all that food and look like he did was beyond me. Somehow, he managed to finish every bite, and a basket of breadsticks, his salad, and a dessert!

"What?" he asked when he noticed me staring at him.

"Nothing. I was just trying to figure out where you put all of it. You ate enough for two, maybe even three people!" I replied on a chuckle after we left the restaurant and were walking back toward my apartment. It was great that everything was within walking distance. Everything I could ever need was right there. It will be a big change for me if things worked out with Jasper, and I moved to Crooked Bend. Small town living would definitely take some getting used to.

"Well, not only do I have a fast metabolism, but I also work out every day so I keep in shape and remain ready for what my job might throw at me. I have a physically demanding job. You know, being a bodyguard is hard, physical work." Jonathan gave me a wink.

I knew he was picking on me just because I didn't understand exactly what it was he did. I didn't like that at all. I needed to talk to Jasper about what exactly it was that Stealth Securities did.

He lessened the dig when I looked at Jonathan and noticed the smile on his face. He really was easy on the eyes. I wasn't really looking for someone. After all, I had Jasper. With *him,* I really wanted to look—a lot.

"Are we going to be able to leave tomorrow like we planned?" I wanted to desperately change the subject.

"That is the plan. It's about a fifteen-hour drive, so we'll probably try doing it in two days instead of one. But, if we get up early enough, we can push through and make it in one day if you like. You left room for me in your car, right?"

"Yeah, there's still room for your things, and Rhett's as long as you don't have much. I only have two suitcases and my laptop. My office is pretty mobile so it's easy to take it with me just about anywhere."

"Rhett's clothes fit into three suitcases. That's all he said he wanted for now. I shipped his books and Blu-rays. They'd fill up your car all by themselves."

"My car is small but has more room than you might think if we lay the back seats down. We should have enough room for all of the suitcases. I plan on coming back to Seattle before Rhett does, so I don't need to take all of my clothes."

"Okay. I don't get why you aren't just moving to California, though. I mean, you plan on spending the next several months with Rhett, right? Why keep paying rent on an apartment here?" Jonathan asked.

That sure made me think. I was close to jumping in with both feet with Jasper. Should I give up my apartment and save money? I should slow down. I made a mistake with Mike; jumping in with both feet got me beat up. Would I be making a mistake if I did the same with Jasper? As it was, I was considering splitting my time between Monterey and Crooked Bend. I knew that Rhett didn't seem to want me around all the time. I had a nagging feeling that on some level I was a reminder to him about what Mike had done to him. What if I got rid of my apartment and Jasper and I didn't work out? Oh, my brain was throbbing!

"Yeah, that makes sense, but I'm not in the position to do that right now. Especially not if we only have until tomorrow. I've been in my apartment a lot longer than Rhett was in his, and I have a lot more shit!" I told Jonathan on a laugh. It was definitely something to consider and think about.

Before I made such a life-changing decision, I should probably talk to Jasper about it, even though he'd already mentioned me moving to Crooked Bend to be closer to him. I could look into finding somewhere to rent there. I knew that Jasper's house was a rental so that meant there were others, right?

We returned to my apartment and Jonathan helped me take my suitcases downstairs and out to the car. Even though I had an apartment, we were both staying in a hotel for the night. I only had one bedroom, and one bed, and Jonathan wasn't going to fit on my couch. We would get an earlier start if we both stay in the same place, and we'd picked a hotel near the interstate, away from the downtown area that I lived. I gave it another look around before deciding that what I had would do for the time being. As long as I met my self-imposed deadlines, and kept my readers happy, I could live anywhere with Internet access. I couldn't imagine a book I couldn't access from Amazon or another vendor. I knew Jasper had Internet access, so that wouldn't be an issue.

When I joined Jonathan downstairs, he took my bags

from me and we loaded up into my baby. I missed Baloo over the past month and I was more than happy to be back behind my baby's wheel. That was, until Jonathan opened the passenger door for me and tried to usher me into the seat.

"What exactly do you think you're doing? You honestly believe I'm gonna let you drive Baloo to the hotel?"

"Blue? Really?"

"No, not Blue. Ba-loo. You know, from *The Jungle Book?* Baloo is a perfectly respectable name for my baby!" Baloo was really my only splurge. When I saw the Ford Focus RS, Nitrous Blue, with a six-speed manual transmission, yeah, I knew I had to have it. Baloo was fun to drive. What I didn't fully think through was that I rarely got to drive him like I should. As I said before, everything was within walking distance. The trip to Monterey and then on to Crooked Bend would give me plenty of time to drive him.

"You're not going to let me drive at all?"

"Can you even drive a manual?" I was grasping at straws, trying to think of everything I could think of to come up with a reason why I couldn't let him drive us to the hotel. It'd been so long since I'd been able to drive Baloo.

"Yes, Liam. I can handle a manual," he said dryly. He had to know I was making excuses "I know my way around a *stick* quite well, so I've been told," Jonathan purred. If there wasn't a double entendre there, I was straight. Holy shit! Was Jonathan gay? Was he *flirting* with me? I had no idea. I just assumed that he was straight.

Giving up, I handed Jonathan the keys and sulked into the passenger seat of *my* car. It wasn't like I wouldn't get to drive tomorrow, right? What I didn't realize was, not only could Jonathan handle a manual, he could *drive* a manual. It was definitely not his first time shifting gears.

"I'd like to hear how you got to learn how to drive like *this*," I commented while relaxing into the passenger seat of my car. I guess I could get used to sitting over here. My car was fun to drive, but also a comfortable ride.

"Europe," Jonathan replied.

"Europe. That's it? Just Europe? What were you doing there?" I asked. I realized I had no business asking so many personal questions, but I was curious.

"I was there on assignment."

"Do I even want to know?"

"I couldn't tell you anyway. Most of what it is that we do is need-to-know, sorry." He winked at me. "I'd have ta kill ya if I told."

Before I knew it, we were at the hotel and it was time to climb out of the car. That seemed to put a curt end to our conversation on the subject of Jonathan's job. Besides, I really wanted to get checked into my room and give Jasper a call. Our earlier conversation was too short. I had a lot to talk about with him after everything that happened this afternoon.

11

JASPER

I certainly learned how to be patient since meeting Liam. I knew he was quite skittish when I first saw him and I couldn't just jump into bed with him like I normally do with men. That was probably for the best. But now, my patience was unraveling.

Liam said he'd be here just as soon as he got Rhett's things dropped off in California. That was over a week ago and still no Liam.

I couldn't blame him; there was no way that he could get to me. We were hit with a blizzard right before Valentine's Day and nobody could get in or out of the area. We were all hunkered down in our homes. All businesses were closed for the duration. Living in town offered some small blessing. I was lucky enough to still have electricity. Sean and Simon weren't as lucky at Wild Creek Ranch. Sean said they had briefly lost power. Thankfully, though, Simon had a generator. After all, it wasn't a rare occurrence in the winter. Still, better them than me.

They had each other to keep warm. I only had FaceTime

Liam, and my right hand. My right hand had much to be desired since having a taste of Liam.

I wanted Liam's hands on my body. I wanted to feel his whisper-soft kisses everywhere; especially on my dick. I regret that we didn't get around to sucking each other off, thought we were close a few times. That was a more intense level of intimacy that I wasn't sure Liam was ready for yet. I regretted not having experienced his plump lips wrapped around my aching shaft while I gently pumped in and out of his mouth. Yeah, I was horny. I couldn't remember a time that I had ever gone so long without having sex. I'm thinking before I started having sex.

It helped make me feel better that Liam was just as frustrated as I was. He seemed every bit as anxious to get back to me as I was to have him here. His texts became much more frequent and so much kinkier. Who knew the little imp was so kinky? Yeah, life was definitely not going to be boring with Liam, that's for sure.

Once the weather cleared up after a week of being snowed in, things were so hectic that it was probably a good thing that Liam wasn't in Crooked Bend. I didn't have time to spend with him. I left before sun-up and worked late into the night. I did it so my brother could help with what needed done at the ranch. Wild Creek was hit especially hard since they were further out and close to the mountains. They didn't have the county to help keep things plowed, and since the ranch was several miles inland, it was probably going to be a few more days before Sean could even leave the ranch. They had their own equipment of course, but the animals came first.

That meant that I was practically living in the office in Jackson. I really needed to talk to Sean about opening a satellite office in Crooked Bend. Maybe it was time to look at adding another architect to the firm as well. One who would work out of the Jackson office. Our business was growing rapidly and we could definitely support another architect. There were a lot of perks to living in a tourist town. I didn't really miss it. I'd grown quite fond of the laid-back environment that Crooked Bend offered.

The last week of February was definitely one that I'd remember for a long time. Sean finally returned to the office allowing me to leave work at a reasonable time. At last, Liam could finally visit. We were talking on the phone while he booked his flight. It was the first of what I hoped would be many long weekend visits. He'd arrive on Thursday and leave the next Monday. I already arranged to have Friday off. I planned on spending the three days with him; hopefully naked and in bed.

When my little imp finally arrived, I was surprised with what I saw. He looked like he hadn't slept in months, which worried me a great deal. I was pleased to see his bruises were gone, but I was aware of that thanks to the past month's video chatting.

What I saw, I thought his eyes might as well have been blackened again; the dark circles under them were so prominent. When he saw me in the baggage claim, all he could do was trudge toward me, exhausted. He crashed into me, rather than falling into my waiting arms. He was so much smaller than I was so I had no problem catching him and supporting his weight. He finally spoke, allaying some of my worry.

"Missed you. Need you," Liam muffled into my chest. His arms were flung lifelessly over my shoulders.

I tightened my arms around his lower torso. I quietly enjoyed the feeling of finally having him back in my arms. "Sweetheart, are you okay? You look exhausted." I pulled back from him enough to look down into his eyes. What I saw made my heart skip a beat.

When Liam looked at me, I saw not only his tiredness, but something else, too. Something I didn't want to think about just yet. I couldn't wrap my mind around what I saw. Did Liam feel for me the way I did for him? Was I ready to acknowledge that I love him? Was I ready for him to love me? I knew that we needed to take things slowly. He just got out of a very bad relationship. I'd never had a relationship so yeah, the fact that I saw what I could only describe as love in Liam's eyes scared me a little.

"Yeah, I'm okay. Just exhausted like you said. It's nothing that a good night's sleep wrapped in your arms won't fix. I haven't been sleeping the best, you can see that. Since you were so slammed with work, I dove in and finished the first draft of my latest manuscript. I brought my laptop but I don't plan on working at all this weekend since my draft is with my editor," Liam told me as we walked over to the carousel. We watched as it started rotating and bags started rolling around it.

"Really?" I know I sounded like an excited kid, but I was excited. "You finished it already? Didn't you just start it?" Liam pointed out the first of his bags on the carousel. I grabbed it before it got away from us. Liam quickly grabbed the second one and then we were off, out the door and into the icy cold Wyoming weather. I was so happy to see him wearing a nice warm sweater under his North Face coat. There was still snow everywhere and it was bitterly cold. The temperature reminded me how much I wanted to get Liam back to my place and snuggle up with him.

"Yeah, I finished it. I've never written a manuscript that fast before and honestly, I probably never will again. I had a lot of free time on my hands." He shrugged. "Rhett spent a lot of time going from one appointment to another. Most of the time Taylor took him so I just spent most of the day writing. With you working long hours, too, I put in a lot of eighteen hour days," Liam explained.

None of what Liam told me sat well in my mind. Not only that Liam was working so much, but also because I didn't realize that Rhett had so many appointments. I really should have taken more time asking him or our dads about Rhett. I probably would have better luck getting information out of Papa than I did Rhett. He'd become reclusive since reaching California.

I put Liam's bags in the back seat of my truck and helped him into the passenger seat before climbing in and starting the engine. "I thought we would stop for dinner in Jackson if that's okay with you? I went shopping so we have plenty of food at the house, but I thought with you being cooped up in an airplane for hours you might just be happier eating out tonight?"

"That sounds great, Jasper. Almost like a date even," Liam said while looking at me.

I still couldn't get over how tired he looked. Reaching toward him, I realized I hadn't yet even given him a hello kiss. "Come here, you." I wrapped my hand around the nape of his neck. The contented sigh he let escape reassured me that I'd made the right choice when I chose to kiss him before we left the airport parking lot. The kiss was soft and gentle, which was exactly how I felt about him right then. He just looked so fragile and it made me want to protect him from everything. "It's a date. The first of many, hopefully," I replied after ending the kiss.

"Is it okay with you if we pick something up quick?" He glanced at me apologetically. "I'm sorry Jasper, I really am beat. All I want to do is curl up with you and sleep for twelve hours. I promise I'll be up for anything come tomorrow."

"I know just the place. There is this amazing diner by my old house. The food is great and the service is quick. It's better than fast food any day and I really don't want to take you to McDonald's for our first date, alright?"

"Sounds good."

Now that I had a destination in mind, I headed toward the diner in hopes of getting Liam fed before he fell asleep. The place was just as I remembered it. Then again, it hadn't been that long since I'd been there. The food was always delicious and the service quick. If the noises Liam was making while devouring his bacon cheeseburger, onion rings, and chocolate milkshake were any indication, he approved of my choice of dinner location.

After paying our check, I ushered Liam back into the truck and headed for Crooked Bend. I couldn't wait to get home and wrap Liam up where he belonged, in my arms. I'd hoped for a more eventful reunion, though I couldn't put him through that when he was so tired. I knew that sexy times were out of the question tonight. I was more than content to hold him in my arms again. It'd been a month since I had and it was just as long since I'd had a decent night's sleep.

Once we got to my place, Liam went to take a quick shower while I made sure everything was locked up for the night. I moved his bags to my bedroom and was in the process of placing them on the bed when he came out of the shower wrapped in a towel.

"I just need some pajama pants from the little one tonight." He paused and gave me an impish grin. "Unless you wanted to sleep naked?" he said with a smirk on his face. There he was, that was my Liam that left with my dads and brother a month ago.

"Naked works for me," I replied. At that, he dropped his towel and climbed into my king-sized bed. I couldn't wait to join him, even if I was only going to hold him all night. He was here and I was going to make the most of it. "I'll be back in just a few minutes, alright?"

"Mmm," Liam mumbled to me as I walked toward the bathroom to have my own shower and brush my teeth. I'd no doubt that he'd be asleep when I came back out of the bathroom. Ten minutes later, I discovered that he had indeed fallen soundly asleep while snuggling into my pillow. I quietly crawled into bed and he immediately latched on to my side. I somehow managed to get my arm under his head so I could wrap around him. When he put his head on my shoulder, I, too, let out a contented sigh and fell asleep faster than I had in the past month. Yeah, definitely needed to figure out how to get him here sooner rather than later.

12

LIAM

*W*aking up in Jasper's arms once again felt like coming home. I'd found my place, and it was with Jasper. Now I just needed to figure out how to get him on board with the idea that I belonged with him. He wanted to take things slow and I was ready to jump all in.

It was all I could do to not fall asleep on the drive between Jackson and Crooked Bend last night. I felt so bad about it but I desperately needed the sleep. After more than ten hours, I was awake and recharged. I urgently needed to pee but Jasper had a death grip on me. I did my best to finagle my way out of his arms as gently as I could without waking him up. Thankfully, I was able to succeed; he was sleeping like the dead. After relieving my bladder and quickly brushing my teeth, I went back into the bedroom and crawled under the covers. Jasper quickly pulled me into his arms and when his warmth enveloped me, I was once again lulled into sleep.

A couple of hours later I was awakened when Jasper's hard cock poked me in the stomach. We were face-to-face. I fought the urge to not wrap my hand around his cock and stroke. It wasn't until he started moaning and rolling his hips that I realized he was most likely dreaming. His hips in motion actually woke me up. I chose to make the most of his dream and morning wood. I untangled myself from his arms. It was long past time that I got a taste of him. Jasper was taking things frustratingly slow. He didn't want to scare me off, I guess, but I was already past fear of anything Jasper might want to do with me. I'd take things into my own hands...and mouth.

The moment I was face-to-face with Jasper's hard cock, I started drooling. He was uncut. I had never had the pleasure of meeting an uncircumcised cock before. I was really going to enjoy sucking and nipping at his foreskin. Going all in, I flattened my tongue out and swiped from his full balls all the way to the exposed head of his cock. When I reached the tip, I couldn't contain my moan when I tasted his sweet pre-cum. Jasper moaned with me. It wasn't until he reached down and wrapped his fingers in my hair and whispered a quiet *yes* that I realized he was no longer sleeping. Happy to fulfill his request, I continued to suck and nibble on his cock and foreskin. This was my first opportunity to suck him and I was going to make the most of it. Tonguing up one side and then licking the slit and tonguing down the opposite side, I couldn't help but chuckle a little when Jasper's grip in my hair tightened and he tried to pull me back to the head.

"Suck it, Liam. Stop playing and suck it like you mean it," he commanded.

Not one to disappoint, I quickly took him down my throat in one motion. His grip in my hair tightened to the point of being painful so I reached up and grabbed his hands to get him to loosen it. He immediately let go of my hair and simply cradled my head in his large hands. The guttural sounds coming from Jasper's throat got progressively louder and the gushes of salty-sweet pre-cum flowed copiously. I was in heaven. I'd wanted to taste him for so long and I was enjoying myself.

"Liam, sweetheart, if you don't stop, I'm going to cum. It's been too long and your mouth is so hot and wet, love. Feels too good."

At Jasper's words, I moaned loudly and doubled my efforts. I wanted him to climax in my mouth. I was desperate to taste him and wasn't going to stop until I did. Lowering my head to pull him into the back of my throat again, I swallowed twice before I hollowed out my cheeks and sucked hard as I slowly pulled up on his cock.

I felt his cock swell and pulse at the same time Jasper groaned and pitched his hips upward toward my mouth. Spurt after spurt of warm cum filled my mouth. I swallowed as fast as I could and didn't move until I licked up every single drop.

Jasper reached down and grabbed me under my armpits and pulled me up to him. He latched on to my mouth as though desperate for my lips, and devoured me. He moaned even louder once he got a taste of himself on my tongue. Knowing it didn't turn him off, I quickly thrust my tongue into his mouth. He immediately sucked, much the same way as I'd done to his cock. Between the blow job I'd given him and this award-winning kiss, I was so hard and ready for my own orgasm by that point. I started thrusting my hips into Jasper's because I needed pressure and friction on my dick, and I needed it right then!

Reaching down between us, Jasper wrapped his warm hand around my aching shaft. It didn't take much to set me off, I was more than ready for my own release. Just a few strokes later, I was painting my own chest as well as Jasper's hand with my release. Gasping for much-needed air, Jasper broke away from my mouth long enough to promise me that we were nowhere near finished, in fact, we were just getting started.

We must have dozed off for a bit again because the next time I opened my eyes, the sun was shining brightly in the room. Gone was the early morning sun. In its place was bright and somewhat painful. Looking over to Jasper, I saw he was already awake and staring at me.

"Sorry, I guess I was more tired than I thought after my drive yesterday."

"Don't apologize. It's okay, I understand." Then Jasper's lips were back on mine again. It didn't take long to get the rest of my body on board with what Jasper had planned. "Tell me now if you don't want this, Liam, because once we take this step, there's no going back. Once I get inside you, I know it's never going to be enough and I'm never going to let you go."

"Please, Jasper, I need to feel you inside of me right now," I pleaded with him. As soon as I said those words, I quickly had Jasper on top of me. He slowly worked his way down my body toward my aching, drooling dick. Jasper didn't disappoint when he got there either. He expertly sucked my dick into his mouth. It was all I could do to hold back from cumming immediately. It had been too long since I was with anyone willingly and even longer since I wanted someone the way I did Jasper.

"Jasper, stop. It feels so good and I'm too excited," I panted. "I don't want to cum until you're buried deep in me," I warned him while pushing on his shoulder to get him to release my throbbing shaft. Thankfully, he pulled off and kissed his way up my abdomen and torso toward my neck. When he latched onto my neck right where it met my shoulder and sucked hard, I lost it, again. Spurt after spurt of sticky cum shot up between us. Jasper made me cum by only sucking on my neck.

The mischievous smile he flashed let me know he knew exactly what he was intending to do, and he just did it. I couldn't really complain. Jasper was the only man that had ever been able to make me cum hands-free. How many men could say their partner could do that? Hell, how many men could do that? I had no clue. Maybe I needed to somehow work something like this into my next book.

"Don't worry, sweetheart, I promise you, we're nowhere near finished. You will cum for me more times than we will be able to count this weekend, I promise."

After that, Jasper worked his way down my chest, licking up the white mess I'd made. His loud groan let me know that he was definitely enjoying himself. When his hard cock brushed my thigh, I realized he was completely hard again. I just hoped it found its way into me, soon.

I thought I'd try whining to convey my desperation. "Please, Jasper. I'm dying here!"

"Patience, my little imp. We'll get there, I promise. First, I'm going to take my time enjoying...Every. Inch. Of. You." He enunciated each word with a kiss.

Before I realized his intentions, I was quickly flipped over onto my stomach and Jasper's face was buried between my cheeks.

I lifted my hips a little to give him better access. "Please don't stop, Jasper. Please don't ever stop!" I pleaded with him. I loved being rimmed but hadn't been given the pleasure for so long I'd forgotten how wonderful it truly felt. Maybe it was because it was Jasper rimming me. No matter why, it was bliss.

I couldn't create a coherent sentence. "Mmm, mfph, aahhh." I couldn't think, everything was sensation. For several minutes, all I felt was Jasper's tongue circling and lapping at my hole. When he stuck a wet finger in me, I hardly noticed, I was so relaxed. He quickly added a second, but I started to feel the burn when a third finger joined the first two. When he gently massaged my prostate, I knew I'd do anything to get him to do it again and again.

"Please, Jasper! Oh. My. God. Don't stop! Please do that again." I was a quivering mass of nerves by the time he pulled his fingers out of my very relaxed hole.

He flipped me back over onto my back with no problem whatsoever, and I couldn't do anything but lie there. My limbs were cooked ramen. I didn't even realize that Jasper suited up and lubed. He was more than ready to finish what he started.

"Last chance, Liam. Stop me now if you don't want this," Jasper told me when he had his rock-hard cock poised at my opening. I could never say no to him.

I twisted so I could look into those beautiful whiskey-colored eyes, I said the only thing I could.

"I'm yours, Jasper, forever."

I was so ready that Jasper pushed into me. He didn't have to pause at all and bottomed out in one steady thrust. When he was completely inside of me, consumed by my slick, wet sheath, we both moaned loudly.

"I'm sorry, sweetheart, I can't..." Jasper told me right before pulling almost all the way out and slamming back into me.

My body hummed, vibrated, and seized without warning. "Jasper!" On the second thrust I exploded like a rocket, painting my chest, neck, and the bed with more cum than I'd ever released at one time.

Jasper continued to thrust through my orgasm, chasing his own. The look of pure ecstasy on his face let me know that he was almost there. He froze for a second then pushed as hard as he could.

"Oh, fuck! Liam!" Jasper managed to shout out before collapsing on top of me. His cock was pulsing while buried deep inside me. My entire body tingled and felt numb at the same time. I was completely blissed out. I'd never experienced such a reaction to someone before.

It seemed like several minutes went by before Jasper's dick finally stopped throbbing. He sighed, lifted a little bit and held the condom on his shaft while gently pulling out.

I immediately felt empty and made a vocal protest that came out in the form of a whimper. Jasper didn't go far; he only managed to flop down beside me. After pulling the condom off and knotting the open end, he dropped it on the floor beside the bed and pulled me to his chest. We were a sticky, sweaty, smelly mess but neither of us seemed to care. Right then, I was completely worn out and couldn't stop my eyes from closing because of my relaxed, pleasured state.

I don't know how long I slept. I awoke to Jasper lightly running his fingers up and down my spine. It was both relaxing and exciting. Especially thrilling when his fingers slightly dipped into my crack at the base of my spine.

"How about a hot, relaxing shower?" Jasper asked once he realized I was awake.

"If my legs are working, I'd love a shower, but I think I'm stuck to you."

Jasper just chuckled at my tired, listless response.

"If I promise to make it worth your while, will that get your legs working?"

Damn, the man was as horny as a teenager! It wasn't that I didn't want to get up, I honestly didn't know if I could. My body was still so relaxed from Jasper fucking me into the bed that I didn't know if my limbs would work.

"I'll definitely take you up on your offer. I just don't know if my legs are working, Jasper. You sure did an excellent number on me!"

Jasper chuckled and grabbed me after he crawled out of bed. I loved how he would man-handle me. With him, it was comforting as well as a turn-on. I found myself placed on his very cold bathroom counter. My gasp just made him laugh so I glared at him. Thankfully, my legs were in working order. I hopped down from the counter in order to relieve my bladder before joining Jasper in the shower.

"You don't mind, do you?" I asked before relieving myself. When Jasper turned away from the shower to respond, he just smiled and walked toward me.

"After what we just did this morning, you honestly think watching you take a leak is going to upset or embarrass me?"

"Well, I just wanted to make sure."

Another benefit of being gay was that you and your partner could both relieve your bladders at the same time. I hadn't done that until Jasper stood on the other side of the toilet and did the same thing I was doing. Yeah, he was definitely laid-back and relaxed about things.

13

JASPER

Once Liam fell asleep after what I could only describe as the best sex of my life, I couldn't shut my mind off long enough to join him in his slumber. Instead, I lay there and enjoyed his warm body snuggled against me, half on top of mine. It wasn't the first time we'd lain in bed like that, nor would it be the last if I got my way.

There were a million things rushing through my brain all at once. The one that screamed at me the loudest though was that Liam was the one. He was it for me. I had to figure out how to keep him without scaring him off, or completely fucking up. I'd never had a relationship before and I wasn't exactly sure how to go about everything. I knew I wanted to try. I desperately wanted to try because I didn't want to be without him for even a minute of time. When he left on Monday, it was going to hurt. I just knew it.

I also knew I needed to tread carefully with Liam. I needed to make sure he was able to handle the kind of relationship that I wanted. I knew I was prone to dominating in bed, and this morning was no exception. I had a very healthy sex drive and I wondered if Liam would be okay with that. Fuck, I sure as hell hoped so.

After about an hour of lying with Liam on top of me, I was no closer to figuring things out than I was when I woke up, or yesterday, or last week. All I knew for certain was that Liam belonged to me. He belonged in Crooked Bend with me. Now to figure out how to tell him. Liam flushing the toilet brought me back to the present, and I realized he was looking at me funny.

"You okay?"

"Yeah, I'm fine. I was just thinking was all. You ready to shower?" I asked while grabbing a pair of washcloths off of the shelf beside the shower. I threw them over the top of the shower door and then ushered Liam into the steamy stall before following him. His loud moan let me know that he enjoyed the hot water on his skin. When he stuck his head under the water and wet his hair, my eyes were drawn to his delectable body. He was short, only about five-and-a-half feet tall, with platinum-blond hair, bright-blue eyes; he was what I would call willowy. He had a beautifully shaped, average dick. It was perfect for his body. Yeah, before the weekend was over, I definitely wanted intimate knowledge of every inch of it.

With Liam facing me, I grabbed the shampoo off of the shelf and tilted Liam's head back and away from me while I lathered his hair, giving him a gentle scalp massage. His moans encouraged me further, going straight to my dick. When my shaft reached forward and touched his stomach, I didn't pull away. I wanted him to know just what effect he had on me. I turned Liam around and rubbed my growing shaft in his wet, slippery crack. That got his attention.

"Again? Didn't you already have two orgasms this morning?"

I was surprised by his response. I thought he'd enjoyed what we did and would be interested in more. I was immensely relieved when I heard him chuckle. He was only kidding.

I bent down and whispered in his ear. "What can I say? You just do it for me, Liam." I felt him shudder against my chest and noticed his cock as it lengthened in front of him. His body let me know that he was just as affected as I was.

I coughed to clear my throat and my mind. It was definitely time to rinse his hair and get us both washed up quickly. I had a good water heater but there was no way it would last long enough for me to do what I wanted to little Liam.

"Close your eyes," I told him after turning him around and tipping his head back away from my chest. When I started rinsing his hair, he surprised me by reaching between us and wrapping his hands around my cock and stroking it. The smile that blossomed on my face couldn't be controlled and once his hair was rinsed, I couldn't help it, I needed to taste his lips again. I grabbed Liam behind his thighs and lifted him up. I slammed my lips down onto his the same time his back hit the tiles of the shower wall. We devoured each other. There was no other term for it. Gone were the soft, gentle kisses, we were too far into each other for those.

In the back of my mind, I reminded myself we needed to get clean. It was so incredibly difficult to pull my mouth away from his. He tried his best to follow my retreating lips. I managed to evade his seeking lips, though it was one of the hardest things I'd ever tried to do.

"Hang on, Liam. We need to finish showering. There's no lube or condoms in here and my hot water heater isn't going to last long enough for us to even give each other blow jobs."

Liam huffed. He was clearly annoyed by me halting our sexy progress. "Buy a bigger water heater, Jasper. Shower sex is hot and sexy. The things I could do to you in the shower!"

"It's not my house, Liam. I can't just upgrade their shit. When I buy a house for us, I can get a bigger heater." I gently set Liam back down on the shower floor and reached for the shampoo again. After a minute, I realized what I'd just said. *Our* house.

Liam stood on his toes and planted a little kiss on my cheek. "Plan on it, Jasper."

I didn't really have a response for him so I gave a subtle nod and quickly scrubbed my hair and rinsed it. My dick was still hard and ready for action. Unfortunately, we needed to get out of the shower first.

I quickly scrubbed my body, using a nice-smelling body gel and loofah and rinsed. I followed up by doing the same to Liam. We changed places and I made sure he was rinsed off. Once we were both acceptably clean and rinsed, I turned off the water and grabbed a big fluffy towel from the rack and wrapped it around Liam.

Liam climbed out of the tub quickly and I grabbed my own towel and followed him out of the bathroom. He was drying off when I joined him in the bedroom. I quickly dried and dropped the towel to the floor. Without any warning, I snatched Liam up and tossed him onto the center of my bed.

He bounced, giggling when he landed. That was a sound I wanted to hear repeatedly. I crawled on top of him like a predator stalking its prey. When I reached his mouth I gave him a gentle kiss before asking, "Now where were we?"

My long weekend with Liam flew by faster than I ever could've imagined. Before I knew it, Sunday night arrived. Our last evening together. I felt sad. He was going to drive Rhett's Jeep back to California and I'd have to say goodbye to my boyfriend. I'd never had one of those, but it was something I wanted with Liam and definitely something I could get used to.

As I'd hoped, we spent most of the weekend fucking like bunnies. Thankfully, after the first night, Liam was well refreshed and ready for anything we tried. We managed to christen every room in the house. We started in the bedroom then moved to the kitchen counter, the living room couch, the dining room table, my office, and ended our exploration in the bathroom.

After the first near-fuck in the shower, I remembered to stash lube and condoms on an empty shelf in the shower.

We did have to pause our love-making once because I had to take a quick phone call from a panicking client. He didn't need to know that I was completely naked, nor that Liam spent the entire phone call giving me one of the best damn blow jobs of my entire life. It was a miracle that I managed to not moan during the call.

After I finally assured my client that everything was alright, I grabbed Liam and proceeded to pound into him on top of my desk. I'll never forget the way he screamed for me to fuck him harder and deeper the entire time. Jesus! He's absolutely perfect for me, no doubt about it! It was like he was made just to love my sexual appetite. I couldn't wait to explore all things sexual with him.

But today, we were lying in bed in a state of orgasmic

bliss. Liam traced something on my chest with his finger while I ran mine up and down his spine. It took me a little while to figure out he was writing words on my chest. When I asked him what he was spelling, he stopped and said, "Nothing."

I felt disappointed when he stopped. I loved what he was doing. I enjoyed feeling him snuggled up beside me. I needed him to keep on writing words on my chest because it was relaxing.

"Don't stop. Like it, sweetheart," I slurred, already more than half asleep.

To my relief, Liam started writing *whatever* on my chest again. "Okay, I won't stop." Liam laid his head down on my shoulder and sighed. If I wasn't already half asleep, I'd have asked him what was wrong. I fell asleep holding him in my arms; right where I knew he belonged.

It was killing me to say goodbye to Liam, but that's what I had to do Monday morning. I begrudgingly helped him load his bag into the Jeep. Each step toward Rhett's car was heavier than the one before. We decided that he should leave the majority of his clothes with me since they were winter clothes. He'd need them here before he'd need them in California. I was not happy that we wouldn't be together again for three or four weeks. Our schedules just didn't allow for more visits.

We hadn't talked about taking things any further or faster. I was still being cautious and moving at what I thought was a respectable pace. What did I have to compare it to? Absolutely nothing. I was completely in the dark when it came to relationships. Liam said he didn't have anything to go by either, as his relationships all ended within a month or two, except for Mike. And *that* sure wasn't exactly a relationship to use to compare.

On the bitterly cold Monday morning in February, I gave Liam one last, lingering kiss. A kiss that spoke of promises yet to be fulfilled. I flicked my tongue over his like I'd done to his cock this morning when we woke up.

"Let's go back inside," Liam moaned into my mouth.

"You know we can't. You have to get on the road and I have a meeting this morning. I'd love nothing more than to repeat this past weekend with you." I pulled away so I could look into his eyes. "We only planned for the weekend, remember?" How the hell was I forming coherent sentences?

"Tell me I can come back. Please, Jasper. This is hard. I don't want to leave."

I rolled my eyes up, lust running through my body and love pounding in my chest. "Please come back, Liam, sweetheart. I'll welcome you with open arms. I'm going to hate going home to an empty house this evening." I looked into his crystal blue eyes. Shit, I was going to miss him like hell. "Be careful, and call me when you stop, alright? I'm going to worry about you until I hear from you, understand?"

"I'll call, I promise. I'm not going to stop unless I hit bad weather. If I do that, I won't reach Monterey until after midnight. You want me to call even if it's that late?"

I growled. Of *course* I wanted him to call! "Yes. Call me every time you stop. When you get food, when you have to fill up the tank. I only have the one meeting this morning, so you won't be interrupting me. I'm just going to be working on plans and blueprints in the office."

Liam squeezed my waist and looked up into my face. "Alright. I'll call every time I stop. Promise."

"Sounds perfect." With one last bear hug and a soft, gentle kiss, I told Liam to take care and watched him drive away with my heart.

14

LIAM

I think the hardest thing I've ever done was drive that Jeep away from Jasper. I made it to the outskirts of Crooked Bend before I was forced to pull off of the road. I tried so hard to keep my tears from falling, but they fell, anyway. They had their own mind, and they were determined that they were going to fall. I gave myself a good ten or so minutes to cry and miss Jasper before I wiped my eyes and blew my nose. I had a long drive ahead of me and if I didn't get it started, I'd never make my destination.

I decided to put on my big boy undies and get to it. The drive was beautiful. It was like I was looking through different eyes. The last time I'd taken this route was Christmastime with Rhett. I was in such a sorry state that I didn't notice much of anything.

I was a beaten and broken mess then. I was under the care of a therapist regularly, and she agreed that I was doing well after what Mike had done to me. My relationship with him had been deteriorating for quite some time, and by the end, I was glad it was over. I could've done without the beating, but it was reassuring that he couldn't hurt me or anyone else ever again.

I drove until my bladder screamed at me and my butt was sore from sitting. It was time for a break so I stopped and refueled both the Jeep and myself. While I sat in the Jeep, I decided to give Jasper a call. I took a bite of my cheeseburger and fries then dialed his number. The options were limited, so McDonald's it was. I smiled when Jasper answered on the second ring.

He took a deep breath before speaking. "Hey, sweetheart, did you stop already?"

I smiled, happy to hear his voice. "My ass couldn't make it any further. Someone gave it a good pounding last night and then Rhett's Jeep did the same thing all morning. Tell me, why does he like this thing?"

The roaring laugh that came through the phone lifted my spirits.

"I couldn't tell you why he likes that old thing." He paused, as though trying to think how to respond to me. "I have to say I don't recall you complaining last night while I was fucking you into the mattress, or against the shower wall."

"Nor will you. You know I was picking on you, but seriously, this Jeep bounces all over the road." I shoved several french fries in my mouth. "I stopped because my bladder was full and my stomach was empty. I decided to stop and take care of myself before heading on my way again. How did your meeting go?"

"It went well. The clients are excited about having their dream home built and they really were pleased with the ideas I had so hopefully we win their contract."

"That's great, Jasper! I should probably get back to driving since my lunch is finished," I said. The last thing I wanted to do was hang up with Jasper. I wanted to talk to him all day.

"I understand, Liam. Please call me next time you stop? I just want to know you're okay. It's a long drive and the weather can be so unpredictable this time of year."

"I will, I promise. Have a good afternoon, Jasper."

"Talk to you soon, Liam. Drive safe." Jasper ended the call. I still had about twelve hours of driving ahead of me. I couldn't waste time sitting in a parking lot. I merged onto the highway and continued my westward journey.

It was well after one in the morning before I finally pulled into the driveway at Jasper's dads' house. I was exhausted. Driving all day nonstop was so tiring! Not that I would ever complain, but I'm sure Jasper keeping me up most of the night before didn't help. I probably should've stopped for the night six hours ago. I was too stubborn and determined to make it back as soon as I could. So there I was, waking Taylor in the middle of the night while trying to sneak into the room they'd given me.

"Sorry, Taylor. I didn't mean to wake you," I whispered to the man that I'd come to realize, though he intimidated me at first, was a complete marshmallow.

"Don't worry about it, Liam. I was already awake. Rhett had another nightmare and I didn't realize that Travis was here before I went running into his room."

"Is he okay?" I asked, worried about my friend. He'd held me and helped me cope those first few weeks after Mike attacked me. I just wished he wanted my help in return.

"He's fine. By the time I got to his room, Travis was

already in bed with him and Rhett was already back asleep. I don't necessarily agree with whatever it is that's going on between those two, but right now, Travis calms Rhett down better than anyone else so I won't complain."

"Taylor, I don't think there's anything going on. I think Travis is a comfort and a source of security for Rhett and nothing else. He tells me they're just friends, and I believe him. Travis is close to our age and he was one of the first people Rhett remembers seeing after he was found in the motel. I'm sure it's a security thing." My assurance seemed to calm Taylor. I found it interesting. Why wouldn't Taylor want Travis involved with his youngest son?

"Look, I know you've had a long day, so why don't you get some sleep. I made sure the blinds were already closed in your room so the sun won't wake you in the morning, okay?"

I know I looked completely wiped. I glanced at Taylor and gave him a look of gratitude. "Thanks so much. Have a good night."

I made my way into the room and kicked off my shoes and dropped my bag at the foot of the bed. I stripped down to my Andrew Christian briefs and dialed Jasper as I collapsed in the bed. I'd have felt bad about waking him up at almost three in the morning except that he was adamant that I call him when I arrived. Besides, he told me earlier that he was going to bed around nine so technically, he'd already been asleep for almost six hours. I was sure he wouldn't be too unhappy that I woke him up. After all, he said he wanted me to call.

"Liam? Are you finally at Dad's?" Jasper's sleepy voice sounded through my phone.

"Yep, I'm in bed. I'm exhausted, but I wanted to be sure I kept my promise that I'd call, so that's what I'm doing. Now

I'm going to say goodnight and I'll call you tomorrow once I wake up, okay?"

"Sounds good, Liam. Sweet dreams, sweetheart." I could tell Jasper was only partially awake. He mumbled through the call.

"You too, Jasper."

I managed to get my phone onto the nightstand before I pulled the blankets up and burrowed into the feather-soft bed.

When I finally woke from my overdue hibernation, it was afternoon and I was voracious. First things first. I texted Jasper to let him know I was awake and that I'd call him after I showered, ate, and joined the living again. After spending close to sixteen hours driving yesterday, I'd already resolved to make the trip in stages the next time. There *would* be a next time.

Jasper returned my text. He informed me that he'd be in meetings all afternoon and that he'd call on his drive home so I had a few hours to kill before we could talk. After my shower and raiding the copious amounts of food in the kitchen, I sought out Rhett. I had to talk to him.

I found my bestie out by the pool, relaxing in a lounger.

"Hey Rhett, how are you doing?" I sat in the lounger beside him.

"Liam! Nobody told me you were back!" Rhett stood and gave me a tight hug. I started to cry uncontrollably as I wrapped my arms around my best friend. Rhett was back. God, I'd missed him! Since the ordeal with Mike, he'd been withdrawn and shied away from physical contact. Before, Rhett was a very touchy-feely kind of guy.

"I got in close to two in the morning and crashed until just a little bit ago. Your Jeep is out front, though, so have fun." I pulled away from the hug and wiped my eyes but not before Rhett noticed.

He cupped my cheek with his hand and wiped an errant tear from my face. "Sorry man, I didn't mean to make you cry."

I shook my head. "It's alright. I know you went through hell. I've missed you. I can't help but feel…"

Rhett grabbed me by the shoulders and shook me. "Stop right there. We've been over this, Liam. What Mike did to me wasn't your fault. I don't blame you, not even a little. The demon's I'm fighting are my own and I'm working on it. I'm sorry I've been so distant. I'm just…"

I waved my hand at my friend. "I get it, Rhett. You don't have to explain anything. I truly do understand. I just want you to get better."

"I will, Liam. I just need more time. It's only been a couple of months so, yeah. Anyway, how was your trip back to Crooked Bend? Did Simon and Sean drive you nuts being all lovey-dovey?" Rhett asked with a dreamy smile on his face. He might tease Sean, but I knew he was immensely happy for his brother. It was time to let him know about my trip and where I stayed. I hoped he'd be happy for me and not have a problem with it. No time like the present to find out.

"About that. I didn't stay with Sean and Simon." I looked up at him through my eyelashes. "I stayed with Jasper."

"Oh yeah? I guess that makes sense. Sean and Simon just got engaged. I bet they are still in that 'all over each other' stage. Did it work out? Jasper didn't drive you crazy, did he?"

I smirked and masked a chuckle "No more so than I wanted. Rhett listen, Jasper and I..."

"Are totally fucking like newlyweds, aren't ya?" Rhett interrupted.

Well, color me shocked! "You know?"

"Dude! It's totally obvious! You have that *just fucked* look written all over your face. Not to mention, you're walking a little funny too." Rhett busted out laughing.

"Hey! It's not funny. Your brother is quite aggressive in bed, among other places."

Rhett pulled back and started laughing. He waved his hands in front of my face. "TMI, man!" He shook his head "I'm happy for you. You're smiling again, I love that." His smile faded just a little. "Just be careful. I'm pretty sure Jasper's never had a serious relationship. I don't know if he knows how. I don't want to see you get hurt again, okay?"

I reached forward and clamped my hand on his shoulder. "Thanks, Rhett. I mean that. I appreciate your concern, but I already know about Jasper's gallivanting ways. He wants to give a relationship a try." I stopped talking and swallowed hard before continuing. "I fell for him, Rhett. Like, seriously hard. Like, my heart is already his, hard."

"Holy shit, Liam! Dude!"

"I know, I know. You don't have to tell me."

"Listen to me, Liam. If you love my brother, that's great. It's amazing. If anyone has a problem with it, to hell with them. If there is anything I've come to realize, it's that you never know what's going to happen tomorrow. If you've got a chance at happiness with my brother, then take it. Take it and run. Grab him and don't let go, Liam. Because you never know if you'll get that chance again."

I was a little surprised at the about-face. He started by warning me and ended by supporting us wholeheartedly.

I looked at him and felt my heart melt for my gentle friend. He was openly crying. That started my own waterworks. I jumped up from my seat and wrapped myself around Rhett. I sat there, just holding him while he trembled.

"Shh. It may not seem like it, but I promise, it'll get better," I whispered in Rhett's ear.

After Rhett was able to calm down, he looked at me and started laughing hysterically. It was the sweetest music I'd ever heard. He hadn't been happy since before his kidnapping. He used to be so cheerful. If he was laughing again, then that was absolutely wonderful.

"If you're sure, if you're serious, Liam, you need to grab Jasper by the balls and don't let go. Don't let him and his bossy ways rule the roost. He can be really pushy."

When Rhett said that, I laughed so hard I fell off of the lounger. Which caused both of us to laugh even harder. It would take more time, but Rhett was going to be okay.

After my chat with Rhett, I decided it would be best if I returned to Seattle and pack up my apartment. He was right; life was too short to wait for what other people thought I should do. Who was to say how long it took to care for someone enough to start a relationship? I may write murder mysteries, but I'm a hopeless romantic. I knew that Jasper was the one for me. He was my chance for love and happiness and I was going to take it.

That's why, two days later, I found myself back in Seattle and supervising the movers about what was going on the truck to Wyoming, and what was going to the local LGBTQ youth shelter. Pretty much everything would go to the shelter. I arranged it with the director. He told me they welcomed all donations. My clothes and small personal items were already packed and loaded in Baloo. All I needed to do was make sure the movers were finished and turn my keys in. I'd checked into a hotel for the night and I would start my trip to Wyoming at first light. I was told my things would arrive in a week, which was well after I would, so if Jasper didn't want me to live with him, I had plenty of time to get a storage facility for my things. I could either find my own place or get another company to move my shit to California. Rhett already agreed to be my backup plan. He and I hoped I wouldn't need it.

After thanking the movers and stopping at the apartment office to drop off my keys, I headed to Salvatore's one last time to enjoy my favorite Alfredo and breadsticks. I'd miss them, but I'd rather have Jasper any day.

After checking into the hotel, I realized it was late enough to call Jasper. Once I'd called him, I could turn in early so I'd have enough rest and get an early start.

"Hey, Cupcake."

"Next time I see you, I'm going to make you pay for deciding *Cupcake* was a good thing to call me, Liam. You've been warned."

"I'm counting on it, *Cupcake*," I teased. "Please make me pay for it. I've been a naughty boy and I need to be spanked," I jokingly said to Jasper. It must have been the right thing to say, if the gasp that I heard followed by heavy breathing was any indication. Knowing I had that effect on Jasper made my dick as hard as granite.

Jasper coughed and growled. "Okay, we have to change the subject, now. How did the packing go?"

"Great. I'm all checked into the hotel. I'll leave for California bright and early tomorrow morning. How was work?"

I hated lying to Jasper. I wasn't going back to California, I was going straight to Wyoming in the morning. I was only able to do it so I wouldn't ruin the surprise. I was taking a big chance and hoped he wouldn't be angry with me.

"Work was just that, work. It was pretty boring." Jasper sighed and continued "I miss you. When is the three weeks up again?" Jasper chuckled.

"You have two more weeks to wait, Jasper. I promise it'll be worth it." It warmed my heart to know he missed me.

"I know," he whined. "I just miss you and want you here. It's not the same without you." I could almost hear the pout in his voice, but he masked it well.

"Who was it who told *me* to have patience?" I replied.

His voice hardened. "I'm patient, and you know it. Get to bed because you have an early start tomorrow. I don't want you driving when you're as tired as you were before, understand?"

"Yes, Cupcake. I understand," I replied, egging him on. He didn't seem to take the bait.

"Goodnight, sweetheart. Drive safe tomorrow."

"I will, I promise. Don't worry, I'll call before I leave and with each stop."

"Okay, goodnight."

"Goodnight."

Two days later, on Monday evening, just a week after I'd left Jasper with the promise to return in three weeks, I was back in Crooked Bend, anxiously knocking on Jasper's door. It was late in the evening. I stood outside for several minutes, but he finally answered. The look of surprise, exchanged for immediate lust when he saw me standing on his porch, let me know I'd made the right choice.

I gave the man of my heart an impish grin. "Hello, Cupcake. Miss me?"

15

JASPER

The absolute *last* person I expected to see standing at my door when I opened it on a Monday evening was Liam, but that's who was standing there. At first, I couldn't do anything except stand and stare at my little imp. I'm not even sure I was breathing. He was here. After only a week away, he'd come back to me. He shivered, standing outside in the cold on my doorstep. Finally, I realized that it was not a dream and double-checked behind him to make sure nobody was watching us before I grabbed him and crashed my mouth against his.

God yes! Definitely Liam. Only Liam could kiss me like that. Only Liam did that little thing with his tongue. I went from flaccid to fully hard in seconds. I backed up and pulled him into the house, closing the door behind us. My hands developed minds of their own, fighting with his layers of clothes without separating our lips. Unsuccessful, I didn't seem to care much. I didn't want to stop kissing him for anything.

Liam pushed gently on my shoulders and turned his head to the side in order to end the kiss. I was so happy to see him that I got carried away. I'd been stifling his ability to talk.

"I missed you too. Terribly," he sighed into my shoulder. It seemed he was hesitant to speak for a moment then he opened his mouth again. "You aren't upset that I came back earlier than we planned, are you?" He looked up at me through his golden eyelashes.

Liam removed his coat. Zipper! I'd have been able to get the damn thing off him if I had enough brain cells left to remember how to pull down the pull tab. That happens every time Liam is near me. All of the blood that's normally in my brain rushes to my dick, leaving me slower than usual.

I shook my head at his ridiculous assumption. "What? Why would I be upset? I didn't want you to leave in the first place! I'm ecstatic that you're back already. How long can you stay this time?" I asked while guiding him further into the house. I made plans for this visit the minute he climbed into the Jeep and drove away. I was trying to figure out the logistics, and how much we could do in whatever time was afforded us.

I finally took a good look at Liam and realized he was tired. He didn't look nearly as tired as the last time, but he still looked like he could use a good night's sleep.

"How long do you want me to stay?"

"Don't tease me, Liam. You know I want you here. Forever." I could even hear the desperation in my voice. "I don't want you to leave. I want you here with me always."

"Done." He seemed to be waiting for my reaction. He sure as hell got one. I was stunned. "Now, see how easy that was?" Liam shouted back to me as he sauntered down the hallway.

I followed him. I had absolutely no idea what was going on

My Choice, My Chance

nor did I know what his destination was. He walked into the bathroom. Well *of course* he did! It was late and there wasn't anything open once he left Jackson. I stopped in the bedroom and sat on the bed. I was hopeful that I hadn't heard him wrong. Did he say he would stay with me forever? I quietly waited for him to come out of the bathroom. I didn't have to wait long.

Liam walked into my waiting arms and stood between my legs. I hugged him tightly, afraid to let him go. I pressed my head into his chest and breathed in his scent.

Liam hummed and I felt the vibration in my head, traveling down my body, and to my own heart. "It's late. I know you have an early meeting tomorrow morning, and I've spent a god-awful amount of the day driving. Can we shower and curl up together to sleep? I know we'll have to talk tomorrow. I guarantee I'll be here when you get home from work tomorrow. I'll even cook you dinner." He pulled back to look me in the eyes with his bloodshot and hollow eyes. "You *do* have food, don't you?"

"Good luck with that. I stocked up when you were here two weekends ago, but that food's long gone. I've not restocked since. I'll stop and get pizza. Sound good?"

I was relieved. "Pizza sounds great." He hugged me again "How about that shower? Care to get all soapy and wet with me?"

I swear, the little imp was asking for it. I knew he was tired. The dark circles under his eyes were more prominent than I realized at first. "A shower sounds wonderful and I promise to behave. Well, I'll do my best. I can't help myself when I'm around your scrumptious body. Especially in the shower."

"You can behave or misbehave as much as you want, Jasper. I don't have much energy left, though, and I might not do much participating." Liam chuckled and licked me on the nose. The little imp.

"Don't worry, I can behave. I'm gonna have fun washing you, though. Come on, let's go." I held Liam's hand as we walked into the bathroom together. I was so ready to get him naked, even if I needed to behave. Tomorrow, all bets were off.

If ever there was something that should always be done, waking up with Liam in my arms was that thing. I wanted to start every morning like that. Could I make it happen? Liam said *done* when I told him I wanted him here always. Could it be that easy? Could I really keep him here with me? I sure hoped so.

This morning, my mind was in the wrong place. I had to get to work, I was scheduled for an early meeting at a ranch on the other side of Jackson. This would be a wonderful time for an additional architect. Sean and I handled it all right now. Damn inconvenient this morning, if you ask me. I whispered a kiss across Liam's temple and gently pulled myself away from my warm, snuggly bedmate. I took care of my morning ablutions, relieving myself, shaving, and combing my hair, to get ready for the day.

He wasn't in the bed when I came out of the bathroom. I could smell fresh-brewed coffee and knew Liam had gone to the kitchen. I smiled, I couldn't help myself. Something as small as making coffee for me meant the world to me. I'd never known anyone that willing to make me coffee except my twin. After quickly getting dressed, I went in search of Liam and coffee, in that order. I found both in the kitchen.

I wrapped my arms around Liam and kissed the back of

his neck while he stood at the stove flipping French toast in a skillet. "Coffee *and* breakfast? What did I ever do to deserve such a treat?"

"Well, for starters, you didn't kick me out last night when I showed up on your doorstep unannounced."

I snorted. "Like that'd ever happen." Surely, he didn't think that I could ever refuse him. We *so* needed to have a talk if he was so insecure about our relationship. Even though it was a fairly new one, he should still know that I would never do that. I looked apologetically at the skillet. "That French toast is a wonderful surprise, but sadly I don't have time to stay for breakfast this morning. I spent too much time after my alarm rang just staring at you sleeping. Now I'm running behind." I poured my coffee in my travel mug. I looked at Liam to judge his reaction.

He shuddered in feigned disgust. "You stare at me while I'm sleeping? I don't know if I find that creepy or if I'm flattered."

"Be flattered, there is nothing creepy about me thinking you're beautiful. I can't stop looking at you. I'm so, so sorry I can't stay for breakfast, but I really have to go or I'll be incredibly late for this meeting and Sean will be pissed if I'm late."

"Go, and don't worry about this." He gestured at the hot skillet toasting the delectable breakfast. "I'll see you this evening after work." He stood on his toes to kiss my cheek. "Is it alright if I set up my laptop here, on your table? I can work on editing my latest manuscript while you're at work."

"You don't have to use the table. You're more than welcome to use the extra desk in the office. Sean left it behind because Simon had a nicer desk in his home office. That means there are two in there. You'll probably have to stack up a pile of papers and crap I've piled on it. Sorry about that."

Liam's face lit up. "Wow. Thanks! Don't worry about it. I can do that easy. It won't be long before I'm lost in the world of *Officer Micah Swanson* and *Detective Nolan Holloway*. I'll see you this evening." Liam once more stood on tiptoes to give me a goodbye kiss.

I could definitely get used to having him here: falling asleep arm in arm, waking up together, goodbye kisses, sharing meals. I was unquestionably ready for that in my life. Now I understood exactly what happened to Sean when he fell in love with Simon. Those thoughts made me stop in my tracks on my way out the door.

I turned around and stared at Liam for a moment before heading on my way. Did I love him? If I didn't already, I was well on my way. Having never been in love before, I wasn't exactly sure what it was or what it felt like.

Knowing that Liam was in my house waiting for me made me happy. It helped make my shitty day better. I needn't have worried about being late for my early meeting. The client himself was over a half hour late. Sean and I weren't happy about that. With such a start to the day, I expected it to go downhill from there. Unfortunately, I was right. The wrong supplies were delivered to the wrong site, blueprints went missing. It seemed that if it could go wrong, it did. If I'd been superstitious, I'd have thought it was fate telling me *no* about Liam, that we shouldn't be together. Thankfully, I'm not. Even if I was, I wouldn't have listened anyway.

I decided to talk to Sean about hiring more people,

A.S.A.P. We had grown so much since we opened our firm. It was past time we hired some staff.

I decided to just go for it. I got out of my chair and walked to his office. "Hey, Sean, you got a minute?"

Sean looked up from a project he was working on. "Sure, Jasper, what do you need?"

"You know, after so much going haywire today, I think we should look into hiring at least an office manager and a third architect. We have more than enough work to justify both. With poor Leslie only able to work part time, we need more personnel. We need someone here full time. Maybe two? I mean, we've talked about a second office in Crooked Bend, too. I am really starting to see the sense in that. I have been thinking. Traveling here can be downright treacherous in the winter. To tell the truth, I'm tired of working late all the time, too. It's starting to wear on me."

Sean laughed at my soliloquy. "Wow, Jasper, tell me how you really feel?" He stopped when he looked at my expression. "What brought all this on? Don't get me wrong, I'm in total agreement. I'm sorry if I've put so much of the workload on you so I can get home to Simon. I'll make sure I pull my weight around here."

"That's not what I'm saying at all. I don't *mind* you cutting out early so you can head home to your man. Not at all. I'm happy for you, Sean. I really am. Since last summer, and especially since Rhett's kidnapping, I've done a lot of thinking. There's so much more to life than work, eat, sleep, lather, rinse, repeat. I'll never find what you found with Simon if all I ever do is work."

"Wow, Jasper. You're completely right." I was glad Sean was taking me seriously now. "We can place an ad for a full-time office manager tomorrow. Hopefully we'll find someone experienced enough that there isn't a learning curve. As for the architect, didn't Jonathan mention something about his cousin being an architect?"

"Maybe? I can't remember. Would he want to leave Monterey to come to Wyoming? Who does that?" Even as I said it, I thought of Liam and smiled a little.

Sean smirked at me. I knew what he was going to say before he said it. "We did. We'd just have to make the proposal appealing enough."

"Alright, I'll see if I can't find out about Jonathan's cousin tonight. I need to call Rhett, anyway. Travis is always near Rhett anymore and Collin is his cousin as well so hopefully I can get some information about him."

"Great! I'll write up an ad for an office manager and forward it to you for approval. When you okay it, we'll have Leslie post it tomorrow, sound good?"

"Sounds great, Sean. Thanks."

I paused before leaving Sean's office. "Do you want to come out to the ranch tonight for dinner? Simon put a stew in the Crock Pot this morning. You know how delicious it is."

I thought about Simon's stew. It *was* delicious. "Thanks, Sean. Not tonight. I just want to go home after this travesty that pretended to be a day."

Sean chuckled. He knew just what I was talking about. "No problem. I'll just go write up that ad and get it forwarded to you before I leave."

"I'll look at it tomorrow. I'm headed home soon with a stop for a pizza and binge-watch some *Supernatural*." I grabbed my keys, phone, coat, and messenger bag and headed out the door. I had a sexy little imp waiting at home for me.

16

LIAM

*S*ince Jasper said he wanted me with him always, I decided to take him at his word and believe that he meant it. After he hurriedly left that morning, I started hauling the stuff from my car into the house. Thankfully, I'd left my clothes here last time so I had clothes to put on. I was most happy about it because Jasper's clothes were way too big for me. His T-shirts were comfortable, sure, but nothing he owned would actually fit.

After getting Baloo unloaded, I distributed the rest of my clothing into the half of the closet Jasper cleared out for me, and into the chest of drawers he offered. He used the dresser, but the bedroom set came with both and he just had it sitting there empty.

Once I finished with that, I went to the office to see what I had to do to clear off a desk. Jasper warned me that there were extra papers piled on the extra desk. That was an understatement! You couldn't even find the desk. It was buried deep under piles and piles of paperwork, blueprints, and miscellaneous everything else. I wouldn't have been surprised to see a kitchen sink there, somewhere. And *that* was just one desk!

The desk he used regularly didn't look much better. His drafting table was in pristine order. You could definitely tell where he spent the majority of his time when he worked at home.

I decided to do my best to make temporary, but neat piles of paper on the couch. I saw a filing cabinet in the corner. When I opened the drawers, I wasn't surprised to see that it was empty, especially considering the state the two desks were in. We were definitely going to have to work on organizing Jasper's office. That level of disorganized chaos, I quickly found, did not allow for me to concentrate on my manuscript.

I wouldn't be able to accomplish anything in the clutter, so I decided to look around the rest of the house. I knew it was a three-bedroom rental. I also knew that both beds in the house were blissfully comfortable because Jasper fucked me on both many times. Other than the office and master bedroom, the house didn't look lived in. Jasper had nice furniture throughout the house, but that was it. There weren't any personal touches anywhere. No pictures, no knick-knacks, nothing. Maybe he either didn't like them or just didn't have any. I wasn't sure.

I'd been to his dads' house. It was huge, but it was *lived in.* It was a home. This appeared to be a place for Jasper to sleep and work. What exactly did that mean? Did Jasper like his life so simplistic that there was no room for anyone permanent? What effect would that have on us? Were we going to be something more?

Unpacking and looking around Jasper's house took a lot longer than I'd anticipated because before I knew it, Jasper was walking in the door with a pizza box with a small bag on top. I hoped there were breadsticks in that bag. I wanted to run over and kiss him but I still wasn't sure what he'd be comfortable with so I just stayed where I stood and watched him. He walked over to me and did exactly what I wanted. He kissed me. It was sweet and tender, and so unlike most of Jasper's previous kisses.

Grasping for anything to say, I blurted out the first thing that came to mind and cringed at how domestic it sounded. "Welcome home. How was work?"

"Damn, I knew I should've shouted 'honey, I'm home' when I opened the door."

I shrugged. I knew I sounded lame. "Sorry, Jasper, I'm just a little nervous. A little unsure right now."

"Why don't we eat pizza and breadsticks and we'll talk about that. Alright?"

"Sounds good. Did you want me to get drinks and plates?"

"That'd be great. I need to put my bag down in the office anyway. Thanks."

When Jasper came back out of the office, I had the plates and drinks already on the table. This wasn't the first meal we shared together so I didn't know why it felt so different; why I felt so unsure. Jasper seemed aware of how I was feeling because he walked to me and hugged me. "Relax. You're here and I'm thrilled. I want you here. Now that you're here, I'm not letting you go so get used to it." I felt goosebumps forming on my skin when he whispered in my ear. He gave me a knee-buckling kiss. If he hadn't had his arms wrapped tightly around me, I bet I'd have fallen. "That's a better welcome home kiss. Now, are you ready to eat?"

All I could do was nod because he once again rendered me speechless. When we sat down to eat we talked about

Jasper's day from hell and about my day spent unpacking and putting off to reorganize the office.

Jasper put his slice of pizza on his plate and looked straight into my eyes. "Not that I'm complaining, but what made you decide to come back to Crooked Bend so soon? How long are you planning on staying this time?"

"Didn't you already ask me that last night?"

Jasper looked perplexed, but nodded. "Yeah, I did, and I told you that I wanted you here always and you said *done*." Ahh. That's why he was perplexed. He wasn't sure what I meant.

I let that sink in for a little bit before I answered Jasper. He said he wanted me there and I knew I wanted to be there with him so hopefully he was serious and would let me stay. If not, I didn't have any foreseeable problems with getting my own place for a while. I knew I could find a place in Jackson. That was a hell of a lot closer to Jasper than Seattle was.

"You're here to stay then? Don't tease, Liam. I'm serious. I want you to be with me. *Here* with me. I know it's fast, but I'm willing to go all in. I hope this means you are too."

"I want to be here with you. I talked to Rhett and he really helped me clear up some things. He made some really good points. Life is short and so unpredictable, Jasper, and we never know what's going to happen tomorrow. Like Rhett said, if we have a chance at something, we should take it. It's not like we're both kids just out of school. I'm twenty-five and you're thirty. We're more established in our careers and I hope I didn't misread things when I say we're both looking for a long-term, serious commitment."

"You didn't misread my intentions, Liam. We're both looking for the same thing. I've never been in a relationship before but with you, there is something about you that won't let me let you go. There's so much I want with you. I'm more than willing to talk about all of it after dinner if you like. We can sit on the couch or cuddle in bed and talk. I'm good with either."

"After dinner works for me. I have to call Rhett though. He made me promise to call him later this evening."

"That's perfect because I needed to call and see if I could talk to Travis for a few minutes, anyway. His cousin is an architect and I wanted to see if he was looking for a new job in a new location, specifically Jackson." Jasper couldn't contain a small laugh; he knew how ridiculous that sounded. But, if they were considering hiring a third architect, that was a good thing. It meant that they were busy and if they had a third architect, Jasper would have more free time.

"That works for me. We'll do that after dinner and then settle down for a chat."

My call was a success. Rhett was happy for both me and Jasper and promised to not tell anyone until we were sure things were going the way we expected. Travis promised to talk to his cousin Collin and give him contact information for the brothers. He was currently working for a firm in Alabama and wasn't happy there so it was promising that he'd be willing to relocate.

I managed to get Jasper into the shower for a long, hot shower. After, we decided to chat in bed. It was warm and comfortable. It wasn't like we weren't going to end up there anyway, so why not? Although I really wasn't expecting the conversation to go the direction it did.

Jasper started us off. "About that *all in* comment I mentioned earlier, what do you think?"

"Well..." Nothing like a pregnant pause to build up the suspense. I giggled when Jasper fidgeted, waiting for my answer. "As I said earlier, I'm all in too, Jasper. I packed up my apartment, turned in the keys, and moved to Wyoming."

"You packed up your apartment and left?" Jasper seemed surprised by this. I nodded and he continued. "Okay, you know this house is a rental. We can stay here, or, and I know it's insanely fast, but what do you think about buying a house? Together. It's a huge step. I'm fully aware. If you're unsure, I'm still going to buy a house. I'll want you with me, even if you aren't ready to commit to buying a house. I want something bigger and more modern. Nothing too crazy but something between here and Jackson would be great. Sean and I have discussed opening a satellite office here in Crooked Bend because the trip to Jackson in the winter can be dangerous, or even impossible sometimes." He paused there. I think he was giving me time to process it. After what he thought was an appropriate amount of time, he continued. "What do you think? Would it be something you might be interested in?"

"Wow, that's so not where I expected this to go." I lifted my head and looked at him, face-to-face. "It's not that I don't want a commitment. I do. I really do. You're so much more established in your career than I am and I don't know that I'd be able to contribute much toward buying a house, Jasper. I have some savings, but you've had more time than I have, and I've been on my own since I was eighteen so everything I've gotten was all on my own and that hasn't really given me a whole lot of time to build up my savings. I'm sorry." By the end of my unfortunate response, I couldn't look Jasper in the eye.

I wasn't ashamed of what I did, nor was I unhappy. I just didn't come from the same type of family as Jasper. I didn't have the same privileges he did growing up. I sure as hell didn't have the capital to be able to afford to purchase a house. I'd only been out of college for three years. Sure, I started writing full time my sophomore year. I'd been publishing books for five years, but I definitely wasn't an architect.

Jasper gently placed a finger under my chin and lifted my face to his. "Hey now, look at me. Seriously, none of that. I didn't ask you because I expected or wanted you to pay for half of the house. Sean, Rhett, and I all have a trust that we can use for that. It was given to us by Dad's parents. I asked because I wanted to know if you wanted to move into a house we could call ours. A home we pick out together. One we can add your furniture to if you want. One that we'll live in together. And, if Sean's rules are to be adhered to, one that has a fireplace. I guess he and Simon use their fireplace a hell of a lot." Jasper smirked at me.

"That sounds perfect. My furniture will be here later this week. I was going to put it into storage until I found somewhere to live if you didn't want me here. I don't know what you had in mind for size of a house, but I don't have a whole lot, anyway. My Seattle apartment was a one-bedroom, and it was full with my things."

"Great! I'll contact the Realtor and see what she has on her radar. I want us to pick it together, okay? It's going to be your home, too. You have just as much say in what we choose as I do, alright?"

"Alright."

Jasper's mood seemed to lighten up a little. He tightened his grip on me and opened his mouth to talk. "Now, you were gone an entire week, exhausted last night, but it's still early and I've this little trouble, well, maybe not *that* little, that I bet you know just how to fix." Jasper rolled over a bit and thrust his hips upward, pressing his steel-hard shaft against my thigh.

"Little issue? Cupcake, I wouldn't say there is anything little about you, at all. You're right though, I know just how to fix it." Without wasting another single minute, I dove under the covers to get reacquainted with Jasper's *little issue.*

17

JASPER

*K*nowing that Liam and I were in a committed, exclusive relationship made me think about a lot of things. He knew I had a past, just like I knew he had one before me. I believed my past was so much worse than his. I hoped it wouldn't be a deal breaker for us. In order for us to be able to truly commit to each other, I felt that I needed to let him know about Rupert and the fallout from that. With that in mind, I set about the best way to approach the difficult conversation.

I knew the sooner we talked the better. The more time I spent with him, the more attached I became and the less I'd be willing to give him up. I figured after a nice dinner I could breach the subject. I made sure to leave work early enough to stop at the store. I had to get some supplies to cook Liam's favorite meal, chicken Alfredo. I knew it wasn't going to be nearly as good as what he was used to getting in Seattle, but I was going to give it my best effort. Hopefully I'd get some points for that.

Dinner turned out to be pretty good thanks to the Food Network app on my phone. Liam thoroughly enjoyed it. I already knew he had a thing for garlic bread sticks so I stopped and picked up a double order of them from the Italian place in town. My guy truly loved bread sticks. I had to chuckle about that. After dinner, I refilled our wine glasses and took the bottle to the living room. I situated myself on the couch and prepared to tell Liam what it was that I needed to. I hoped and prayed that this didn't backfire on me. For the first time in my life, I wanted a relationship. I know I'd asked Rupert if we could be in a relationship, but now, a decade later, I realize that I didn't want a relationship with him. He was my first and the nature of our arrangement definitely wasn't healthy.

Once Liam joined me on the couch, my stomach roiled and it took effort to keep dinner down. Maybe we should've done this before we ate. I couldn't remember the last time I was this nervous. Liam seemed to pick up on it because he was asking me if I was alright. I should be asking him that. I probably would be by the time I was finished.

Liam frowned and scooted close to me. "Are you okay? You seem a little nervous. You know we don't have to do this if you don't want to. We both know we had a past before. We don't have to do this. I'm okay with leaving the past in the past and going on from when we met."

"I know, and I appreciate that, but I need to clear the air on some shitty things in my past. If I don't, it's always going to be in the back of my mind bothering me. I just hope, by the time I'm finished, you still want to be with me."

Liam pulled back. He looked upset. "Seriously, Jasper? You think that hearing about the guys you've slept with will make me want to not be with you? I know you were, as Rhett put it, a *complete commitment phobe who brought several guys home each month.*"

I couldn't help the snort that came out of my mouth at

hearing the phrase several guys each month. I knew it was way more than just several guys each month. "We'll get to that in just a bit, alright? For now, I want to start at the beginning. One that started while Sean and I were at university. Growing up, we went to private school. After graduation, we enrolled directly into a university. I had my first sexual encounters while in college. I wouldn't call myself a late bloomer." I chuckled. "I was quite acquainted with my hand, as well as toys, but I hadn't found a guy that I wanted sexually until I saw Rupert for the first time.

"Rupert wasn't what you would've thought I'd be attracted to. He was one of the architecture professors. He was older, well into his forties, sophisticated, and very commanding. I made it known immediately that I found him attractive. He didn't return my interest at first. I tried for months and months to get his attention but, nothing. Then, one day right before winter break, he asked me to meet him in his office during office hours to discuss my final assignment. I worked hard on that assignment and was worried about my grade so I was nervous when I went to his office during the allotted time."

"He didn't want to talk about your assignment, did he?" Liam asked when I paused to think about how best to describe what was about to happen in Rupert's office.

"No, he didn't. When I got there he got up and locked the office door while I sat. That made me so nervous. After he sat behind his desk, he stared at me for the longest time. I later came to realize that he was stroking his cock through his pants to get it hard while looking at me. I noticed what he was doing when he told me to get up and come to him on the other side of the desk. He pointed to the floor and commanded me to get on my knees and suck him off.

"Without a single objection, I did. I'd been so enamored

with him for the past four months that I didn't really think anything of it. It was the first time I'd given anyone a blowjob and according to him it was okay but needed work. He was willing to train me but I had to keep quiet about it. Being the young, naive, horny eighteen-year-old that I was, I readily agreed. What I didn't realize was what exactly I was agreeing to. That day in his office I agreed, without knowing, to become his submissive, his sex toy.

"For two years I thought that what Rupert and I were doing was what I wanted. For two years I let him do just about everything imaginable to me. About a year into our 'agreement,' he started asking me to top him. It was the first time I was ever allowed to top, and I loved it. I thought that meant that he loved me and I was sure I loved him by that point. I was wrong. So, so wrong. For a year, I was at his beck and call and fucked him after he took me roughly. I thought that's how it worked. I thought that was just how our relationship worked.

"I found out that it wasn't a relationship at all. The house he always told me to meet him at? He rented it under another name. I was just one of many of his students who he was fucking. We didn't know about each other because we were only ever allowed to come to the house on our assigned day. There were only a few he let fuck him, and I was one of them, but that didn't mean anything. It just meant I had a big enough dick for him. When I asked him two years in if we could take our relationship to the next level and come out together as a couple, he laughed at me and told me we weren't in a relationship at all.

"That's when I found out he was married to a woman. She was from what you'd call old money. He popped out a few kids with her and kept her happy enough that she didn't really care that he *taught night classes* when in truth he was fucking several of his students while he was supposedly teaching. Anyway, after he tied me to his bed and fucked me with so little lube that I was quickly sore, then rode me until I was completely spent and lost my erection, for whatever reason I thought it would be a good time to ask about our relationship. I was wrong."

Liam seemed tremendously upset with what I was telling him, but not upset with me. He was upset *for* me. "What happened? Were you alright? You said he fucked you raw, as in without lube or it took so long that you got sore? You know what? Never mind. Forget I asked because I really don't need to know."

"I don't mind telling you. It was both. He was fond of using very little lube when topping and using none when bottoming. He liked pain and didn't care if his partners did or not. Since I was so young, it wasn't difficult to get me hard, nor for me to stay hard once he put a cock ring on me. The point is he used me, just like he used everyone else. He was a closet gay that was only interested in himself and what he wanted. When I found out he was married, I just about puked. I'd never knowingly cheat or be the *other person*. That really messed with my head. That part affected me deeper than knowing he'd used other students like he'd used me. He liked students that were young and gullible. I was both.

"I'd heard enough and stood to leave. He grabbed me and wouldn't let me. He'd gotten rough with me over the past two years but never like that. He tried to force me to give him a blowjob before I left and I told him no, that I was finished and we were through. I tried again to leave and he grabbed me again. This time he punched me on the side of the head and told me we were only through when he said so and then again demanded a blowjob. Since he'd hit me, I fell to my knees. When I was knocked off balance and he grabbed my chin and tried to shove his dick in my mouth, I reached up and grabbed his balls and twisted, hard. He screamed like a stuck pig and let go. He fell to the floor. I managed to get out of the room and dressed enough to leave."

I stopped talking. I needed a break, and I needed some more courage. I downed another glass of wine in several large gulps, I looked over to Liam to see if I could gauge his reaction to what I'd just told him. The last thing I expected was to see tears in his eyes. Worried about him, I shakily reached for his arm and asked what was wrong. I was worried he was disgusted and upset but he completely shocked me when he told me how he was feeling.

"Oh, Jasper. None of that was your fault. You were young and naive, just like you said. You didn't really know what he was doing," Liam told me while giving me a tight hug.

"Yeah, but that's not the worst part of my history, Liam. Because of the betrayal that Rupert put me through, I refused to commit to anyone for the next ten years. I've been with lots and lots of men, Liam. And I do mean lots. I've never let another man dominate me like that again and I only ever fuck men once, maybe twice if they're really good and then that's it. I've become him. I used men for my own pleasure."

"Tell me something, Jasper. Did you tell any of those men you hooked up with that you were looking for anything other than just that, a hook up?"

"No, I was always very upfront about what we were doing. I always let them know it was for one night and one night only and that was it. They all seemed okay with that."

"Then what's the problem? They knew the situation and still participated. Is it because there had been so many?"

"In part, yes. That doesn't bother you?"

"Well, you were safe, right? You're tested regularly, right?"

"Yes. Plus, I've always used a condom; even with Rupert we always used condoms. I've gotten tested every four to six months. I'm on PrEP, just because you never know. Condoms break. Things happen and it is better to be safe than sorry. Better to *be prepared*." I put up the first three fingers of my right hand in a Boy Scout salute when I quoted their slogan.

"So you're negative then?"

"I've always tested negative. My last test was in December, right before I met you and the results were negative then as well. Since I first saw you, I haven't even wanted another man, let alone *been* with one."

"Then I don't see what the problem is. You have a past, Jasper. For ten years, you slept with lots and lots of men. As long as you keep it to you and me while we're in this relationship and nobody else, then just leave the past in the past. You said you would never knowingly cheat. Well, don't cheat on me. That is the deal breaker in my book. No cheating? No problem. If I catch you cheating on me, I'll castrate you like you tried to do to Rupert."

I couldn't help but cringe and cover my balls when Liam threatened that. I happened to be quite fond of them and prefer them right where they are. I wouldn't give him any reason to do anything of the sort. I was with Liam by choice. I wanted to be in a relationship with him and only him.

I was a little behind my brother Sean. He'd done the same as me last summer, He'd grown tired of the countless number of hook-ups and one-night stands. Finally, I was tired of the clubs and the barely legal boys that didn't know what the hell they were doing. I wanted something permanent. I wanted something stable. I wanted quiet dinners at home, and long soaks in the tub. I wanted to binge-watch *Game of Thrones* while cuddling on the couch. I wanted all of that, but only Liam. I know I've only known him for a few months, but just like when Dad met Papa and Sean met Simon, I knew. He was it for me, my choice, and my chance.

I'd waited too long to get a taste of him. I grabbed Liam around the waist and pulled him onto my lap. He willingly followed, quickly straddling my legs. Once I placed one hand at the nape of his neck, the other cupping his cheek, I pulled his lips to mine and got my taste. He tasted exactly like I expected. Like garlic bread sticks, red wine, and something else that was just Liam. "How did I ever get so lucky to find a guy like you?"

18

LIAM

I would never get enough of Jasper's kisses. Whether they were gentle and sweet or an all-consuming claiming, I'd never say no to them. He had kissing down. He knew how to do it. Lucky me! I was the one he was kissing. But, I knew it was a night to come clean. I knew that I needed to tell him about my past. After all, he told me about his, it was only fair that he heard about mine. He knew about Mike, but he didn't know about my other boyfriends. Or any of the hook-ups in between. He needed to. He needed to know that I hadn't been an angel, and that I wasn't as inexperienced as it seemed he thought I was. With great reluctance, I pulled away from the jock strap melting kiss and crawled off of his lap.

"Hey, come back here," Jasper said while reaching for me when I crawled to the other end of the couch.

I shook my head and pushed his hands away. "Not yet. You talked, now I get to."

Of course, Jasper took the high ground and didn't want me to feel compelled to tell him about my past. "Liam, you don't have to. I wanted you to know about my past because I wanted to be sure you could live with it. I don't care about your past. You're here now and to me, that's all that matters."

I knew, however, that I needed to get things off my chest, too. Full disclosure. "I felt the same about your past, Jasper. It didn't matter to me but I listened when you told me your story. Now I'm going to insist that you hear about mine. Sit there and listen, okay?" The last thing I wanted was to get pushy, but I could if I needed to. Rhett told me to make sure that I didn't let Jasper steamroll me. This was me keeping control. He got to talk, now it was my turn.

"You already know about my parents and how they dumped me when I went to college at seventeen." Jasper acknowledged with a nod. It was a topic we breached after Rhett had been kidnapped. He didn't interrupt so I continued. "Well, what I didn't say at the time was that, they dropped me off with just my bags for college and about a thousand dollars cash and told me that they'd done their part and kept me alive. They were adamant that I needed to be straight for them. Since I wasn't, they disowned me. They called me an abomination. *An abomination!* They seemed to have a complete unabridged dictionary of derogatory names for me and used every one of them. There was no way *they* could have a gay son. They had been disappointed enough when I turned out to be so much smaller than my father and look less masculine. When they found out I'm gay and was never going to marry the girl they picked out for me it was more than they would tolerate. I was dumped off at the front of the college and haven't heard from or talked to them since then. That is perfectly fine with me though. I felt lucky enough and was thankful that they at least took me to the college before dumping me. They could've just kicked me out onto the streets and they didn't.

"I went to the admin office to see what I could do about changing my degree and to ensure I could keep my room in the dorm. I was fortunate and won a scholarship that covered almost all of my tuition and boarding. I'd already lined up a work-study gig in the library, without my parents knowing. It would cover what the scholarship didn't. Because of all of that, because my parents disowned me, I was on my own from that point to this. Being alone and without real help, I started writing. At first just little short stories. After those, I got into fan-fiction-type stories. Then I advanced and wrote my first novella. To date I have over twenty novels that follow Officer Swanson, Detective Holloway, and their associates. I make a very comfortable living but I'm still frugal.

"Now you have the back story, but it doesn't tell you about how I went a little crazy in college. When someone is stifled for so long, and they're finally given freedom, I did what a lot of people do, I went the complete opposite of stifled and went overboard. I carried a reputation for being easy. There were always guys looking for a quick fuck or blow job and I was *always* ready and willing." I stopped because of the shocked look on Jasper's face. I guess he really did think I was an angel or something.

"Did you really think I'd only ever had sex with the three boyfriends you heard about? Think again, Cupcake." I paused before continuing. "That's not the point though. The point is, I've had threesomes and foursomes, and I was a willing participant in a couple of orgies. All kinds of freakiness goes on at some of those frat parties and I was always looking to party.

"After about a year, I decided that life wasn't really what I wanted. My grades started slipping and that meant my scholarship could be in jeopardy. I quit partying cold turkey.

I started focusing on school and on my writing. My channeled energy and frustration enabled me to come up with my best-selling characters."

Jasper gasped. He looked like he was having a really hard time wrapping his head around what I was telling him. "Wait a minute, you're telling me that you've slept with more than the three guys I thought you slept with?" I thought his head was going to explode. His face turned red and he looked like he was constipated for lack of a better word.

His reaction made me angry. No, I was *pissed*. "What? You're allowed to have a past and I'm not? That's a little hypocritical, isn't it?"

He looked at me with a blank stare, this time. "That's not it. I'm just...processing."

I wasn't in the mood to calm down, but I forced myself to, anyway. "Well, process in a hurry, because I'm not finished."

He took several deep breaths and his puce face turned a light pink before he spoke. "Alright, go on."

I looked at him to be sure he was ready for me and started back up. "As I was *saying*, I calmed down and refocused. A few months later, I had my first real relationship. It lasted six whole months, but it was just the two of us. He moved on to someone who was *a little more fun*. Those were his words, not mine. I spent the next year without a boyfriend. I didn't go out looking for, any hook ups, either. One day while I was re-shelving books at the library, I met my second boyfriend. He was lost and was trying to find a book. I later found out that he used the story as a cover to talk to me. I spent the next year with him until we both graduated. After graduation, I went to Seattle to live and work and he went on to grad school in California. We tried to make things work. Well, *I* did. He was in California with lots of willing guys. He decided I wasn't there, wasn't willing to move there, so he'd just sleep with those willing guys. There went dirt-bag number two." I stopped for a minute to gauge Jasper's facial expressions before continuing.

"I stayed single for the next year, working my ass off at a local bookstore while writing full time. I finally found someone willing to take a chance on my manuscript and things took off from there. I kept the job at the bookstore for a little longer as a precaution. I met Mike at the bookstore. We were together for almost two years before I met Rhett. For those first two years, he was a great boyfriend.

"There were signs but I just ignored them. There were times he'd get a little rough with sex, but he'd always apologize afterwards and say he was sorry that he got carried away. I always believed him. He was 'out' to his co-workers but he didn't want them to know that he was dating me so I was never invited to any of his work functions. He always went with 'friends.'" I used finger quotes for the end of my sentence.

"Are you saying that the people he took were more than friends?" Jasper asked after I mentioned Mike and all of the times he took another guy, Chris, to his work functions instead of me.

"Yeah, I imagine they probably were." I shook my head. "I *know* they were. Like with the roughness, there were signs that things weren't what I thought they were. There were several times that Chris would be over at Mike's place when I got there. Mike always wanted to leave as soon as I arrived, to head to my apartment instead of staying at his. There were even times he wouldn't let me in his apartment when the two of them were there together. Thinking back, that's probably because they had just fucked in Mike's bed and he didn't have a chance to change the sheets yet. Chris was openly bi and in a relationship with a woman. I think Mike saw that as a challenge. He was one of those men who believed you were either gay or you weren't; that a person couldn't like both. I didn't know that at first. He probably fucked Chris any chance he got."

"You and Mike never lived together?"

"No, I always had my own place and he always had his. Like I said, there were signs that things weren't right, but I chose to ignore them."

"I agree. There was a real possibility that he was fucking Chris. Don't be hard on yourself. It happens. I can tell you this, Liam. I'll *never* cheat on you. Ever. That's not who I am. I want you to know that right now."

I smiled up at my new boyfriend. "I believe you, Jasper."

"When did things go bad? You said it had something to do with Rhett?"

"Yeah. Up until I met Rhett, Mike got all of my attention when I wasn't working. When I met your brother, we clicked so well and became friends, I started hanging out with him in the evenings. Rhett and I'd go to the movies or we'd order pizza and hang out and watch crap TV or play video games. Mike turned overbearing and controlling when I wasn't available every time he wanted to see me in the evenings. The more controlling he got, the more abusive he got.

"I tried my best to deal with his abrupt personality change for several more months. I didn't even break up with him until he beat me unconscious because Rhett and I wanted to go see a play. I was so lucky that Rhett found me.

"I couldn't remember what happened to put me in the hospital. I remember having an argument with Mike about going to the movies with Rhett and then he hit me and then nothing. I woke up in the hospital, Rhett was there with me. He found me when he came by so we could go to the movies. That was my wake-up call though. I told Mike we were through when I saw him next. I hadn't heard from nor seen him for about a month when he forced his way into my apartment and beat and raped me. Again, Rhett found me. That time, I remembered everything until I was knocked unconscious. I pressed charges when I once again woke up in the hospital. The rest you know, because I ran here to Wyoming two weeks later." After all of that, I really needed a drink. A strong one, I wondered if Jasper had anything.

I felt my head spinning and my mouth turn dry. "By chance, do you happen to have anything stronger than the wine to drink? I could use a shot of something."

"I've got some scotch if you want. That's all I have though."

"That works."

"Alright, I'll be right back in a sec."

While Jasper was in the kitchen to get my drink, I took several deep breaths and thought about everything we disclosed. It was a lot. A whole hell of a lot. Most of it was ugly. I did admit that it was refreshing and quite cleansing to get things out in the open. I only prayed that Jasper could get past my former indiscretions as easily as I could his. If he couldn't, there would be no us. He came back with two tumblers and a bottle of high-end scotch. He poured us each one and then held his up so I did the same. What he said both shocked and delighted me.

"Here's to the past, and to leaving it there like you said we should. Here's to the future. Our future, together. We both have made the choice to go into this all in and with our eyes wide open. Here's to us, Liam." He clinked his glass to mine and threw back his shot of scotch. I did the same and then did the only think I could think of. I threw myself at him and attacked his mouth, his neck, anything I could reach.

Jasper picked me up easily and walked us to the bedroom with me wrapped around him. Once there, clothes seemed to fall off and we proceeded to show each other just how much we wanted each other.

19
JASPER

Life was amazingly good when you shared it with someone. It didn't take long for Liam and me to find a routine. He'd never lived with someone before but I had, even if it was with my brother and we *definitely* didn't share a bedroom past our university years. I didn't have any issues whatsoever with sharing a room with Liam. To tell the truth, I rather enjoyed it. It was nice to have someone to eat dinner with. I enjoyed having someone to talk to when I came home from work. It was wonderful having someone to sleep with and wake up next to. Because Liam worked from home, I made sure we had plenty of evenings out of the house. On the weekends, we always made plans to go places and do things.

There was always something to do in Jackson, so that's where we spent a lot of our time. I found it ironic. After all, I'd left Jackson in order to get away from the club scene and everything that went with it.

Liam and I didn't visit clubs. I'd asked him once if he wanted to go and he said no. I left it at that. We spent a lot of time on various ski slopes in the area. Growing up in Seattle gave Liam plenty of opportunity to ski, and he'd taken it.

We put off looking for a house because we kept busy with work and outings. There really was no rush, but after discussing it more than once, it was something that we agreed we wanted to do, eventually. We even discussed the possibility of having a little cabin built for us. There was plenty of time to decide. We enjoyed hunkering down in the little rental house outside of Crooked Bend.

Spring arrived, and with it warmer weather. It was still cold, but no longer freezing unless you were on the slopes. With the warmer weather came more work. People didn't understand that in order to get plans drawn up, you had to allow time. We were already loaded down with a steady stream of work, but in the spring, things became hectic. We *really* needed a third architect.

Simon asked me if he could take Sean away for a week or two in a few weeks before things became too crazy out at the ranch. I guess the stress Cammie put on him to plan the wedding was getting to him, and Sean needed a break, too. We managed to hire a full-time office manager, but Travis' cousin Collin was under contract and couldn't join our firm until around mid-July so that meant it was up to Sean and me until then. Since it was still only just the two of us, that meant I'd be the one running the show when Sean was away so I was looking at extra-long hours for a week or two.

I had seen the amount of stress Sean was feeling and I couldn't say no. I knew he and Simon needed to get away for a bit.

Of course, no Sean meant longer hours at the office. I didn't like the idea of being away from Liam so much. Not only did Simon and Sean not know that I was in a relationship with Liam, we weren't exactly sure how to tell them. We weren't hiding. After all, Rhett knew. We went out and about all over Jackson doing things.

When it came to Sean, I had a mental block that kept me from telling my twin that I was falling in love. We shared almost everything; we didn't keep secrets for the most part —until Liam. I didn't know if I could handle seeing the disappointment or wariness in Sean's eyes when I told him. Since Rupert, I'd only ever had meaningless hookups. Liam was so much more than that. He was my everything. If Sean didn't approve, it would destroy me because I knew I'd choose Liam.

Because I was about to become insanely busy, I told Sean I was taking a long weekend. It might seem unfair to Sean at first, but he didn't know what Simon planned for the two of them. Liam and I deserved three days alone without phone calls and email interrupting us. I booked a room at one of the ski resorts. It seemed odd since we lived right there, but I wanted to take him away for the weekend. With short notice, I didn't have much time to plan. I stumbled through planning a romantic weekend staycation. All I had to do now was go home and tell Liam.

Just like always, when I arrived home that evening, Liam was in the office, glued to his laptop typing away. I learned early on to not interrupt. When I interrupted, he got pissed. When he got pissed, his inner-diva came out. When his inner diva came out, I was in trouble. Who knew that my little imp was so sassy? I sure didn't, until I interrupted him one evening. He didn't take too kindly to me interrupting his train of thought right in the middle of writing a steamy scene between Micah and Nolan. I didn't realize at the time that his two characters were also in a relationship together. I more than made up for it when I dragged Liam to the floor of the office and showed him exactly what his two characters could get up to.

Instead of having a pissed-off boyfriend, I diverted myself to the kitchen to fix dinner. I wasn't nearly the cook Rhett was, or even Sean, but I did okay. Hopefully, if I made Liam's favorite, the smells of garlic and chicken would bring him out of his writing cave. If not, I'd have to bribe him with garlic bread sticks. If *that* didn't work, I could always just throw him over my shoulder. Come to think of it, that wasn't a bad idea.

I hadn't really gotten overly dominant with him in the bedroom yet. I didn't want to force the issue, nor did I want to cause any negative memories to resurface. I hadn't pushed the subject even though Liam had hinted that he wanted to try to do some of the things we'd discussed early in our relationship. Maybe this weekend would be the perfect time to explore that side.

"Something smells good in here." Liam approached me and kissed me on the shoulder. "When did you get home?" Liam then reached up, pulled my head down, and kissed me on the lips.

"Let's see." I put my finger to my chin and looked up as though I had to calculate time. "I've been home long enough to peek in on you in the office, then I came in here to cook dinner. About a half hour I guess. Did you finish whatever you were frantically typing?"

"Yep, I sure did! What's even better is that I've got this new idea for some spin-off characters. They're super chatty right now so I'm just going to go with it. As long as they're chatting, I'm going to be glued to my laptop typing. I should get a ways into the story this weekend if I keep at it. That will work out great because I've really wanted to come up with new characters for a while."

That was the absolute last thing I wanted to hear. I had plans for this weekend and I hoped that Liam would agree with them. I couldn't ask if he needed to work. I knew it was important to him. I just smiled and turned back to the Alfredo sauce, hoping it hadn't burned.

My silence didn't go unnoticed, though. "Hey, what's up?"

I shook my head and gave him a noncommittal answer. "Nothing, just finishing up dinner. Why do you ask?"

Liam stood back and fisted his hands on his waist. "Maybe because after living with you for almost three months, I know you? I know that was a fake smile. What gives?"

I took in a couple deep breaths before I answered Liam's question. "Nothing gives. I just didn't realize you were working this weekend. I took tomorrow off so we could spend three days together, but since you're working, oomph." I didn't get my sentence finished, because I had one hundred and forty pounds of Liam in my arms after he jumped on me and started peppering me with kisses. My heart soared.

"I can finish next week, no problems. I have, like, four chapters and an epilogue to write, that's it. The new characters can definitely wait. Now what were you saying about a weekend together?"

I had no choice but to put Liam down, otherwise dinner would be ruined. I reluctantly set him on the counter next to me while I finished the pasta. The Alfredo sauce was done so dinner would be done when the pasta was.

"Let's talk over dinner, okay? For now, the short version. I took tomorrow off so we could go away for a few days. We aren't going far, just to one of the lodges in Jackson. I thought it would be nice to get away where nobody could bug us for a weekend."

Liam helped me plate the food and carry it to the table. Once we settled in, I told him what I planned, at least part of it. There were some things I wanted to surprise him with.

"Simon called me today. Sean's really stressed out about the wedding and everything at work. He wants to take Sean away for a week or two soon. I told him sure. That means in a few weeks I'm going to be really busy with work. I told Sean I was taking tomorrow off. I want to spend the weekend with you. I know a weekend away won't make up for how long Sean's going to be gone, but I've noticed how stressed he is. He needs this."

Liam reached over and palmed his hand over the back of mine. "Hey, don't worry about it. I completely understand. There is no way I could ever plan a wedding. Just the thought makes me cringe. When you are working those long hours, I'll work long hours, too! I need to keep going on those supporting characters my readers are asking about. It'll work out great for both of us."

I looked at my perfect little understanding imp. "Are you sure? I know things have already started picking up and I'm already not spending as much time with you as I want."

Liam gave me a million-dollar grin and nodded, his blond hair flopping over his forehead. "It really is okay and I understand. I know things will get better once the new architect arrives in July. You always make sure you're home early enough that we can talk before you pass out." Liam smirked as he made his last statement. I caught on right away and couldn't help teasing right along with him.

"Pass out, is it? Is that what we're calling it now?"

"Hey, you know how it is for men of your advanced years, Cupcake."

"Advanced years? Are you implying that I'm old, Liam? I'm going to make you pay this weekend for every time you've called me *Cupcake*. You've been warned you little imp." I gave Liam's lips a small kiss. I loved our banter. It was comfortable, fun, and enjoyable.

Liam's face lit up like I'd just promised him a month on the French Riviera. "Promise? I've been waiting for you to punish me, you know. Yet, my ass is still as unspanked as it's always been. Don't tease if you don't promise to follow through."

"Trust me, Liam. I plan on fulfilling all kinds of promises this weekend," I whispered in Liam's ear right before I walked off toward the kitchen to get another bottle of wine. When I came back, he was doing his fish impersonation once again. I was unprepared, for the second time that evening, for Liam to throw himself at me, but that's exactly what he did. We never got to that second bottle of wine.

20

LIAM

I won the lottery when I got Jasper for a boyfriend. At least, that was my opinion! I was happier than I'd ever been. It might not have seemed like a big deal to go away for the weekend and stay local, but it was the thought that counted. He was the first guy I ever dated that had done anything like that for me, ever. I thought it was fucking fantastic!

After an amazing night of slow, sweet, lovemaking, we got up early to pack and drive to the slopes. We had gone skiing and snowboarding a few times over the past couple of months, but this time would be different. Personally, I was more a skier than snowboarder, but Jasper preferred to snowboard. I was learning, but it was slow going. Since it was already well into spring, my days of practicing with a snowboard were numbered. Not only was the weather warming up, but Jasper was about to get insanely busy with work.

For now, I would enjoy what would probably be the last time we were on the slopes until late in the fall. I knew going into the relationship that Jasper would be busier in the summer months than the winter. That didn't mean he wasn't busy in the winter, though. Architecture was a full-time job. Sean and Jasper spent the winter months designing and working on inside construction. Summer and early fall was when they included any outside construction. My boyfriend was about to become incredibly busy.

After a day spent on the slopes, I was more than ready for our ensuite hot tub. When Jasper told me we were going to a lodge, I didn't realize he'd booked one of the higher-end rooms. We had a massive king-size bed just like we did at home, with our very own private hot tub out on our private patio. I had quite a few plans for *that* amenity. First, a good, long, soak seemed the most appropriate action. I think I spent more time on my ass than I did on the snowboard so I really wanted to soak my sore muscles.

We stopped in the lodge's restaurant to eat dinner before retiring to our room. Once Jasper and I got back to the room, I told him I'd be in the hot tub if he wanted to join me. I left a trail of clothing along the way to my destination. I was just sitting down when an equally naked and quite excited Jasper joined me on the patio and climbed in. The moan he let out as he sunk down into the steaming water let me know I wasn't the only one that was sore. Good. I didn't think it would be fair if only one of us was suffering.

"Damn, this water feels amazing. I didn't realize how sore and tired I'd be after only a few hours of snowboarding," Jasper said once he laid his head back against the side of the tub.

Looking over at him, I couldn't resist poking a stick at him once again. "Must be your advanced age catching up with you," I said while doing my best to look completely innocent. It didn't work, but then again, I didn't expect it to either. I squeaked when Jasper reached over and grabbed me by the waist and hauled me onto his lap. My squeak quickly turned into a moan when my hard shaft met his equally hard one.

"What did I tell you about that?" Jasper asked with a playful gleam in his eyes.

"That you would make me pay for it? But, Cupcake, you still haven't so I don't think you'll do it. You're all bark and no bite. That's okay, I'm still crazy about you."

"If I hadn't just gotten in, I'd drag you to the bedroom and show you just how much I can *bite*. For now, I think I'll show you how dirty my mind has been all day while thinking about getting you into this hot tub."

I was aghast with feigned shock. "All afternoon? Why in the hell did you wait *all afternoon*? I've been ready to come back to the room for hours!"

Jasper stopped nibbling on my collarbone long enough to look up at me. "Why didn't you say something? I only planned on spending today on the slopes because I thought you enjoyed it. I want to spend the rest of the weekend here in the room ordering room service."

I shook my head. It was amazing to me. Why didn't we ever just communicate? We both did a lot of assuming. "I didn't say anything because I knew you love to snowboard. I prefer to ski. It's just easier for me. I didn't mind going. I had fun but the fun ended after a couple of hours of falling on my ass."

Jasper chuckled and inched even closer to me. "Liam, sweetheart, you should've said something. We could've left when you were ready to leave. I can't read your mind, although that'd probably be quite interesting. Please, in the future, speak up. Alright?"

"Okay, Jasper. Now that we have *that* cleared up, is it possible for you to go back to doing what you were doing? I rather liked it." I turned my head and presented my collarbone to Jasper so he would have easier access. He sure didn't need it; he always seemed to have no problems getting to parts of me he was after.

"Bossy bottom." He nudged his nose into my throat. "I like it. You know you're really asking for it? I promise, tonight, you're going to get it. For now, I'm going to go easy on you."

Jasper grabbed my ass and pulled our groins together hard. The water provided just enough to make things slippery, it sure wasn't nearly as good as lube. Things were a little floaty if we weren't pressed together tightly. Who was it that decided that sex in a hot tub was a good thing? I sure wasn't about to agree with them. Although, I wasn't going to complain about the things Jasper was doing to my neck. It was a major hot spot for me and he knew it.

After a few minutes of being frustratingly turned on, I pulled back from Jasper and looked into his eyes to ask if we could go inside. I wanted to take this to the next level, whatever that would be. I wanted to finish what we started so long ago. I was ready to finally get all of Jasper in the bedroom.

Jasper carefully stood up and I let my legs drop from around his waist. I had no doubts that he could have climbed out carrying me, but I didn't want to take any chances. It was so chilly! We quickly made our way in from the patio. I was a little surprised when Jasper pulled me into the bathroom instead of toward the bed.

"Let's shower first. Even though the hot tub is supposed to be clean, who really knows?"

I scrunched up my nose, thinking about what mystery bacteria may have been lingering in the outside Jacuzzi. "Eewww. Yeah, let's. I didn't even think about that!" I was happy to jump into the shower and get clean with Jasper. After all, it was *always* fun to get clean before I got dirty with him.

After a quick shower, we dried off and Jasper walked with me toward the bed. I was so excited, which was ridiculous because we'd had sex dozens of times over the past several months. This wasn't anything new. But for some reason, this time felt different.

"Are you sure this is what you want, Liam? Remember, this isn't necessary. You can change your mind or can stop at any time. Understand?"

"Yes, it's what I want, Jasper. I've been waiting for this. You're the one who kept saying *not yet.*"

"I want to make it clear that I want *you* no matter what, Liam. This isn't required, remember that."

I put my hands on Jasper's cheeks and held his face in place, pointing toward mine. "I remember. I know. I'm anxious and more than ready for this. However this goes, Jasper, I want this. I want you, with or without this. I'm *so* willing and now you've got me rambling so kiss me so I can shut up."

Thankfully Jasper obliged and I was able to stop talking. I hoped I didn't embarrass myself too much. My erection deflated just a touch, but was quickly back at full mast after just a few of Jasper's amazing kisses. He definitely did it for me. He never had any trouble arousing me. Hell, the man could make me cum by sucking on my neck. He had, several times.

Jasper stopped kissing me and I felt disappointed. He had some important things to tell me and I should be listening. "Alright, Liam. We have to set up some safe words. A good standard is red, yellow, and green. If you're okay with them, this is how they work. Just like a traffic light, red means stop, yellow means you need to slow down, and green means you are okay to continue. I'm going to ask you several times what color you are, if you don't answer, we stop, okay? The last thing I want to do is cause you any harm or pain. Understand?"

I hadn't even thought about *safe words* before, so I accepted what he was telling me. I was still processing all that Jasper had just said, so I just nodded. That wasn't what he wanted.

Jasper put his hands on my shoulders and guided my head up so I was looking into his face. "Nope, I need you to talk, Liam. I need to hear you say what you want. No nodding. Words, I need to hear them."

I inhaled a deep breath of air before answering. "Yes, I understand. Red-stop, yellow-wait, green-I'm good. I'm ready, Jasper."

"Alright then, if you're sure." Jasper walked over to a bag he'd brought and put it on the bed. "I want you on your back on the bed for me, Liam. Remember, you can stop at any time."

I did as he asked and walked to the bed and crawled into the center of the bed and flopped down on my back. I was beginning to feel tension and thought the flop would help lighten the mood. It worked because Jasper chuckled at me.

I couldn't see what Jasper was doing in his bag, but I noticed he was putting several things on the nightstand. Lube, check. Some sort of little black thing, check. Rope, check. Wait, rope? Did that mean?

Jasper must have seen the confused look on my face because he picked up that little black thing. "Alright, Liam, this is to make sure you last long enough to enjoy what we're about to do." I didn't know what it was. It just looked like a strip of leather.

"What *is* that?" I gave up trying to guess and asked.

"This? It's a Velcro adjustable cock ring. It'll make sure you don't cum before we get started, my little imp." With that, Jasper bent over and took my cock to the back of his throat. I couldn't contain the moan that emerged from my throat; it felt so good. All too soon, he popped his mouth off my head.

"Enough of that. Now that you're hard enough, let's get this on, shall we? Color, Liam."

"Green. Definitely green."

21

JASPER

When Liam gave me the green light, I had a fleeting thought to put the cock ring on myself instead. I was excited to finally get to play with him. We had a very healthy sexual relationship but I wanted to make sure he was comfortable with me and felt safe. I always wanted him to feel safe. I waited. Patiently. Because he was more than worth the wait. If playing around like this didn't work, then that was okay. I wanted Liam any way that he was comfortable.

Getting the cock ring on him was easy. I quickly had him strapped in. I moaned when I looked down at the sight before me. His cock was a beautiful thing to begin with, but when it was strapped in with his balls like that it was breathtaking. I needed another taste of him so I took one. Bobbing my head, moving my mouth up and down on his shaft, I don't know who moaned louder, me or him. I had so much skin to explore that night that I needed to get going. I could always come back if I wanted. I sure planned on it.

"Still green?"

"Yes, green."

"I want you to sit up and straddle my lap facing me," I told Liam. I got up and sat on the bench at the foot of the bed. Once Liam was on my lap, I pushed him away from my body a bit. I needed him to sit further back on my thighs for what I had planned. I spread my legs. That caused his to spread even more and left his ass open and exposed between my thighs. I distracted Liam by devouring his mouth and running my hands all over his body.

I wrapped my left arm around Liam's waist to hold him in place and snaked my right hand down to his firm ass and gave it a good squeeze. I ran my finger along his crease and applied a little pressure when I got to his hole but didn't stop to play there for long. No, I had a promise to keep, and I was going to fulfill it. Liam was plenty distracted. My lips and tongue kept moving continuously between his lips, to his neck, then his ear. Once I reached his neck, I gave a gentle bite at the same time I struck.

Smack!

Liam's yelp and startled look were my reward for spanking his no longer unspanked ass for the first time. I pulled back enough to look at him and the damn little imp smirked while saying one word.

"Green."

Green. He said green. I went back to rubbing all over his body distracting him again. I wrapped my hand around his red cock and started gently stroking it. In the midst of my stroke and his moan, I struck again.

Smack!

That time, Liam moaned after I swatted his ass so I immediately swatted him again.

Smack!

He whimpered before he moaned. The little imp

squirmed while he thrust his ass back toward my hand as much as he could.

"Green. Oh, God, green! More. Don't stop. Oh my God, Jasper. That feels fucking fantastic."

I was only too happy to oblige.

Smack!

Smack!

Smack!

"Jasper!" Liam panted. I looked down to see his cock turned an angry red as it twitched continuously. I knew he would cum if I hadn't strapped him in. That was the reason why I did. I wanted him to learn some self-control. He could go all night, having multiple orgasms and never seeming to tire out, but I wanted him to have one intense orgasm, not multiple great ones.

"Color, Liam."

"Green. Fuck me now, please. I need you!"

"Not yet. I'm not finished. We've only just started. There's so much more to do."

He wriggled on my lap, silently complaining before formulating a coherent sentence. "I need to cum, Jasper. Please."

I leaned forward and tongued his earlobe before whispering in his ear. "Not yet, sweetheart. I promised I'd make you pay for calling me Cupcake. This is the punishment."

Liam's eyes sparkled when he looked at me. "Does that mean every time I call you Cupcake, you'll spank me?"

I couldn't help myself. I busted out laughing. The look on Liam's face was one of pure mischief and excitement. My little imp loved getting his ass spanked and wanted to know how to get it spanked again. When I finally stopped laughing long enough to talk, I replied. "We'll see. We can probably arrange something."

I went back to nibbling Liam's neck and grabbed both ass cheeks with one hand and gave them a good squeeze. Liam's gasp let me know that he was well tenderized.

Smack!

Smack!

That was four swats per cheek. I couldn't wait to see how beautifully red they were. The moans and whimpers coming out of Liam's mouth were about to send me over the edge so I decided to move on to the next little event I planned for my troublemaker.

Grabbing Liam's ass again, I stood up and walked around to the side of the bed and released him onto the bed. Without warning, I flipped him over and lifted his hips so his ass was up in the air. At the same time, I gently pushed between his shoulder blades so he'd put his head down. What a beautiful view. He was perfect; his ass was rosy red, and his fluttering hole was just begging to be kissed. Before I grabbed both red cheeks and squeezed them, I tucked a pillow under his hips to help him with balance. The ass squeeze earned me another moan from Liam. I dove right in. I used my tongue to swipe upward, starting at Liam's balls and trailing all the way to the small of his back.

He loved being rimmed, and I was always pleased to oblige my imp. It always relaxed him and I needed him relaxed for what I planned. After tongue-fucking Liam's hole for several minutes, I inserted a spit-slick finger and went spelunking for his prostate. It didn't take long for me to find it. Liam gave me the sweetest yelp to let me know I hit the jackpot. I intended to give Liam the longest, most erotic foreplay session ever.

Finding the bottle of lube, after pulling my finger out of Liam, I poured a generous amount of lube onto my fingers and reinserted first one then two fingers into Liam's tight channel. When two fingers thrust in and out with ease, I added a third. After I had three fingers buried in Liam's ass, I flipped him over and took his leaking cock back into my mouth. The salty-sweet pre-cum seeping from his slit was what I was after, and I couldn't help but moan with his cock buried deep in my throat. Liam was a whimpering, quaking, begging mess by that point. I wanted to prepare him. I wanted him to go higher than he ever had before. With each whimper, with each plea, with each *green* that passed his lips, I needed him. I needed him to feel things he's never felt before. I needed to be the one to take him to new heights.

I pulled off his throbbing and pulsing cock. "Color, Liam." I didn't want to pull off, but I needed to know he was still okay.

"Green. Please. Please, Jasper. Please let me cum. I need to so bad. Please. Green!"

Liam begged. He'd be begging more before the evening was over. He'd cum, eventually. Multiple times if I had my way. I wasn't close to letting him cum, yet.

Smack!

Smack!

I gave his ass two quick smacks to bring some of the color back. His skin was so fair that it didn't take much to bring back the rosy color. Climbing off of the bed, I picked up the rope and held it up to show Liam.

"Color, Liam?"

After a few whimpers and several blinks, he weakly answered. "Green."

"I'm only going to tie your hands together, okay? Nothing else. Only together, not to anything. You're still going to be loose and able to move, alright?"

"Green, Jasper. Green, green, green. Just fuck me already, dammit!"

I grabbed Liam's hips and flipped him over quickly and gave his ass two more swats.

"Who's in charge here, Liam?"

"Fuck! Green! You are, Jasper. Please, fuck me already. I'm dying here."

I growled to let Liam know I was dissatisfied with him as he continued to ignore my command that he could not tell me what to do.

I watched Liam's ass as he started humping the pillow holding his hips elevated. That was exactly why I wanted him to have limited use of his hands. I didn't want him helping himself along. I'd give him everything he needed. He just needed to be patient and trust me.

Flipping him back over, I gave him a look and he had enough thought to look apologetic for his error.

"Now you know why I don't want you to use your hands. I promise, Liam. You are going to get to cum many times. Just be patient."

Liam had tears in his eyes when he answered me. "Okay, Jasper. Please. Green." My poor little imp was suffering so beautifully, but he wasn't asking me to stop, either.

When Liam provided another green light, I wrapped the rope around his wrists. I made sure they weren't too tight and that he could still wiggle his fingers. I did make sure it was tight enough that he couldn't get loose. He was not to use his hands. When I finished securing his hands I lifted his arms to place them on the pillow above his head, "Leave them there."

He wriggled and whimpered in response to my command.

"I mean it, Liam. Don't move your hands. Understand?"

"Yes, Jasper. Still green."

I nodded and crawled off the bed. I walked away and

grabbed lube and a condom. I rolled the condom down my throbbing cock and poured copious amounts of lube into my palm. I moaned when I rubbed my lube-covered palm down the length of my rock-hard shaft. It felt so good to finally feel friction and pressure on my cock. I reminded myself that tonight was about Liam and making *him* feel amazing. I stopped pleasuring myself and returned to his angry cock. It was so dark red it was almost purple at that point. Soon, I told myself. Soon he'd have his first of many orgasms for the night.

After a few strokes, Liam started thrusting up into my fist. I didn't waste time while I worked the rest of the lube around his opening and then inserted three fingers back into him without warning. His back arched off of the bed and I knew he was ready. I wanted him more at that moment than I ever had before. I was at my wit's end, so I crawled between his open thighs and pushed his legs up towards his chest and positioned myself at his entrance. Instead of thrusting myself inside, I impaled him by pulling him onto my cock.

"Color?"

"Green," Liam whispered.

"Cum for me Liam, cum now," I rasped out as I slammed home at the same time I pulled the cock ring off him. That was all it took. He came immediately and he came hard. So hard his sperm landed on his head and all over the pillow he was lying on. Liam let out an orgasmic wail that was absolutely beautiful. His diminutive body shuddered and jerked throughout his orgasm. I just sat there buried balls-deep inside him and watched him fall apart. It was a breathtaking sight.

As soon as I knew he had come down from orgasmic bliss, I pulled almost all the way out and slammed back in, hard. I didn't hold back. I took what I wanted, and I wanted Liam. I wanted all of him. Not just his body, I wanted everything that made him Liam.

I fell on top of him and grabbed his bound wrists with one hand while supporting myself on the other arm and then I devoured Liam's mouth. I nipped at his lips gently and then I plunged my tongue into his mouth and mated with his tongue. A sheen of sweat formed on both our bodies, thanks to the time and effort I took thrusting in and out of Liam.

I released Liam's bound hands. I needed to feel his hands on me. I needed him to dig his fingers into my back while I pounded into him.

I pulled his arms around me and commanded him. "Grab my back and don't let go."

He didn't need to be told twice. He quickly tightened his arms around me, digging his fingers into my muscles. I rubbed my stomach against Liam's cock while I pounded his prostate with mine. I was getting close and I wanted Liam to finish with me. I listened to the noises he was making and the way he was clawing at my back. After all the times we'd made love, I could tell his signals and knew he was almost there as well. I knew exactly what would flip the switch and take him over the edge. When I felt the telling tingle at the base of my spine, I moved over to Liam's neck and sucked hard where his neck met his shoulder on his left side. He screamed through his orgasm and when his channel clamped tightly around my cock, I joined him and came harder than ever before. I didn't know where his shouts ended and mine began.

22

LIAM

My holy Jesus God! I couldn't move. I just panted. That was the most intense sexual experience ever! I felt almost paralyzed with pleasure. I was completely numb. Jasper seemed to be no better because his weight was pressed down on me, panting just like I was. When it became too much of an effort to continue holding on to him, I let my legs and arms drop, lifeless, onto the bed. I was most definitely truly and thoroughly fucked. Quite well, too. I'd never felt like this, ever.

After several minutes of panting and trying to catch my breath, I was finally able to look at the man who just shattered any previous orgasm records I'd ever had and muttered just one word to him.

"Green." Then I promptly fell asleep.

When I woke up a little while later, I was wrapped in Jasper's arms and he was staring at me.

"Was I out long?"

"Not long. Here, drink this." He handed me a bottle of water. I gladly took it and practically inhaled the water. While I was drinking the water I realized that Jasper must have cleaned me up while I was asleep. There were no traces of lube or cum on me. If I wasn't delightfully sore in all the right places, I'd have sworn that I dreamed everything.

When the bottle was empty I lowered it and looked sheepishly at my handsome lover. "Sorry, I guess I passed out. Was I out long?"

He chuckled and squeezed me tighter for a moment. "You could say that. I guess I wore you out. You were out only about a half hour. Are you okay? I wasn't too rough, was I?"

The look of concern in Jasper's eyes melted my heart, and he stole what little bit he didn't already have possession of.

I gave him a warm smile and shook my head. "No, Jasper, you weren't too rough. I loved every minute of everything you did. I'd like it if we could soak in the hot tub again. My muscles would sure appreciate it."

He couldn't contain his chuckle and I quickly joined him.

When the bottle was empty I lowered it. "I'm gonna make you promise to behave in the hot tub, though." I nodded, my hair flopping down over my eyelids. He reached over and brushed it out of my face.

"I promise. Right now, I just want a good, long soak. After that, probably another shower. It was a long day. Then once we accomplish that, I just want to snuggle beside you and sleep."

"Well, how about you curl up in my arms in the hot tub first, and we can go from there?"

I gave him a sigh before I replied, blinking my eyes up at him flirtatiously. "That sounds heavenly."

Jasper crawled out of the bed and picked me up. "Alright, hot tub it is then." He carried me to the patio door. I reached down and opened the door and closed it after he stepped through, me still in his arms. He gently set me down in the steaming water. I moaned in delight as my muscles thanked us both, the warm water seeping into my joints and aching muscles. Jasper climbed in behind me and I leaned against his chest. When he wrapped his strong arms around me, I knew I could have easily fallen asleep.

I hummed while I sat there with the water rushing over our bodies. "Probably better if we don't stay out here too long. I'm so warm and comfortable. I think I might fall asleep."

"Don't worry, I'll keep you from drowning. I promise I won't keep us out here that long. Just relax and enjoy. I'm sorry if I overdid it. I forget sometimes just how forceful I can be."

I rolled my head lazily against his chest. "Don't apologize. I meant it when I said I loved every minute of it. I really did. I'm looking forward to doing it again. I don't know that I'd be able to have such enthusiastic playing every single time. That was intense and amazing. I've never felt like that before, Jasper. Ever."

Jasper tightened his grip and chuckled before leaning over and kissing my ear. "Relax. I'm glad you enjoyed it. Believe me when I say I don't want things that intense every time, either. Occasionally will be great."

"Occasionally would be amazing," I hummed. I was dozing off. I woke when Jasper stood up carrying me into the bathroom for another shower. I knew we really needed to rinse off the Jacuzzi water, but all my body wanted to do was curl up next to my lover's warm body and sleep.

Jasper made quick work of our shower. Before I knew it, he dried me off and was tucking me into bed. I'm glad he thought to flip the pillows since I made a mess of them. He tore the top blanket off of the bed, too. We wouldn't need it anyway. Jasper was my own personal thermal blanket. The man was a furnace. I was never cold while sleeping next to him.

"'Night, Jasper," I said, well on my way to dreamland.

"Goodnight, Liam. Sweet dreams, sweetheart." Jasper kissed my forehead. That's the last thing I can remember before I fell into slumberville.

The next time I awoke, it was bright in the room and I was alone. I must have been really exhausted to sleep through the night. My concern, though, was why I was alone? Where did Jasper go? My answer came soon enough in a vision of Jasper, wearing nothing but low-hanging gray sweatpants, pushing a room-service cart.

"Please tell me you didn't answer the door dressed like that," I croaked. What the hell was wrong with my voice? I actually *croaked*!

With one of those signature smiles that made me tingly, Jasper handed me a glass of juice.

"Here, drink. Yes, I answered the door dressed like this." He gestured from his chest to his groin. "Would you have preferred I answered naked?"

The juice was exactly what I needed because my voice sounded normal the next time I spoke.

I huffed. I was not happy that he'd opened the door so exposed. "No, but I'd have preferred it if you'd put a shirt on." I was surprised with the level of possessiveness in my voice. Jasper was mine, and I didn't want to share him.

Jasper slapped himself in the forehead. "A shirt! That's what I forgot! No wonder the room service guy was looking at me funny. You should've seen his eyes bug out of his head when I asked him if he liked the claw marks my boyfriend gave me last night when I fucked him into the mattress. This, of course, was after he hit on me."

I gasped and felt my ire rising. I was so jealous! "What! He hit on you?"

Jasper shook his head with a smirk on his face that turned into a chuckle. "Did you *not* hear the rest of what I said, Liam?"

"Yes. But, still."

The sigh Jasper gave me was more of a groaned growl. He put his hands on his waist and shook his head at me. "Liam, when are you going to realize that you have absolutely nothing to worry about? You're it for me. I want you and nobody else. Got it?"

"Yeah. I get what you're saying but why me, Jasper?"

"You mean other than I know how amazing you are? How about loving. Perhaps it is because you're sexy. Oh, I know! You're a great friend and person. Possibly because I find you completely adorable. Should I go on?" Jasper just smiled at me and rolled his eyes.

I was in awe that this perfect man thought so highly of me. "You think I'm sexy?"

"Out of all of that, you only got sexy? Seriously?" He laughed. I guess I did sound a little ridiculous.

"No, it's just the first thing I wanted to discuss." I smiled up into Jasper's face. Damn, *he* was the sexy one.

Jasper crawled toward me on the bed and gave me a small kiss before he sat down beside me. "Of *course* I think you're sexy. How could I not? Tell me the truth. Do you think you don't do it for me? Especially after last night? What's it going to take, Liam?" I could tell he was getting exasperated with my low self-esteem.

I was unhappy with myself, now. "I'm sorry, Jasper. Just give me some time, okay? I know you like me and are attracted to me. I'm just a little insecure and it has nothing to do with you, okay?"

He seemed to find some peace with my reply, but I could tell he wasn't completely over his frustration. "Alright. How about some breakfast?"

"Breakfast sounds great. Just let me go to the bathroom first."

While I was in the bathroom, Jasper took that time to wheel the room service cart over to the little table in the room and set the food out. I stepped to the table and he lifted the lids on the trays like he was a server. I had no idea that I was even remotely hungry until I smelled the delicious breakfast in front of me. My stomach was certainly ready for breakfast; my stomach growled in complaint that I wasn't already putting something in there.

We ate everything quickly. I was *famished*! When we finished, I went to take a long, hot shower. I vaguely remembered showering with Jasper last night but I wanted a long soak this morning. The hot water heater at the rental we lived in wasn't the greatest and didn't allow for very long showers so I intended to take advantage of the water supply at the lodge while I could.

We spent all day Saturday, and until checkout time on Sunday, in our room, naked. So different from Friday night, Saturday morning Jasper and I didn't have sex; we made love.

There were no other words for the slow, gentle way he worshipped my body with his. Though we'd had gentle sex before, it had always felt like fucking, or releasing tension. When he looked down into my eyes as he slowly stroked in and out of my body, I knew. Without a doubt, I was completely and totally in love with Jasper.

It was too soon to tell him, I knew that. I could show him

though. I could show him with my body, my actions, my choices, with words other than those three little words that weren't so little. They were a big deal. I'd only ever said them to one other person before and look how that turned out. But was I ever really in love with Mike? My feelings for Jasper felt so different. They felt so much more. Now I just needed to find the right time and place to do it. For now, I was content just being with him.

All too soon our time at the lodge ended and we were forced to return to reality. Those three days with Jasper, spent away from our hectic lives, was wonderful and exactly what we needed. Not only did we connect in a new, more intense way sexually, but we spent hours and hours talking. It was during the times that we were talking I felt that our relationship grew. I've never known anyone as well as I did Jasper and that was reassuring. He held nothing back, kept no secrets from me. When we weren't fucking each other to an exhausted stupor, we were talking about any and everything. When we got tired of talking, we'd make slow, sensual love to each other.

All good things come to an end, though, and too soon we packed our bags and left our escape behind. We walked to Jasper's truck and started the forty-minute drive back to our house. When we arrived, real life came crashing down on us by way of dozens of voicemails, texts, and emails. It was probably too much to expect just one more evening without having to deal with reality, but we were given no choice. We were both extremely busy and we knew getting away for just a few days would be all we could manage anyway, but our few days weren't up yet. Well, not in my summation.

I returned to the chaos that was my life by returning emails to my editor, while Jasper took his phone and went into the living room to call Sean. When I finally got to my texts and voicemails, the ones that seemed most important were from Rhett. I had either texted or called him every day since I moved to Crooked Bend but I had only been back to visit once. I expected to have visited more, but once I left, he seemed to become increasingly distant. When I asked Taylor about it, he reassured me it was to be expected and that Rhett would, hopefully soon, be more his old self again. I decided I needed to call my friend and see if there was anything I could do to offer support for him. Luckily, he picked up right away. I never expected him to be as excited as he was when I called. I was happy he was excited and sounded happy, for a change.

"Liam! I'm so glad you finally called back! You're never going to guess who just called me!"

"You're right, I'm not. Who?" I paused. I should explain why it took me so long. "Sorry for not getting right back with you. I was away for the weekend with Jasper."

I heard Rhett groan. "Shit, I forgot you said you were going away. How did that go?"

I smiled to myself before I answered. "Don't worry about that. But, just so you know, you're brother is a sex god. Now tell me who called you!"

"Logan!" He was clearly beside himself with excitement at that bit of news. "I just about shit my pants when the phone rang and caller ID told me it was him!"

I was excited *for* Rhett at that news. "Holy shit, Rhett! You're right. I never would've guessed that. Tell me everything. I mean everything!"

23

JASPER

To say that life had returned in full force would be an understatement. Technically, I was only gone for two and a half days, but with all the work that was piling up, it felt more like two and a half weeks. We desperately needed Collin to come aboard before July. We also needed more than one full-time and one part-time office manager. We never envisioned that things would take off as well as they did. I couldn't complain, but it *was* getting out of hand.

It looked like things were going to be crazy for the next couple of weeks. Since Sean would be gone, things were going to get downright *insane*. I could foresee a lot of hours at work, which meant Liam would be at home alone a lot. When I was finally able to drag my ass home, I'd be too exhausted to do anything other than shower and fall asleep.

Times like these often made me wonder why we did what we did. Was it worth it? In the end, I knew it was. I was already used to sleeping wrapped around Liam each night after mutual orgasms of various types. Those mutual nightly orgasms were looking like they were going to be less frequent.

I still had tonight at home with Liam before I was back at it. I was definitely going to enjoy the time we have left. On our way home, we stopped at the store in Jackson. I wanted to be sure we would have groceries for the week. Tonight we planned to cook dinner together and finish up the night cuddling on the couch. That one benign act always led to sexy times. I hoped I could convince Liam to cuddle in bed instead, and be done with it.

His birthday was coming up next month and I needed to figure out what to get him. He said he had everything he could want when I asked him but I knew there had to be something that he'd like—or love. Maybe there was something he could love. I know that he likes kittens. The background on his laptop was kittens and he was always watching cat videos on YouTube. Maybe I could get him a kitten. He'd like a kitten, wouldn't he? I guess I could always hint around about it and see. The last thing I wanted to do was get him something he hated. We always had dogs growing up. Never cats. Cats were new territory for me. I knew that we didn't have time for a dog. Isaac had one, but he worked at the ranch and it was with him all day. I wasn't home all day and I've seen Liam get so engrossed in his work that he didn't realize that eight hours had gone by. Yeah, definitely not a dog. But...a cat? Possibly.

With that decided, I went in search of Liam. I found him lying on the bed, talking to Rhett. I really needed to talk to my little brother more often so I plopped onto the bed beside Liam and got in on the conversation. They both just laughed at me. It was so good to hear Rhett laugh again. He was coming around, slowly. I told him about Simon's plans and he was excited to see them both when they went west. We talked about work and how he was doing.

He told me how good a friend Travis was becoming and

how he felt comfortable around him. I asked if it was more than that, and he said no, that Travis was into older partners, and preferably more than one at a time. There was no way he ever wanted to be involved with someone like that. That cleared up any questions I had about Rhett and Travis. It was so good to talk to my little brother, and I made a vow to call him at least once a week, if not more.

Leaving Liam to finish his call with Rhett, I wandered into the kitchen. I really didn't feel like cooking so I called the local Italian restaurant and placed an order for pizza and breadsticks. Tomorrow would be soon enough to return to our routine—cooking and being all domestic and shit.

Tonight, I wanted as much time with Liam as I could get, so pizza it was. I left a note for Liam to tell him where I was going and grabbed my coat and keys and left to pick up our dinner. When I got home again, I realized that I didn't need to. Liam hadn't moved. He was right where I left him. When I showed him the pizza box, he gave Rhett an abrupt parting comment and joined me at the table.

The evening was perfectly ideal. We ate dinner, cuddled on the couch until Liam realized he was horny. He straddled my hips and rode my dick while hanging on to the back of the couch. After taking a shower where we again worked each other to orgasm with mutual blowjobs, we collapsed into bed.

All too soon, the Monday morning alarm was going off and Liam was crawling out of bed to start coffee while I got ready for work. What I wanted to do was pull him back under the covers and forget about our jobs for a few more days but I couldn't so I got up and got ready for the day. I knew it was going to be a crazy day, but I couldn't have prepared myself for how hectic it really had turned out to be. Monday was just the start of a hectic week, too! I think I saw Liam a whopping total of five or six hours that entire week. Not nearly enough. God, we needed Collin, now! The end of July was much too late. I'd have to add that to my to-do list. I needed to call and see if he could get out of his contract earlier.

After an insane week of work, I finally had a day off. I spent it at home, doing absolutely nothing, except spending time with Liam, naked. It was my favorite state to be in around Liam. I needed some Liam time after the week I went through.

In my covert questioning about feline companions, I found out he'd always wanted a cat but his parents wouldn't allow pets. Eureka! Now, I just needed to find a rescue cat that I could adopt.

I hoped my plan didn't backfire on me. Being in a relationship was new for me and I was sure I was screwing things up. I called Rhett to see what he thought of my idea. Surprisingly, he thought it was a great idea and told me that Liam almost got a cat when they were living in Seattle but that he didn't because of his ex. Rhett's information sealed my decision in concrete. The majority of planning Liam's birthday surprise would be a "during the workweek" event, so it would have to wait until I got back to the office and away from Liam.

Over the next couple of weeks, we were slammed at work but I made it a priority to text Liam as often as I could. I was working long hours, but so was Sean, and I knew he had the added stress of trying to plan a wedding, too. I wanted to make sure I let Liam know I missed him and was constantly thinking about him. I only managed little bits of free time here and there, so, I texted in lieu of calling.

Me: Hey there.
Liam: Hey yourself.
Me: I just wanted to say hi. Hi.
Liam: Hi back.
Me: I miss you. I'll see you tonight for dinner.
Liam: Really?
Me: Yes, really. Gotta go. See you at 6:00!

Shortly after five, I was walking toward the door. I met Sean on the way.

"Where are you headed to so early?"

"Home. I have a dinner date tonight."

"Really? Since when do you date?"

"Since I met someone."

"Is that why you've been taking long weekends?"

"Yes, now why don't you go home to Simon instead of bugging me? I'm sure your guy would love it if you went home and gave him dessert *before* dinner for a change."

It took a moment, but Sean finally caught on. If his blush was anything to go by, he caught my meaning and liked the idea. If I didn't leave soon, I was going to be late for dinner. I told Liam I'd be home at six and I was *going* to be there by six. I rushed off, waving to my twin and leaving him with a funny look on his face. I didn't have time to think about his confusion or curiosity. I needed to get home to my boyfriend.

I made it, with ten minutes to spare. Liam seemed so surprised. That told me things needed to change between us. If I told him I'd be home, it shouldn't surprise him when I was. He should've accepted that I'd be there. I knew I was working long hours, but we were busy and he knew spring and especially summertime was busy for us. Because Sean was leaving next week for his romantic getaway and I'd be all alone, I had planned another surprise. Liam didn't know it yet but he and I were headed to Bozeman, Montana for the weekend.

Alright, actually, it was for a four-day weekend. We didn't schedule any meetings for the next two weeks and I was taking Friday and Monday off. I found a Pixie-bob rescue that had a litter of kittens that were ready to go home. I applied and they approved me for adoption. We would need to drive to Montana to retrieve our new fur baby. It was still too cold for pets to fly in the cargo hold. I was trusting that Rhett told me accurately that this would be a good thing. If not, then Rhett would become the daddy to a new kitten.

After dinner and enough sex to wear Liam out, I snuck out of bed and packed a bag for our trip in the morning. I truly hoped Liam would be happy with his surprise. I set the alarm for a little later than usual and crawled back into bed and curled around Liam. He sighed in his sleep and I quickly joined him.

All too soon, the alarm was waking us up. When Liam reached over to turn it off, his screeching woke me the rest of the way up.

"Jasper! Hurry up! You're late! The alarm went off late and now you're late for work!"

I grabbed my sides as I burst out into gut-wrenching laughter. I almost felt bad about not telling him, but dammit, I wanted to surprise him. I did the only thing I could think of to calm him down. I pulled him back into bed and crawled on top of him. I dove under the covers and swallowed his still half-hard cock down my throat. Liam's worry quickly turned to moans.

Pulling off his now fully erect cock, I reassured him that

I wasn't late at all. "We're going out of town for your birthday. We have to go pick up your present. Surprise! Now, do you want to cum in my mouth, or do you want me to fuck you?"

It seemed like Liam needed to think about his reply at first, but I guess he was probably trying to think about what I'd just said more than anything. He seemed to have a problem concentrating when I was sucking his cock but I finally got my answer. "As if there is a choice! Fuck me, hard!"

"Gladly." I reached over to the nightstand and grabbed a condom and the lube and quickly suited up. I prepped Liam and then did exactly what he asked. I fucked him. Hard.

After a quick shower, we were out the door and on our way to Montana to meet our new fur baby. I planned ahead and bought everything we would need for him or her, and stashed it at the house. I had a kennel hidden in the back seat of the truck under an extra blanket. I really hoped this didn't backfire.

I'd been to Montana once before but never to Bozeman. When we finally reached Bozeman, I drove to the hotel I booked and checked in. We were only staying the one night. We would be collecting our newest family member tomorrow morning and then go right back home to Wyoming. It took everything in me to not spill the surprise but somehow I managed. Liam was easily distracted with sex so it really was a win-win for me.

When he discovered his birthday surprise was a kitten, saying he was excited about the idea would be an understatement. He screamed like a little girl. I had no idea his voice could hit that pitch, at that decibel. I worried my eardrum would burst!

"Seriously! We're adopting a kitten? Oh. My. God. You are the absolute best boyfriend. Ever!"

The director of the rescue just stood off to the side and stared at us. When Liam finally calmed down, she introduced herself and took us to the kittens. Liam plopped down on the floor and played with as many as he could.

"Are you sure you only want one?" she asked.

At Liam's hopeful look, I almost caved, but I stood my ground and told her that we were only looking for one right now. I hated leaving them there, but Liam never had a kitten before. I knew he'd give one all the attention it would need so I stood firm with my original response. I thought more than one would be too distracting for him.

"No, just the one. Liam's never had a pet. I grew up with dogs but Liam works from home and will be home with it most of the time, but I think just one is the best start for us."

"That's a responsible answer. Okay then, Liam, now the hard question. Which one do you want?"

In the end, it took Liam over an hour of playing with the kittens to pick a brown spotted tawny tabby. Of *course* he chose a unique kitty that also happened to be polydactyl with six toes on each front foot. He was a cute little thing with gray eyes. I was so relieved that my idea didn't backfire.

I paid the adoption fee and gave the agency an additional donation and thanked them. Finally, I got Liam and our newest family member out the door. It was still pretty cold in Montana, even though it was May. I didn't want to be outside for long with our little bundle of fur. After we were all back in the truck, I looked at Liam and asked, "You ready to head home?"

"Yes!"

24

LIAM

"He's so adorable, Jasper! What are we going to name him? I can't believe you got me a kitten for my birthday! He's the best present ever! You are *so* getting laid tonight. Not that you weren't anyway, but you're *definitely* getting extra. Maybe we should call him Spot. No, that's a bad name for a cat. Tiger? No, every cat is named Tiger. Shit! We don't have anything he's going to need at home!"

"Liam!" Jasper had to raise his voice to get my attention. I'll admit, I was overly excited and rambling. He did get my attention, though, and I sheepishly looked over at him.

"Sorry. I guess you could say I'm a little excited."

"A little?" Jasper smiled at me and I knew he was only picking on me. It made me feel a little better about rambling.

"Let's see if I can remember all of the questions. We have everything he needs at home already. I picked everything up this week. It's all stored out in the garage. We have food here with us, but you'll have to run to the pet store and get more later in the week. I'm sure you'll want to pick out some more toys for him, anyway. I got the basics. Litter box, scratching post, some sort of tree tower climbing thing, and food bowls." He took a deep breath before continuing. "As for getting laid. I'm never going to turn *that* down. Please don't ever feel obligated to have sex with me, Liam. That's not why I got the kitten. I got him because you told Rhett you always wanted a kitten growing up but your parents wouldn't let you have pets. As for a name, I'm sure you'll come up with something."

I knew my voice was shaky, and that there were tears in my eyes but I couldn't help myself. It took everything in me to not tell Jasper then and there just how much I loved him. I did. I knew I did, but it wasn't the right time. Not then. Not yet. I'd figure out a time to tell him. I was going to have to figure out something soon before it slipped. I told him how grateful I was, instead.

"You got everything he needs? That's *amazing*, Jasper! Thank you so much!" I did a major no-no and unbuckled my belt so I could reach him across the bench seat and give him a quick kiss on the cheek. I quickly got back into my seat and buckled my seatbelt. "As for sex with you, Jasper, you're amazing in bed. I never feel obligated to have sex with you. I enjoy it. A *lot*. You make me feel things I've never felt before. Trust me when I say it's absolutely no hardship at all."

I cuddled my little purring fur ball in my lap and thought about how long I'd wanted a cat and how for my twenty-sixth birthday that I was finally getting one. The little fluff ball reminded me of something I'd heard about Ernest Hemingway and his house in Key West. The property still has descendants of his original cats. The cats were mostly all polydactyl like our new kitten.

"I've got it!"

Looking over at me, Jasper asked, "Got what?"

"The perfect name. Let's call him Hemingway!"

"Hemingway. Is he one of your favorite authors or something?"

"I admire his work. But it's because of his toes. Hemingway's house in Key West has several descendants of his original cats living there. They're polydactyl just like our kitten. It's a perfect name!"

"I told you, you could name him whatever you wanted. Hemingway is a fine name. But how do you know his cats are polydactyl?"

"The cats in Key West are polydactyl because of inbreeding actually. It's a mutation that they've developed. I only know because I'm obviously a Hemingway fan and have read about him. The cats on the island around his home are a huge tourist attraction."

I cuddled little Hemingway for a bit longer before I put him in his kennel and relaxed, enjoying the drive. Jasper talked about everything happening at work and I told him about my latest work in progress. I was making great progress on a pair of spin-off characters that I introduced in my last book. I was stepping outside my normal genre and was writing more of a romance than a murder mystery. I guess what they said about writing what you know was true. I found romance and love and now I was writing about it. Although, including what Jasper and I did between the sheets, and anywhere else we happened to get busy, I might have to classify it as erotica rather than romance. It was hot. I hoped it would be well received because I was having a ton of fun writing it.

I rolled my head on the headrest and looked at Jasper.

He cleared his throat and started talking. "Hey, I've been thinking. I know we said we'd wait a little bit, but what do you think about looking for a house again? It's warmer and we've been together for almost six months now. I know it's not that long but like I've said before, you're it for me, Liam. I think it would be good to find a home for ourselves. What do you think?"

"I think it's a great idea. We can call the Realtor and see what she has available and go from there. When we get home we can go over what we both want and tell her when we call. I know that houses are more limited in Wyoming than where we grew up, but hopefully we can find something suited for us. My *biggest* requirement is a larger water heater." I laughed, remembering our first shower together and how short we had to make it. "I want to take a long, hot shower. Preferably with you in there with me. With one or both of us on our knees, mouths full."

Jasper pushed on the front of his jeans and sent me a lascivious look. I knew exactly what I was doing. Although, I didn't necessarily want to turn him on when he was driving down the highway and I couldn't help him with his intended erection. Sheepishly, I looked at him and offered an apology.

"Sorry. I'll behave until we get home. Then I'll pounce."

"Promise?"

"Yep!"

It took five hours to get home but we finally made it and I was happy to be back. Jasper had all day Sunday and Monday off and I was excited to spend as much naked-time with him as I could. I didn't know how that was exactly going to work out anymore with a kitten. Dangling parts. Kitten with sharp claws. We might have to throw on underwear or sweats or something before roaming around. The thought of Hemingway attacking my balls made me cringe. We'd hopefully be able to teach him. Hemingway took off to explore his new digs while I grabbed a notepad from the office. We had a list to make and I wanted to get it finished before I got too distracted and forgot.

The list was easy enough. We both pretty much wanted the same thing. At least three bedrooms. One for us, a guest room and one for an office. Two bathrooms were a must. A modern kitchen would be nice since we were being all domestic and shit and cooked more nights than not. I never thought this would be my life. I had an amazing boyfriend, a job I loved, we just adopted a kitten together, and were discussing buying a house. This was definitely something I never imagined.

We discovered that finding a house wasn't difficult at all. Our choice to wait until late May seemed to have provided us with the ideal time for house hunting. The Realtor showed us a substantive list of houses to review. I was charged with sorting through them to find the ones in our price range that met our requirements. Not too difficult a task, and I quickly narrowed it down to three. Jasper was coming home early, if you could call six early, tonight because it was my birthday. I wasn't upset, nor did I have any complaints. I did everything I could to reassure Jasper I understood that he was busy and it was not a big deal. I honestly understood and was okay with it. I worked long hours, too, and was making great progress on my manuscript.

Although, I'll admit that I worked considerably fewer hours after Hemingway joined us. He was just so damn cute. The tower that Jasper got for him was his favorite thing. We put it in front of the window in the office. He'd lie on it most of the day and watch the birds in the yard. When he wanted attention he had no problem letting me know. He'd just jump onto my laptop and lie down on the keyboard. That was a good way of getting the attention he expected. If I couldn't do my work, he'd get petted.

I was excited that Jasper was coming home early tonight. He promised to bring home a pizza, my idea, and we'd celebrate. He already gifted me with the best present ever. I was excited to tell him about the houses the Realtor found for us. There were three, but one definitely caught my eye. It was a small, four-bedroom log cabin. It had an extra bedroom but maybe we could each have our own office, or we could turn one of the bedrooms into a library. I loved that idea! I had so many books in storage. Right now I didn't have anywhere for them, so they were far away in Jackson.

The sound of a key in the lock let me know that Jasper was home, and he was even earlier than I expected.

"Honey! I'm home!"

I couldn't help it, I busted out laughing at Jasper's greeting. He just smiled at me when I walked out of the office with Hemingway behind me.

"It appears that your shadow shrunk a bit."

"Huh?"

Jasper pointed to the floor behind me. I looked down to see Hemingway following me. He had been doing that all day and I didn't know why.

"I don't know why he's following me. He's been doing it all day." I walked up to Jasper and gave him a welcome home kiss. What started out as a gentle peck quickly turned into so much more when Jasper swiped his tongue across my bottom lip and I readily opened for him. It was second nature at that point. His tongue gently explored my mouth and all I wanted to do was forget the pizza and drag him back to the bedroom. With a few gentle nips and kisses to my lower lip, Jasper pulled back and ended the kiss.

"Happy birthday, Liam."

"Thanks. You already wished me a happy birthday this morning when we woke up."

"I know, but I wanted to say it again. I've never spent a birthday with a boyfriend and it's new, so I want to keep saying it."

I shrugged but decided he deserved a little teasing, anyway. "What about next year? Aren't you planning on spending my next birthday with me too?"

"That was the plan. Just humor me, alright?"

"Okay, I suppose that's not too difficult a request." I took a deep breath and smelled marinara sauce and fresh-baked crust. "The pizza smells so good. Thanks for picking it up."

Jasper walked toward the kitchen with the pizza. I followed him, and Hemingway followed me. "Not a problem. It's literally on the way home so it's not a problem to pull in and grab a pizza. It's your birthday, so you should get to pick what you want for dinner."

"Pizza is perfect. Shall we eat?"

We went to the table and sat down to dinner. We didn't even bother with plates. We just ate out of the box. Between the two of us, it wasn't difficult to finish off the large pizza and the double order of breadsticks. I *so* loved their breadsticks.

I swallowed my last bite when I remembered to tell Jasper about the house listings. "Oh, hey, I almost forgot. I was going through the listings the Becca the Realtor sent to us. I found three that we would agree on. There is this one, though, that I really want to see. I need to know when you're available to view it so I can get it scheduled. We should probably see all three, right?"

He took a drink of wine and swallowed before responding. "If you want to see all three, we can. If you want to see just one, that's fine too. I can join you anytime this week during my lunch break or any time after six in the evening. Set up the appointments and I'll make it work."

That was easy. "Are you sure?"

"Yes, I'm sure. I'll put it down as a meeting and make sure I'm there. Just let me know when and where."

"Awesome." I made a mental note to set up an appointment. "How was work without Sean?"

"Busy. Crazy. Thankfully, we don't have any new-client meetings this week or next. Simon decided to keep Sean away for a week and a half so that helps. I have to run from site to site checking on not only my projects, but Sean's as well. It's going to be a lot of driving from one place to another. Nothing I can't handle."

While I listened to Jasper, something occurred to me. "Once Collin joins you, will you take on more clients?"

"God no! We already have enough work for at least three full-time architects. When Collin gets here, we'll each have very manageable schedules. That in itself will be a huge relief."

"You finished talking yet?" I asked while looking at the empty pizza box between us. I had plans for the rest of the evening, and they involved getting Jasper naked as fast as I could.

Jasper seemed to be reading my mind. He had a smirk on his face before he asked me a question. "Yep. What did you have in mind?"

"You. Me. Naked. Sweaty. At *least* two orgasms each."

"If that's your plan, can you tell me *why* we're still sitting at the table?"

In unison, we stood. Our clothes were history by the

time we reached the bedroom. The trail of clothing in the hallway was the last thing on our minds. I'd pick it up later. At that particular moment, all I wanted was a naked Jasper. Apparently, he wanted me equally naked. It was good to be the birthday boy this year. Jasper brought me to orgasm three times!

25

JASPER

*L*iam was right. He found absolutely the most perfect house. He scheduled a viewing for all three houses for the same evening. We went from one to the next, ending with the one he was most interested in. It didn't take me long to understand why. The house had four bedrooms and three bathrooms with an open floor plan and a nice-sized kitchen. It wasn't even an old home. We found out the seller's wife hated winters in Wyoming and wanted to move back to Texas so he was selling his dream home. I kind of felt bad for the guy. Kind of, but not really. His loss was our gain.

I could tell Liam was excited about the house as soon as we pulled up. He was bouncing in the seat. His seatbelt was off and he was out the door before I even put the truck in park.

"Calm down, Liam." I couldn't help but laugh at his excitement. I was excited too, but I knew I needed to stay calm. We needed to view the house, and we needed to do it with an open mind. I definitely shared some of Liam's excitement, though. I had a good feeling about the house.

Becca, our Realtor, walked us through the house and did her little routine, like she had with the first two houses. When we met in the kitchen after looking through the home, she asked us what we thought, Liam spoke up, catching me by surprise.

He was still bouncing on the balls of his feet. It was like he'd just been given the best gift ever. "Can we go through it again, real quick?"

"Of course, take your time. I'll be here. You two can make your way back here and let me know what you think, okay?" she responded to him.

Liam snatched my hand up and started walking toward the stairs. After we reached the top, he pulled me into the master bedroom, stopped and sighed. I felt an immediate urge to wrap my arms around him and pull him back against my chest. I rested my chin on the top of his head. We stood there in silence, enjoying the moment, before I asked a question I already knew the answer for.

"This is the one, isn't it?"

"Is it that obvious?"

"Only because I feel the same way. It's perfect, Liam. I can definitely see the three of us living here for a long time."

"Three?"

"Hemingway. Were you planning on leaving our fur baby behind in Crooked Bend?"

He snorted before he replied. "No. I do find it cute that you constantly refer to him as our fur baby." I tightened my grip around him. "Technically, this house is still in Crooked Bend. It has a Crooked Bend address."

I stuck to the fur baby comment and explained why I called Hemingway that. "I don't know if I would ever want the other kind. I don't know how good a dad I'd be. I'm a little selfish and work so many hours."

Liam's chest rumbled with laughter that I could feel through my chest. "Oh hell no! Can you imagine us with a kid? I get so lost in writing the poor thing would starve! Don't worry, Jasper. I don't see kids in my future either. I'd like to see this amazing house in our future. Can you imagine all of the sexy times we could have here?"

"Yes, yes, I absolutely can. You ready to give Becca our offer?"

Liam sighed with a satisfied whisper of breath. "Yes. Hopefully they'll accept our offer." Another sigh escaped Liam's lips. He looked longingly into the bedroom once more before we left.

We took our time returning to downstairs to the kitchen. The rental we lived in was ranch-style. My imagination was already working on overdrive, considering everything I could do to Liam on those stairs. Jesus! I needed to change my thoughts, and now! The last thing I wanted to do was return to the kitchen with a hard-on protruding from my jeans. By the time we made it back to the kitchen, I had my dick under control. Liam just gave me a sexy look that let me know he knew exactly what I was struggling with, and why I was struggling. Hopefully, his thoughts were of a similar nature.

Becca was waiting at the kitchen table when we entered. "What did you think? Did any of the houses you saw today speak to you?" She looked directly at Liam, not me. She sure had us pegged correctly. What Liam wanted, Liam was going to get.

I redirected her attention back to me. "Sure did! We're interested in this house. You said the owners were anxious to sell?" I asked.

"That's right. They're very anxious to sell. I usually don't do this, but for you, I'll tell you that you should put a bid in at fifteen percent below their asking price. That will leave room to negotiate if they don't accept your first offer."

I looked at Liam. I needed to be sure he agreed with me. "You're sure this is the one?"

"Absolutely. Green all the way."

"We'll make an offer five percent below their asking price. Liam wants this house and I want him to be happy. What makes him happy makes me happy," I replied, never taking my eyes off of Liam's. His grew as big as saucers. The sellers were definitely motivated to get out of the house; the asking price was below what my grandparents had put into trust fund accounts for Sean, Rhett, and me to buy a house. Sean was going to use his to pay off the loan Simon and his family had taken out to have their new arena built that we were building for them. Although Simon didn't know it yet.

"Very good. If you two could follow me back to the office, we can take care of the paperwork and get it sent off to the sellers and see what they think."

"Sounds good to me," I replied, finally taking my eyes off of Liam long enough to look at the Realtor to give her a smile.

We left and followed her back to her office. By the time we got the paperwork together and left the check for the earnest money, we were both starving and decided to eat at the diner in town. We normally went to Jackson to eat but I didn't care if anyone saw me with Liam. I wasn't hiding him, or us.

Our food arrived and my phone rang at the same time. Becca was calling. She told me the sellers accepted our offer. I grinned at Liam and gave him a thumbs up sign. He started bouncing in his seat with excitement. So damn cute!

We arranged it so we'd meet her at her office the following day to finalize the sale. I'd need to call the bank and get the funds transferred once I knew where to send them. Since it was a cash sale, things moved quickly. We'd close on our house by the end of June. *Our* house!

Damn! I guess I was growing up. I was in a serious, monogamous relationship, I was buying a house with him, and we adopted a kitten together. Would we be getting engaged next? Shit! Would Liam want to get married? I sure could see myself married to Liam. I was crazy about him and knew I loved him. So far, I hadn't been able to say those three words to him. The timing always felt wrong. I made sure I showed him all the time how I felt about him. It was probably time to tell him. I was getting into a habit of planning surprises for Liam, too! One more to go.

We finished our dinner and headed home to Hemingway. I made a mental note to contact Collin and let him know I'd be moving the end of June. He'd still be welcome to stay with Liam and me. We would still have a spare bedroom that he could stay in until he found a place. Hopefully, he'd managed to find a way out of his contract sooner. We really needed him and he wanted out of Alabama desperately. It's a complete win-win.

Sean and Simon would return next week. With Sean back at work, hopefully things would level out some. I really needed to tell him about the house, not to mention Liam. He knew I was seeing someone, just not who *someone* was.

There never seemed to be a good time to tell him. He was overly stressed about the wedding. His future mother-in-law was adding a lot of pressure on the two of them about getting things scheduled and organized. She was a sweet woman normally, but she acted as though she wanted to take over the wedding planning. Sometimes, Sean would come into the office and I could just tell that Cammie had been at it. I was so glad I wasn't in his shoes.

After spending a little while playing with Hemingway, Liam and I called it a night and went to bed after getting dirtier and then clean in the shower. I had a good life, and I knew it. Liam changed so much about how I looked at life. Sean started the "improve Jasper's life" process almost a year ago when we left Wild Creek, but it was Rhett bringing Liam to Wyoming for Christmas that turned my life a complete one-eighty. Who knew a little blond imp could be so powerful?

Work was par for the course, which meant insanely hectic. I hated being spread so thin but there wasn't much that could be done until Collin arrived from Alabama. We made him a generous offer and he accepted. It seems that finding out that our little town of Crooked Bend openly accepted gay men didn't hurt him in making a decision to come to Wyoming. I guess they weren't so accepting where he lived in Alabama. Not that it mattered, but we had no idea of Collin's sexual orientation when we offered the position to him. His professional portfolio spoke for itself. He sounded happily surprised when we told him that Sean was engaged to a man, and that I, too, was openly gay. I told him we had never experienced any negative behavior in town at all. That seemed to seal the deal for him. He'd be so much closer to his brothers and cousins, too.

I was relieved to find out that Collin would be able to use accumulated vacation time and leave earlier than anticipated. He'd be arriving in Crooked Bend the first week of July. Thank God! That meant we only had to do without his help for just over a month. He was still looking for housing. After getting assurance from both Liam and me, he finally agreed to accept the offer to stay in our guest room while he looked for places. We would need to make sure we behaved ourselves until we were in our bedroom. That wouldn't be too difficult, right?

When I saw Sean after he returned from his romantic getaway, he looked relaxed and very well fucked. It was a good look on him. He had so much to discuss. He told me that they decided on a location for their wedding. They chose the vineyard they visited in California. They hired the on-site wedding planner, no more wedding stress! I was so happy for him. He was relieved and it showed. He also told me that his second visit to Rhett was much better than the first. He was still with our dads, but was doing a lot better. I was happy to hear that.

Liam reported that Rhett fell into a slight state of depression when he hadn't heard from Logan in over a month. I guess Liam took it upon himself to go out to Wild Creek and rip Logan a new one for it. That's something I would've *loved* to see. Whatever it was that Liam said, worked, because according to Rhett, Logan called him every other day after that. I honestly didn't care what it took to get my little brother back. If being friends with Logan helped, then that friendship better flourish! I thought that Logan might be looking for more than just friendship.

Since Collin was a shoo-in, and after I told Sean about my soon to be homeowner status, we started looking for properties in Crooked Bend for a satellite office. It would be so much closer for the two of us, and Collin was more than willing to work out of the Jackson office location on a daily basis. It seems he had become accustomed to a long commute.

Try as I might, I couldn't find time to tell Sean that not only was I living with a guy but was also in love with him and that the guy was Liam. Why did it seem that my timing always sucked when it came to saying important things to those that meant the most to me? I decided that I'd plan a romantic evening with Liam and tell him those three important words before I told Sean about us. I needed to make sure he felt the same way before I told Sean. I didn't know if I could handle Sean seeing me fall apart over a man, again, if he rejected my declaration of love. If he rejected me and didn't love me in return, it would devastate me irreparably.

26
LIAM

June

I absolutely couldn't believe it. We were going to get the house of my dreams! The sellers were quick to accept Jasper's offer and were eager to close on the house. Apparently, the seller's wife had already gone back to Texas without him. He'd only stayed in Wyoming to sell the house and was eager to get back to her. We were closing in just a few hours and would be moving into our home tomorrow. I was excited, but also nervous. I had plans for tonight. I sure hoped that Jasper didn't freak out on me.

I mean, we were there. I knew it in my heart that we were to that point. I could tell that Jasper felt something more than just affection every time we made love. There was no other word for it when he kissed me from head to toe and stroked himself into me slowly while linking his fingers with mine. The look in his eyes when he did that just made my heart palpitate with emotion. Maybe he hadn't said the words, but he did with his body. God, I hoped my plan for tonight's romantic dinner worked out.

I had it figured out. I would stage a romantic dinner for Jasper in our new house. Somehow, I hadn't really figured out how yet, I'd work it into the conversation that I love him.

I used words for a living! You'd think it would be easy to tell the man I loved that I was in love with him. I have never struggled with something so much in my life! I'd only ever said it to one other person and that was a dangerous mistake. *That* man almost killed me. Jasper was nothing like Mike. The mind is a funny thing. Even though it had been over six months since I last saw him, there were still times that I cringed when Mike would cross my mind.

I still had a few things to stage before I met Jasper to close the sale and get our keys. I'd be happy to finally establish myself somewhere permanently. I was tired of living out of boxes. We only had just a few boxes left to finish packing and tape up. Things that we needed on a daily basis were last to go into boxes. We completely gave up trying to keep kitchen items unpacked. We were living the true bachelor life, eating out twice a day. I was so sick of fast food it wasn't even funny. I'd come to love cooking with Jasper so much! It had become one of my favorite parts of the day.

Come to think about it, I enjoyed everything that we did together. We did so many little things together and it was amazing. A year ago I was miserable. I was amazed with how much had changed in such a short amount of time. It was even better when you knew you'd found the right person like I had.

Closing on the house was quick and virtually painless. It did require Jasper and me to sign our names dozens of times. I argued against having my name on the house repeatedly. I didn't think Jasper should put my name on the deed to the house. He was the one buying it, it should go in his name. He finally won when he gave me an ultimatum; it goes in both names or he wasn't going to buy it. That was underhanded and unfair, but I wanted that house so I begrudgingly agreed. I felt he shouldn't put my name on it if he was using his trust money to buy the place. I wasn't putting any money into the purchase. He told me we could put all of the utilities in my name if it made me feel any better. It didn't.

After we finished signing the papers, Jasper said he needed to run off to the office. I didn't mind. With him gone, I had the perfect opportunity to run to the rental house and grab the stuff I needed for my surprise. I couldn't believe my luck!

I finally made it to our new house with everything. I wanted to cry when I pulled into the driveway and saw Jasper's truck there. How in the hell was I going to set everything up for my romantic picnic surprise if he was already there?

Admitting defeat and coming to the conclusion that tonight was not going to be the night to tell Jasper that I loved him, I got out of Baloo and walked up to the house to search for Jasper.

I was floored when I walked into the house. Jasper made a trail of lit candles. They started at the front door inviting me to continue inward. I followed the small flames, making my way to the living room. The sight before me made me gasp and start to cry. There, in the middle of the living room, surrounded by candles, and with a blanket and several pillows laid out on the floor was Jasper. It seems my man had the exact same idea as me! He obviously came straight here from the Realtor's office instead of going to his office in Jackson like he'd told me.

I didn't move at first. I noticed Jasper started to look

uncomfortable so I slowly made my way toward him and the little picnic he had put together for us.

"Jasper, what..."

"Liam, just give me a minute here, alright?"

I had no idea what Jasper planned but I knew that there was absolutely no way I was going to let him go another night without telling him exactly how I felt. With as wonderful and sweet as this all was, this was *my* plan. Did I talk in my sleep? Nobody ever mentioned me talking in my sleep before so probably not. How was it that Jasper came up with the exact same idea as me? I took a big breath and did my best to calm myself and stepped into the room. I didn't stop there. Nope! In true Liam fashion I walked right up to Jasper and hauled off and whacked him on the shoulder. Not the most romantic move ever.

"Liam! What the hell?"

"How dare you, Jasper!"

"How dare I what? You're mad I try to be romantic for you? What? You want me to be an asshole or something?"

"No! I love it when you're romantic. I love it when you plan trips and dinners and send me flowers and candy and stuff. It's an amazing feeling knowing that you care enough about me to do all of those things for me."

"Then why in the hell did you just hit me?"

"Because! You ruined my surprise!"

"How did I ruin *your* surprise? I haven't even told you your surprise yet!"

We were both upset and started raising our voices, shouting at each other by that point. Not one of our best moments.

"What do you mean you haven't given me my surprise yet? I had everything all planned and you beat me to it! I was going to come in and set up a romantic dinner for you, but you beat me to it, Jasper!" I was openly bawling by then. It was not a pretty sight. I know, I've seen me when I cried in the past. My face gets red and splotchy when I cry.

"Liam, I haven't given you your surprise yet because the dinner isn't your surprise. I wanted to give you a perfect romantic dinner so I could tell you just how much you mean to me. I wanted the timing to finally be right so I could tell you that I've fallen completely and totally in love with you."

I opened my mouth to wail out more of my frustration when his words sunk in. "Wait, what?" Did Jasper just tell me that he loves me? Out loud? Surely I'm mistaken. My ears were playing tricks on me. They had to have been. Could I be so lucky to fall in love with a man that loved me back?

Wrapping his arms around me, Jasper said those three wonderfully beautiful words to me again. "I said I love you, Liam. I love everything about you. I love the way you get lost in the stories that you write. I love the way you bite your bottom lip when you get turned on like you are right now." He tweaked my chin with his index finger. "I love the way you dance around the house in nothing but your underwear. I love the way you smile at me when you first wake up in the morning. I love the way you drag your cute little ass out of bed to make coffee for me while I get ready for work. I love the way you are devoted to your friendship with Rhett and always drop whatever you're doing when he calls or texts you. I love everything about you, Liam. You are an amazing person and for whatever reason, you chose to give me a chance. I'll be forever thankful and grateful that I have this chance to spend time with you. I can do this all night. Should I go on?"

Clinging to Jasper, I still had difficulties articulating

those three little words. I knew more than anything that he wanted to hear them from me. It wasn't a hardship and it sure wouldn't be a lie. I'd been in love with Jasper for months. "I...I...oh my God, Jasper. I can't. You can't possibly be real. There is no way that you, oh my God!" Wrong three words. I took a deep breath and finally, wrapping my arms and legs around Jasper after climbing him like a tree, I looked into his beautiful whiskey-colored eyes and said the most important four words back to Jasper.

When they started, it seemed I wasn't lost for words, after all. "I love you too. I have for so long, Jasper. I just couldn't find the right time to tell you either. I wanted to tell you when you took me to the ski lodge but it didn't seem like the right time. I wanted to tell you when you took me to Montana to pick up Hemingway, but again, the timing seemed off. I had a similar evening planned for you to do this exact same thing. I planned a romantic dinner for you. I wanted to tell you how amazing you are. How wonderful you are. How happy you make me. You beat me to it!" I knew I was whining, but there you have it! I took a breath, regrouped, and continued. "You are the most amazing man I've ever known and I'm so thankful that you love me. I promise, I'll never take that love for granted."

Jasper clamped his lips against mine in what I could only describe as a toe-curling kiss. He somehow managed to lower us to the blanket and pillows on the floor. There must have been several blankets because I only felt softness below me. I knew that hardwood floors weren't soft at all. The love of my life gently licked, nipped, nibbled, and kissed my lips, chin, neck, earlobes, and shoulders. I was a quivering mass of noodles by the time he stopped and pulled back enough to look at me.

"I love you, Liam. With everything I have and am. You're

everything for me. I've never felt this way about anyone ever before and I never want to with anyone else. You're my choice and I don't ever want to lose you."

I looked into his eyes and saw the truth in his words. "You won't. I promise. You're my chance at love and happiness, Jasper. I'm so thankful that I took a chance with you. I've never been happier, or felt more loved than I do with you."

I pulled Jasper's head forward to mine, because it was Jasper and I would never get enough of his kisses. The man was a master at kissing and I loved that he loved to kiss me as much as he could. Somehow, Jasper got us both completely naked and was frotting against me. Before we could get too carried away, he rolled us over so I was on top, straddling his hips. I explored his body. He'd given me the opportunity like that, so I took advantage. I leaned forward and touched, kissed, licked, and sucked, starting at his neck and working my way down his body.

I gave his nipples extra attention, gently nipping at them until they were hard peaks. I must have been doing something right; he was pressing his hips upward into mine. I continued downward, paying special attention to the ridges and valleys sculpted into his abs. I trailed onward using my tongue toward my prize. I loved Jasper's cock. I'd never been with a man who had an uncut cock before Jasper. My Jasper would be the last, too, because he was it for me as well.

I loved to play with the foreskin on his cock. He loved it when I sucked and nibbled on it. After several months together, I was able to deep throat Jasper without gagging. He wasn't overly large or thick. In my opinion, he was perfection. I loved that he was all mine. I wanted to make sure we got to the main event soon because I had a deep-rooted ached for him. I reached over and grabbed the condom, opened it, and quickly rolled it down Jasper's rock-hard, velvety length. He gave me the lube and I poured a generous amount directly onto his erect length and then used my hand to cover him from tip to base. I wiped the excess across my hole but didn't bother prepping. I needed Jasper, and I needed to feel him inside me immediately.

I leaned forward and positioned myself above him but when I started to lower myself, Jasper stopped me. I looked at him with an exasperated expression.

"Wait. I need to prep you."

"No, it'll be fine. We had sex right before we went to the Realtor's office. I'll be okay, I promise," I slowly sunk down onto Jasper's cock. It felt so wonderful. Once he was consumed to the hilt, I stopped and looked down at him and repeated my three favorite words to him again. I love you. So, so much."

He softly ran his hands from my hips to my shoulders and back down. "I love you too, Liam. More than I'll ever be able to tell you."

"You tell me all the time, Jasper. You've been telling me for months in the way you look at me. In the way you make love to me. Do it again, Jasper. Make love to me and show me how much you love me."

Jasper held me firmly at the hips and lifted me almost all the way off of his cock. He held me there while he thrust his hips up into me repeatedly. When his arms got tired, I took over and rolled my hips.

That action gave us a completely different feeling, one that hit my prostate with every rotation. It drove me absolutely wild. Jasper couldn't hold his orgasm long. Before I knew what he was doing, he sat up and latched onto my neck and bit down and sucked on that magical spot where my neck and shoulder met on my left side. That spot always makes me cum. Without disappointing, I came. Jasper told me several times that he loved me that night. Both by saying those beautiful words as well as showing me by the way he made love to me. It was a night that I'll never forget and always cherish.

JASPER

Never in a million years would I have ever thought that Liam would have the same idea I did to tell me he loved me. The night we closed on the house turned out to be the best night of my life. Never before had I told a man I loved him, other than my fathers and brothers. They didn't really count. I didn't want to spend my life with them. I did with Liam. I was so happy with where we were in our relationship. I knew that one day and probably soon, I was going to ask him to marry me. For now, I was happy and content to just be in love with my boyfriend.

We had so much stuff to move. Everything was packed and ready to go, we just needed to transport it. I cheated though. I hired a few of the guys from one of our crews to help us load and unload all the boxes and furniture from both the house we'd been renting and Liam's storage unit. Between the two of us, we had more than enough stuff to fill our new home. What we didn't have or what Liam didn't want or like, he'd just get rid of and go out and buy something else. For the most part, we both had similar tastes in décor. We both liked comfortable furniture, neutral colors, and nothing too fancy or overly modern. We wanted our house to feel warm and welcoming.

When we first got together, we'd bought a king-sized bed. That's where we slept. We moved my old bed into the spare bedroom. I had no reservations with buying the new bed. Liam didn't even bring the bed he used in Seattle with him. Moving two king-sized mattresses was not something I wanted to try and do by myself so I bribed the crew with a promise of pizza and beer. I even paid them a little cash for help. I received more than enough volunteers to get everything moved in just a few hours. That left Liam and me in a maze of boxes at our new place.

Hemingway was pissed that we locked him in one of the upstairs bathrooms while we were moving, but quickly forgave us when we offered pets and some cubes of chicken. Yeah, Liam spoiled that cat.

We lived among boxes for a week while we slowly unpacked everything. Things were still incredibly busy at work which didn't help. I needed to be home earlier than I was so I could help Liam unpack. It wasn't fair to him that I only had a few hours each evening to commit to it.

I owned just as much stuff as Liam did, if not more. He said he didn't mind, but I still felt guilty for leaving him to do most of it. I tried to make it up to him by bringing home dinner or offering to take him out but he said he was tired of fast food. So was I, honestly. I'd gotten used to cooking dinner with Liam each night and I missed that.

Sean must have noticed a change in my mood because he mentioned it to me one day at the office in between meetings. "What's got you so cranky? You'd been so happy and eager to get home or run off for a date. What happened? Did things not work out?"

"No, things are great. I'm just trying to juggle everything and I haven't even unpacked yet. It's just getting to me. That's all."

"Unpacked? Wait, you moved already? Why didn't you let me know?"

I looked at my brother in disbelief. "Umm, I did. You've been so busy with planning that thing, you know, your wedding. It's all good. I paid a few of the guys from one of the crews and bought pizza and beer. We got everything moved in just a few hours. Easy. Now I'm just annoyed with living among walls and cubicles of boxes. I need a day off to unpack but things are so busy here. Collin said he'd be here next week sometime so I really need to get things going on getting my place ready."

"Collin is staying with you? When did that happen?"

"When I offered? Is it a problem that I offered for him to stay with me until he finds a place? I honestly didn't think you'd have a problem with it."

"I normally wouldn't. I don't. It's just...just don't sleep with him, alright?"

If he wasn't my twin brother, I might have slugged him. "What the actual fuck, Sean! Why would I sleep with him? You know I'm seeing someone and have been for a while."

Sean quickly backtracked. "Sorry, Jasper. I'm stressed and you haven't ever dated someone, especially as long as you have this guy so I keep forgetting about him."

I sighed—loudly. "Why are you stressed?"

"Mostly, my future mother-in-law. She's great. She's wonderful. Though, all of a sudden she's turned into someone we don't know. It's like she's become possessed or something with this wedding. She's fighting everything about it, the location, the colors, everything. Simon is so busy at the ranch with all of the new foals, I hardly see him. There's so much for him to do so she keeps bugging me about everything. Also, trying to plan the bachelor party. Deciding where to go on our honeymoon. Like you said, work. Things are crazy here. So there's plenty to be stressed about."

"Hold it!" I stopped him right there. "Rhett and I are planning the bachelor party. We've got that covered. Last time I talked to him, Liam had some good ideas for that, too. Mark that off of your to-do list. You're on your own for planning the wedding though. As for the honeymoon, I recommend going somewhere warm. That way you and Simon won't need many clothes, at all."

"That's not a bad idea about the honeymoon. Actually Ana is helping out tremendously with the wedding planning. Then again, that's what we hired her for."

"About Cammie, tell Simon. Let him know his mother is still hounding you about the wedding. I know he told you to tell him if she tried to take over again. Let. Him. Know."

"Ugh, you're right. I just don't want to cause any tension between them."

"You may not want to but you have to realize she's causing tension for you. It's *your* wedding. Remind her, or have Simon do it."

We were interrupted when Sean's phone rang. Luckily for him, it was Simon saying he was in town. He wanted to meet for lunch. He seemed hesitant to leave the office, so I waved him out the door. Things were hectic and busy, but we both needed to eat. I decided it was the perfect time to eat the lunch Liam packed for me and get caught up on work so I could leave earlier than usual.

Wanting and doing were two different things. I didn't make it home until almost nine. I was so busy at work and didn't realize it was so late until my phone rang. It was Liam wondering if he should hold dinner for me. It was only then that I realized how late it was. I felt horrible that I'd done that to Liam. Not only had we not been intimate since the day we closed on the house and told each other that we loved each other, but I'd worked late every night since. I was really winning when it came to showing Liam how much I loved him lately.

Grabbing only part of what I needed, I ran out the door, only barely remembering to set the alarm and lock the office. I stopped and grabbed a burger on my way out of town and made it home in just under forty minutes, my regular time frame. It was late and I felt like shit for being so late. Running inside after I parked the truck, I stopped in my tracks when I spotted Liam and Hemingway curled up on the couch.

"Hey, Cupcake. I'd ask how work was but I already know it was busy. I got about a dozen boxes unpacked today. I wrote for several hours, too! I'd say that it was definitely a productive day for me. How are you doing?"

There he was, my Liam, sitting on the couch and acting like nothing was wrong. What did I ever do to deserve him? I needed to make sure he knew I was completely committed to us. I was starting right that minute. I walked up to my man and picked him up off of the sofa and swung him over my shoulder. The giggle that accompanied him grabbing my ass let me know I made at least one right decision today.

"While you're back there, reach into my pocket and text Sean and let him know I'm going to be in late tomorrow, if at all. It's Saturday for fuck's sake. Then turn the phone off, got it?"

"Yep! It's going to be a red and green night?" Liam asked while hanging down my back. He slipped my phone back in my pocket about halfway up the stairs to our bedroom.

"Nope. Tonight, I'm just going to worship your body as long as you'll let me."

"Okay. If I happen to want you to fuck me into the mattress instead?"

"That can definitely be arranged."

Liam nodded his head enthusiastically. "That. Yes, please. Fuck me. Hard. Multiple times. Worship next week. Tonight, make me scream."

With his request well defined, I tossed Liam onto our bed and set about making each of his wishes come true. It was a very good night.

I absolutely loved our new house. Liam seemed just as happy with it as I was. We unpacked boxes. It seems we did nothing else! I had a plan for the extra bedroom. Liam would have one for his own office. I was going to have a bunch of custom bookcases built for it. We kept several custom woodworkers on speed dial for special projects and I knew that getting a wall of book shelves wouldn't be a problem. When we moved, we put both desks in the same room like they'd been in the rental. That wasn't really working out because I knew it bugged Liam when I was in the office with him when he was writing. I had no problem giving him the extra bedroom. He definitely deserved it.

While we were unpacking the last few boxes, we started talking about my most recent conversation with Sean. I let Liam know that I was a little concerned about Sean and how much

Cammie was stressing him out. I didn't know what I could do to get her to back off, other than to call Simon and let him know. Liam suggested that it sounded like the only option. I agreed.

When the conversation migrated to Collin's impending arrival, the conversation turned a different corner.

"You're really okay with Collin staying here, right?"

Liam looked at me with confusion. "Of course I am. Why wouldn't I be? The poor guy is moving all the way from Alabama to join your firm. He doesn't know anybody. Why would I have an issue with him staying here?"

"I was just making sure. When I mentioned it to Sean, he seemed shocked that Collin was staying here and told me to make sure I didn't fuck him."

"Why would he say that?"

I shrugged. "I don't know. Maybe because after Rupert and before you, I only wanted no-strings hook ups and almost never any repeats. I was a bit disrespectful, I guess. I reminded him that I was seeing someone and he seemed shocked that I was still seeing someone. I should've told him it was you then, but Simon called and he was lost to anything but him after that."

"Hey, don't worry about it. I think it's best if we wait until after their wedding to tell him it's me you're seeing. He is under enough stress. Since I'm such a close friend of Rhett's, I don't want to add stress. Knowing Sean, he'd stress because of your history with Rupert and everything you went through after that. Even though Rhett is the one who told me to come back to you and give us a try, Sean would still be worried about my friendship with Rhett if we didn't work out. I think you definitely did the right thing by not pushing the subject."

"I agree with you, Liam, but I hate that Sean doesn't

know that it's you that I'm seeing. It makes me feel like we're hiding or something."

Liam looked me straight in the eye. He had a determined expression on his face. "If it bothers you that much, we can call him right now and tell him. I'm not hiding and I know you aren't hiding us. He knows you're seeing someone. He knows you have been for a while. He just doesn't know my name. How about you tell him in increments? First let him know you've gotten serious, then tell him we've moved in together, then tell him who you've been seeing. Whether it's me or someone else. That you went through all those milestones in your relationship should be what matters most."

"You're so smart! I want to make sure you know how important you are to me. That's all. I'll tell him if that's what you want, or I'll hold off if you think that's the way to go."

"Trust me, Jasper, I know. Collin gets here tomorrow. That means you only have tonight to fuck me on those stairs until after he leaves. I've been thinking about you pounding into me from behind on them since we woke up this morning."

I leered at Liam with my most intrigued expression. "Since this morning, huh? Why didn't you say something sooner?"

"Because if I had, we wouldn't have gotten everything unpacked and ready for our house guest tomorrow. Now, what's a man gotta do to get his boyfriend to fuck him on the stairs in their new house? It has to be intense enough that he feels it tomorrow."

I winked at my boyfriend. "Simple, ask."

Liam didn't ask. He did something even better. He stripped completely naked and he crawled up the stairs, wiggling his ass with each step. I couldn't take my eyes off his perfect backside. When his cheeks parted, I could see his rosebud winking at me. I grabbed the throw blanket off of the couch to cushion his knees before I joined him and did exactly what he asked. If he was walking a little funny when he met Collin the next day, well, Collin was a gay man as well so I was sure he'd understand.

28

LIAM

*H*oly Shit! When I asked Jasper to fuck me on the stairs, I had absolutely no idea that he'd be at the absolute perfect height to do such a thorough job from below. I was undeniably feeling it the next day. I wasn't complaining, though. It's exactly what I asked for.

Jasper spoiled me something awful. No matter what it was, if I wanted something, all I had to do was ask. If he was able to, he gave it to me. I hit the jackpot when Jasper decided he wanted me for keeps. I would never take him or his love for granted.

Collin called a few minutes ago. He let us know he was going to be arriving soon. I know that Jasper and I were both anxious, though for different reasons. I was anxious because it had been just the two of us for the past six months. Jasper was anxious because it meant they were going to have a much needed third architect. Although, I'd benefit from that aspect of it for sure. Jasper already said they wouldn't be taking on more work just because they acquired another architect. They already had more than enough client projects for three. By adding Collin, they would be able to lighten both his and Sean's workloads. That'd be nice. I might get to see Jasper for dinner on a more regular basis again.

I don't know what I expected when Collin arrived, but it definitely wasn't the taller version of Jonathan and Travis. The blond-haired, blue-eyed, six-foot-five giant wasn't what I was expecting. I'd met a couple of his cousins; he was slimmer than they were. I expected him to look like his brother Daniel.

I found out that Collin was the oldest and the only blond among his brothers. The others were all brunette. Collin was so friendly! Even though he was almost as tall as Taylor, he had an easy-going way about him, nothing intimidating at all. He was likeable. After spending some time talking to Collin and finding out more about him, I knew that he would be an asset to Sean and Jasper at the firm.

I thought we'd have an awkward first evening together but it was comfortable. We spent hours talking and getting to know one another over dinner. We kept the conversation going well after we'd finished eating, too. Even Hemingway made nice and graced Collin with some lap time. We understood that the three-day trip had exhausted Collin. By ten he was more than ready for the king-sized bed in our guest room. We said our goodnights and turned in shortly after he did. Because we had absolutely no way of knowing how well sound traveled in our house, we made sure to keep the noise down while Jasper made love to me that night. I loved that he was just as content to make slow, sensual love to me as he was to fuck me into the mattress or the stairs when I asked.

It was July and we still had no real concrete plans for the bachelor party for Sean and Simon. When they came back from their week away, they told everyone they'd found a perfect location. They also hired a wedding planner who was part of the staff at the vineyard. There was only a little over a month until their wedding, so we really needed to get our act together and figure out what we were going to do for their combined bachelor party.

Jasper and I were on speakerphone with Rhett one evening trying to come up with ideas. It wasn't until Collin walked in during our conversation that we really got anywhere.

"Sorry, guys, I didn't realize you were on the phone," Collin said while turning to quickly leave the kitchen.

"Hey, wait!" Jasper said to Collin's retreating back. "It's really no big deal. We're just chatting with my brother Rhett, trying to plan Simon and Sean's bachelor party. Unfortunately we're getting nowhere."

"Bachelor party, huh? When is the wedding?"

"August twentieth," we all said in unison.

"Do you have any plans or ideas for the bachelor party at all?" Collin asked us.

"Not really, no," I told him.

"Then what about Vegas? I went there with my brothers and cousins for Travis' twenty-first birthday and it was a total riot. There will definitely be lodging, and plenty of entertainment," Collin suggested.

I just stared at Collin. That was an amazing suggestion. I finally snapped out of my stupor. "Okay, why didn't any of us think of Vegas?" I looked at Jasper and then my phone, as if Rhett could see me scowling through the receiver.

I heard Rhett groan before replying. "I don't know, but it's perfect,"

"I agree. There are so many things to do in Vegas. Rooms definitely won't be an issue, either," Jasper agreed.

I picked up the planning conversation again. "Okay, so now that we have a location, we need to work out the entertainment."

Collin spoke up, again. "Well, if you want to go to a strip club, I could suggest Poles. It's where we took Travis. It's a gay strip club right off of the strip. By itself, it was definitely worth the trip."

Rhett interrupted. "Damn, Collin, you're on a roll tonight. Guys, why didn't we ask him to plan the bachelor party for us before now? Alright, I've got rooms booked at the Bellagio. I'm sending both of you links for the room confirmation as well as the one for Poles. My God." He gasped. "You guys gotta see this lineup! Seriously, if these are the current dancers there, I'm going even if Sean and Simon don't want to."

Jasper rolled his eyes. Apparently hearing his little brother talk about hot strippers was a bit too much for him. "Oh my God, Rhett. TMI, little brother. I didn't need to know that," Jasper complained into the phone. Collin chuckled and gave me a big smile while Jasper thumped his head down on the kitchen island.

Rhett continued, defending his comment. "What? Not all of us are getting laid on a nightly basis like you and Liam. I haven't even seen another naked man that wasn't on video since last year!"

Cringing even more, Jasper picked up the phone to reply to Rhett. "Alright. Seriously. Too much information. I don't want to hear about your sex life. We'll call you tomorrow, Rhett. I love you. Bye." Then he hung up before Rhett or I could get a word in on the conversation.

Collin and I completely lost it and both busted out laughing.

Jasper looked like he was watching a confusing tennis match, moving his head from me to Collin and back again. "What?'

I giggled and winked at Collin before answering him. "You're something, Jasper. I can't believe that, with as much as you like sex, you cringe when thinking about Rhett having it."

"He's my little brother, Liam. Sometimes I have problems remembering he's twenty-two and no longer eleven. I realize he's an adult. That he's had sex. That doesn't mean that I have to like it or that I want to think about it."

"Aww, that's so sweet," Collin said, picking on Jasper.

"Are you saying you don't feel that way about your younger brothers?"

"Jasper, my brothers and I are each only a year apart. My parents got busy and popped us out one right after the other. The youngest in the family is Travis, but he's got his brothers to worry about him. I've never really thought about or worried about my brothers having sex."

"Oh to be so lucky," Jasper replied.

"Anyway, I'm glad I could help with the bachelor party. Hopefully you guys find a bunch of things to do there. If not, it's always fun to eat tons of food and hit the casinos. It's a win-win no matter how you look at it," Collin said right before walking out of the kitchen with a water bottle.

Now that we had ideas for the bachelor party set, we sent off a group text to everyone that said they wanted to attend. It was going to be a fun weekend for sure.

I was surprised when Rhett called the next day. We said we'd call him, but we usually called in the evening after Jasper got home.

"Hey. Did you not want to talk to Jasper or something? He's not home from work yet, he had a late afternoon meeting."

"No, I'll call him back later. This isn't about the party. I need your advice. Logan texted and said he's going to Vegas but for me to not read too much into it. What the hell, Liam. Why would he say something like that? I just don't get him. He runs hot and cold with me all the time. What did I do wrong?" Clearly, this text from Logan was really upsetting my best friend.

"Wow, I honestly don't know, Rhett. About the only thing I know is he's been super busy at the ranch. I know very little about Logan. He's always been so quiet and kind of standoffish every time I've ever been around him. Have you thought about calling Simon and asking him about it?"

Rhett, clearly upset, continued his end of the conversation. "No. I'm honestly thinking about just giving up all together. He's so sweet when he calls and some days he even texts. Then he's cold and distant others. I just don't get it."

I didn't really have a good answer for Rhett. Instead, I gave him a suggestion he might not like. "Well, okay, if you're thinking about giving up, do you have anyone in mind? I mean, you and Travis seem cozy. What about him? He's really close to my age so he's only a year or two older than you."

"Ugh, no. Travis, although hot, is a total no. He has a thing for older guys. I'm younger than him. He creeped me out, actually. He said he'd gladly fuck me if in a threesome with Logan. I told him to get out and I haven't seen him since."

Color me *disgusted!* "Seriously?"

"Yeah. Can you believe it?" His voice raised half an octave. He was clearly unhappy "I just want out of Monterey.

I love my dads. I really do. They've been great, and I've really needed them but help, Liam. They're suffocating me!"

"Have you thought any more about moving back to Seattle?"

"You're in Crooked Bend. Why would I go to Seattle?"

"You went to Seattle alone before. Why not again?"

"I don't know. I'd have to find a new job and a new place to live and right now that's more than I can handle."

"Okay, what about Crooked Bend?" Rhett had mentioned it for *some* reason. "We still need a bakery. The building is still empty, and still for sale. You could totally come here and open your own bakery." Then I realized that we had our own single, attractive gay man right under our roof. "You could meet Collin. He's hot. Like, seriously hot. Tall, blond hair, blue eyes. He's a taller, hotter version of Travis. He's super sweet. I'm sure he could definitely put you into orgasmic bliss."

"Who is it I'm giving multiple orgasms to?" Collin startled me when he came into the living room.

"Oh shit," I replied. "Rhett, I'll talk to you after Jasper gets home, bye." I quickly hung up the phone and stared up at a smiling Collin.

"Do you really think that Jasper wants me to fuck his little brother? Are you sure I'm even a top?"

"Are you telling me you're a bottom?"

"No, I go either way but that wasn't the point. There *were* several points *to* talk about. You think I'm hot do you?"

I hope I didn't fuck up and send the wrong signals to Collin. I turned a nice shade of red. I knew I did because I could feel my face heating up. "Seriously, Collin? You've seen your family, right? The ones I've met have all been hot. You're no different."

Collin winked at me. "Well, thanks for that. I still don't

think Jasper would approve of me sniffing around his little brother."

"He's cute. He's a few inches taller than me, but not much taller. He can cook like it's cool. Bake. Oh my God can he ever bake."

"Yeah, but you're forgetting something."

"What?"

"From what I heard, he's hung up on someone named Logan."

"Yeah, well, Logan has been giving him the run around since Christmas. I think he's tired of his emotions being yo-yoed back and forth."

"Still don't think it's a good idea to get involved with my boss' little brother. That just has disaster written all over it."

"Okay, fine. But if I get him to move here, you'd see just how cute and wonderful he is. He deserves someone that will love him unconditionally."

"I don't doubt it, Liam. I'll just stick to being single, for now. I came in to let you know that Jasper told me to tell you that he'd bring supper home after his meeting."

"Alright. I guess that means we get pizza and breadsticks tonight. There aren't but the two places in Crooked Bend. You either have the pizza place or the diner and that's it."

"Hey, pizza works for me. I'll be in the office working on some plans if you need me." Collin walked off toward the stairs. He was definitely hot. But Jasper was so much hotter.

29

JASPER

Vegas. I'd only been there once before and I don't remember much about it. I remember it was loud and busy and bright. If things went as planned, this time around it would be pretty much the same. Only this time, I had every intention of remembering the trip. I planned on having a good time with my brothers, but especially Liam.

Sean was excited about having the bachelor party in Vegas. He wanted to surprise Simon at the party. He made arrangements with the owner of the club so that he would be the one to give Simon a lap dance after they were called up onto the stage. But, unfortunately, he felt nervous about how he'd perform. Like the good twin that I was, I offered to help.

Collin found us comical when he walked in on us in the office one day. Sean was sitting in a chair and I was doing my best to try to show him what he needed to do. In the end, Collin was a better teacher than I was. The guy definitely had some moves.

After a few preliminary lessons, we suggested several

videos for Sean to watch and learn from. Poor Simon, or *lucky* Simon? He wasn't going to know what hit him.

Sean had always been the quieter, calmer twin, so hearing what he planned took me aback, but I was happy for him and I knew that he'd do just fine. Even knowing he wasn't professional level, I knew that Simon would love it! Simon was as crazy about Sean as I was about Liam. Who could have predicted that both of us would find love in a tiny town in Wyoming? Neither one of us thought there would be many prospects and weren't looking for love. Sean, though, *knew* he wanted someone to love. I thought I wanted to stay as far away from love as possible but Liam changed that. There was no way I could ever imagine my life without him.

The end of July wasn't the best time to go to Las Vegas. It was hot in Wyoming in the mountains. In the desert in Vegas? Ugh. I was about to ask whose idea it was to come to the desert at the end of July when I remembered that it was mine. It was Collin who suggested Vegas, but Rhett, Liam, and I readily agreed. There really was nobody to blame but myself.

When we arrived, it was like heaven when we stepped inside the Bellagio to check in. Not only were the casino and hotel beautiful, the environment was also blessedly cool! Liam had been texting Rhett since we deplaned. Apparently my little brother was already here and already checked in. We flew on the same flight as Tyler and Isaac. Simon, Sean, Graham, and Logan were all booked on a later flight. That was Rhett and Liam's doing. There was something going on between the two, and I decided to go with it.

I'd only met Tyler once or twice before. He seemed like a nice guy, but somehow a little sad, too. Maybe a weekend away in Las Vegas would help cheer him up.

Hell, since Sean started seeing Simon, I had a whole new respect for cowboys and what all they did. Ranching was hard work. With animals that outweighed you, often with stubborn attitudes, the men who managed them deserved a lot more respect than they ever got. A weekend away was definitely earned as far as I was concerned.

Not two minutes after arriving at our room, Rhett was knocking on the door. I knew it was Rhett because Liam was expecting him. Besides, who else could it have been? After I got a quick hug from my brother, those two went to the bedroom of our suite to chat. God only knew when I'd see them again. I was happy to see Rhett smiling again. He had come a long way since he was kidnapped and I was so thankful for that.

Deciding to find out what those two were up to, I took a chance and went to the bedroom to join them. I found them both sprawled on our bed, talking. It didn't take long to figure out they were talking about Logan and what was going on between him and Rhett.

"I just don't know what to think anymore, Liam. He still calls me every other day. It's great, sometimes. The calls can be warm and personal; those make me feel good. Other times it's almost like I'm talking to a different person, I'm left feeling cold. I feel like I'm talking to two different people." Rhett sighed heavily while venting to Liam who just looked at me with a lost look on his face.

"I don't think he's two different people, Rhett, I just think he's working through some issues," I told Rhett after deciding to interject my two cents' worth. "Do you want me to ask him? I'd totally go all *big brother* on him. Even though he *is* about four inches taller than me and he's impressively ripped from hefting hay bales and grain bags around, I'll totally rip him a new one if you want me to. Just say the word and it's done."

Liam and Rhett both laughed at me. That was exactly what I intended. I *was* serious though. I'd already decided I was going to have a chat with Logan no matter what, but I'd definitely feel a lot better about butting in if Rhett gave his approval.

"You know what, Jasper? I'd love it if you could talk to him. Maybe you can get some answers. I know I can't. All I know is that he goes back and forth about being with me. Sometimes he says he wants to, then he seems to be hesitant. I know he's struggling with the fact that I'm so much younger than him. I'm twenty-two and he's thirty-six. Fourteen years is a difference, but hell, it's not like I act immature. I'm not, you know that."

"Is this why you two scheduled us for different flights?" I asked on a chuckle.

"No, honestly, there wasn't enough room available on the early morning flight for all of us so I decided to send Logan with Simon and Sean. Tyler said he didn't want to fly on the same plane as Graham so I added him to the early flight."

"Wonder what's going on with that? I get it that Graham is his boss, technically, but still. I thought they all got along."

"Oh. My. God. Did you not know?" Rhett directed his eyes to Liam. "How could he not know?"

"I don't know what you're talking about, Rhett. I'm just as clueless as Jasper is," Liam replied.

"Sean didn't tell you? What the hell happened to you two? You and Sean used to tell each other everything!" Rhett shouted.

"Well, things changed in college. I guess when we moved to Wyoming we matured and started our own lives. We just aren't as close as we used to be. You know I've kept things from him, it's only reasonable to assume that he's done the same. What are you talking about?"

"Okay, but you can't say anything!" I looked at Rhett. I didn't want him spilling any secrets, but I also wanted to know what was going on. He continued telling the story. "Sean told me after Simon told him. Anyway. I was told that Graham and Tyler were sleeping together. Like, they were getting it on. Simon was completely shocked because he could've sworn that Graham was straight!"

"Seriously? How does Simon know?"

"I guess he caught them. Well, kind of. He called one morning or something and woke them up. Instead of Graham answering his phone, it was Tyler. It was quite obvious that his call woke them up."

"Damn. I didn't see that one coming. I'll have to agree with Simon. I could've sworn that Graham was straight. Seriously? Graham and Tyler? Are they still a thing?" I asked Rhett hoping he knew.

"I don't know. Sean hasn't mentioned anything about them since. Neither of them really denied it nor fessed up."

"Wow. I just don't. Nope, still not seeing that one. Do you think that something happened and that's why Ty didn't want to be on the same plane as Graham? Wait a minute! Didn't we see Graham out with what's-her-name a few days ago in Jackson when we went out to dinner with Collin?" I asked Liam, remembering our trip to one of the restaurants in Jackson. We saw Graham with a lady friend. They seemed quite cozy.

"I remember that. I didn't think anything of it. I always thought he was straight. Maybe he is? I don't know. I guess we could watch the two of them closely and see if we notice anything," Liam replied, while getting off of the bed to go to his bag.

Liam pulled two shirts out of his bag. They were black with the word *Groom* on the front, and *I'm his* on the back. Arrows pointed in opposite directions under the words. "Okay, anyway, we need to make sure that we take these shirts for Simon and Sean to wear tonight." We definitely needed to make sure we get pictures of the grooms in their shirts.

"When do you think we should expect the grooms and the rest of our party?" I asked looking at my watch. We had a tentative schedule to keep. There were reservations tonight at the club and I wanted to make sure we kept them.

"They should've checked in by now. Why don't you text Sean and see?" Rhett looked at his own phone.

I don't think I've ever seen my little brother wear a watch. Liam didn't either. Honestly, the only reason why *I* did was because I needed to be able to tell the time during meetings and it wasn't professional to whip out my phone to check the time. I wore a watch, and over the years it has become a habit to glance at my wrist to check the time instead of checking on my phone.

Rhett's phone dinging meant that he at least got a response. "Alright, they're here. Let's go. I just sent a group text to the rest of the party. Let's go have fun and see some sexy guys taking it off and strutting it for us! Damn, I really think I need to get laid or something."

"Are you sure you're ready for that?" Liam asked what I couldn't.

Rhett's expression flashed to a little fear but he straightened it out quickly. He shrugged before answering. "I honestly don't know. I think so. I've come a long way thanks to my therapist. I'm never going to find out if I don't try, you know?"

"Alright, so Jasper and I aren't drinking tonight, well, maybe a shot or two, but that's it. Let's start with one here and we can work on getting you a little loosened up. That way you can get out there and be less inhibited and flirt with some of those dancers. While that's happening, Jasper is going to talk to Logan to let him know it's time to man up or move on." With the look Liam was giving me, I knew I didn't have any choice but to do what he said. I was going to be having a heart-to-heart with Logan tonight.

Liam grabbed the bottle of whiskey and poured three shots just as there was a knock at the door. I walked over to see who was there and was greeted by a smiling Isaac, a glaring Tyler, a sheepish-looking Graham, and a distressed Logan. The distress on Logan's face immediately cleared when he saw Rhett. Yeah, there was definitely something there. The look of distress quickly turned to one of concern when he saw Rhett take not one but two shots of whiskey in quick succession. Yeah, my little brother earned a little relaxation if you asked me. There were plenty of people to watch out for him tonight. He'd be alright.

"Do any of you want to join us in a shot before we collect the grooms-to-be?" I asked the rest of the group.

Everyone but Logan joined. I discovered that Logan didn't drink. Ever. That was commendable. Since he wasn't going to join us in drinking shots, I decided the time couldn't be better to have my chat with him. I figured now was probably the best time because later, we'd be at the strip club, highly distracted.

I asked Logan to walk with me to the lobby. I wanted to check on the cars we hired. He seemed anxious to accept and agreed to join me. We left the rest of the group in Liam's care.

After we verified the cars, I stalled Logan long enough to tell him I didn't think it was cool that he was playing with Rhett's feelings. He needed to either man up and claim him or he needed to cut all contact and let him be. I also hinted that Liam and I had shown a pic of Rhett to Collin and that Collin was interested in meeting Rhett once he moved to Crooked Bend. Logan didn't like the idea of Collin anywhere near Rhett, nor had he known that Rhett decided to move to Crooked Bend. That was a mistake on my part but I figured Rhett would forgive me for spilling his secret if it got him his guy. All in all, I felt the chat went well considering I was given so little time to do it in. We made our way back upstairs and joined the rest of the group outside Sean and Simon's room. It was time to get the bachelor party started.

30

LIAM

When we arrived at Simon and Sean's door, it was obvious that we'd interrupted something. I wish Jasper and I could be so open about our relationship but we couldn't. Not yet. I understood that. In just a few weeks, everyone would know that we were together. I couldn't wait for that wonderful day!

We collected the two grooms and headed toward the club. I was anxious to see Simon's reaction once Sean got on stage and surprised him with a lap dance. I knew Jasper possessed some moves and I could only assume that Sean did as well. More than once, I'd seen Simon with a satisfied smile on his face. So I could only assume that Sean had some moves that he used on his fiancé on more than one occasion.

Rhett's several shots of whiskey kicked in while we were in the car. He was starting to get that blissed-out look that he got when he was either well on his way to drunk or had just been thoroughly fucked. Since I knew he hadn't just been thoroughly fucked and I just watched him take three shots of whiskey back to back, I knew it was from whiskey and not a good fucking. He could surely use the latter. Just for good measure, I decided to turn a death glare on Logan. He looked shocked and apologetic in response. Good. He should feel sorry. He's been messing with Rhett's feelings the past few months. My friend Rhett did *not* need that shit. He needed someone to love him unconditionally, no matter what age or circumstances.

When we pulled up at the club, Sean discreetly looked over toward me and gave either me or Rhett, or both, a sly wink. I was anxious about what he had planned. When he got out and Simon plowed into the back of him because he suddenly stopped, it was all Jasper and I could do to not laugh at the show Sean was putting on. He mentioned the name of the club and it being Poles and sounded utterly shocked, but we both knew he already knew the name of the club. He was in on a set up with the owner for Simon's surprise. Trying to get things rolling, I shouted to the group to get things started. Jasper played along and scolded me for being too excited. This was going to be an interesting night.

We could smell alcohol, coconut oil, and sex from the minute we stepped into the club. I immediately considered dragging Jasper back to our room and lubing him up with oil and rubbing my body all over his. I was always horny around Jasper. Add alcohol and strippers and I was ready to go. He was a master at getting me to cum whenever he wanted and if the looks he was throwing my way were anything to go by, he knew just what state my dick was in; a painful one. Luckily, we were in a strip club and it wouldn't be inappropriate for me to obviously adjust myself. There was absolutely nothing supportive about the Andrew Christian jocks that I favored, but Jasper loved me in them and the easy access they afforded was definitely a plus.

We made our way to our reserved table, center stage. We

had an amazing time. The dancers at Poles definitely knew how to work the pole. I observed a lot of impressive and interesting positions. My mind wandered to Jasper and how adventurous he would get with me.

After about an hour of nonstop dancing and gyrating, the DJ asked for the two grooms to please come to the stage. Sean looked excited but Simon looked like he was ready to murder someone. I just tried not to laugh too hard. This was perfect and I was so glad we would have it on video for future blackmail purposes. Well, not really, we just wanted Simon and Sean to have a little something to remember their bachelor party by.

Simon and Sean made their way to the stage and took their seats like they were instructed by the two jock-wearing dancers. It wasn't until the music started and no dancers came out that Simon began to look confused. That was, until Sean looked over at him and gave him a devious smirk and winked before getting out of his chair and dancing his way over to Simon. The show that Sean put on for Simon was hot. There was no other word for it. At the same time, it was a bit awkward for us since we knew both of them and neither of them really did it for any of us. Instead, we all started taking shots and discussing what else we had planned for this weekend while Sean did his best to seduce Simon with a lap dance up on stage. Tonight was the big night of our weekend and the rest was pretty much open.

Before we knew it, the song was over and Simon was dragging Sean off of the stage. They did manage to stop by the table long enough for Jasper to give a half-ass toast to the couple before they were again on their way out of the club. That was to be expected though, because Sean just spent four minutes half-naked grinding his cock against

Simon's. Yeah, they were going to have fun back in their hotel room. If they made it that far.

The rest of us decided to stay, even though the two grooms left early. New dancers came out onto the floor in either jeans or skin-tight shorts that hid absolutely nothing. They roamed around so we could chat and mingle with them. It was a good plan; get the patrons even more excited and they'll tip the dancers even more. Going with our earlier plan, Rhett and I made our way over to one of the dancers who was drool-worthy. Rhett made it clear that he was interested and winking at me, the guy decided to play it up and slid his hands around both me and Rhett. He then reached down and squeezed our asses. Rhett moaned, I squeaked.

When I felt the hairs on the back of my neck stand on end, I turned around to see Jasper glaring at the dancer and before I knew it, he grabbed me by the shoulders and jerked me away and loudly, in front of everyone there declared, "Mine!"

He didn't stop there though. He planted a soul-stealing kiss on me in order to stake his claim, as if he needed to. I was already his and had been for a long time. When the kiss ended, I noticed that a very drunk Rhett was being dragged out of the club by a very pissed off looking Logan. Either Rhett was finally going to get what he wanted or he managed to piss Logan off enough that he no longer wanted anything to do with him. I had my money on option number one.

Once they were gone, that left me, Jasper, Isaac, Tyler, and Graham. Jasper told the others that we were headed out to see the sights of Vegas and we would see them tomorrow, and we headed out the door. It wasn't until we got into a cab that was waiting curbside that I realized that Jasper was pissed.

"Hey, what's wrong with you?"

"Seriously, Liam? You have to ask what's wrong with me? I'll tell you what's wrong. You were cuddling up with a stripper and he had his hand on your ass! That's what's wrong with me! I told you before, I. Don't. Share. Period."

I was stunned. I'd never seen Jasper angry like this. "Whoa, Jasper. I get it his hand was on my ass, but I didn't ask for him to put it there. If you were closer, you would've known that I didn't want it, didn't like it, and was about to shove away right before you walked up and made a show of things. He was supposed to cuddle up with Rhett, not me!"

"Damn, fucking sexy strippers," Jasper muttered quietly.

"Hey, look at me," I implored to Jasper. When he finally looked at me, the look in his eyes was not one that I wanted to see on a regular basis. He was so pissed off. "Are you pissed at me or the stripper? I need to know what's going on, Jasper."

"You're mine, Liam. He grabbed your ass and smirked when he did it."

"Okay. I'm sorry, Jasper. Again, I didn't want him to grab my ass. I was with a quite drunk Rhett and he was supposed to cuddle up to Rhett, not both of us. Really, Cupcake, I'm sorry. You know I love you and I don't want anyone else but you. Please, Jasper. I didn't ask for it and it meant absolutely nothing to me. Please, don't end us because of that."

Jasper's expression turned to shock, but he was still angry under that. "What? You think I'd break up with you because of that? I'm pissed, but you're stuck with me, Liam."

I still felt horrible. My stomach was beginning to churn with nerves. "Why are you pissed at me?"

"I'm not." He groused. "I'm pissed at him for grabbing you and I'm pissed at myself because I should've openly claimed you a long time ago."

"Okay, so claim me. You'll get no complaints from me."

"Alright, wait here. I'll be back in a few minutes."

It was then that I noticed our cab had taken us back to the Bellagio. Jasper was out of the cab before I had a chance to say anything. I did as he said and sat there, waiting for him to return. When he did a few minutes later, he looked exactly like he did when he left. I didn't know what was going on so I decided to find out and ask.

"What's going on? Why are we back at the casino and now leaving again? I don't understand, Jasper."

"I know, but you will. I was checking on Rhett. Logan answered his door so I know he'll be alright. As for you, you little imp, I've got a surprise for you."

"Really, you know I love surprises! You're so good at them too! Hemingway was the absolute best surprise!"

"Well, hopefully this will top Hemingway."

"Do I get any hints?"

"Nope. You'll know soon enough. What I said, Liam. I meant it. You're mine. I love you and I'm claiming you."

"I've got no issues with that, Jasper. I love you too."

"Good. I sure as hell hope so because that's about to be tested, Liam."

Now *I* was feeling pissed. I huffed and looked out the window before looking back at Jasper. "What do you mean, *tested*? What's happening? Do you doubt that I love you? Seriously? I changed everything for you, Jasper! I agreed to wait to tell your twin about us! Seriously? Do you seriously doubt that I'm in love with you?" I couldn't believe what I thought Jasper was saying. What the fucking hell? Was he serious? How did we go from adopting a kitten and buying a house together to my love for him being tested in Vegas?

"Liam, look at me," Jasper said while grabbing my chin and forcing me to look him directly in the eyes. I loved looking at his eyes. They were the exact color of the whiskey that we'd had earlier in the room. They held so much expression. They told me his moods and his thoughts. I could literally spend hours staring at them. I loved to look into his eyes when he made love to me. It connected us more than anything. "No, I don't doubt that you love me. I know you love me. I just hope you love me as much as I do you."

I was still unhappy with this conversation, though I did calm down. "Jasper, I love you more than anything. I thought you knew that. If you don't, I'm sorry I haven't made that clear enough."

"You can make it very clear right now, Liam. Come with me."

I didn't even realize the car stopped at first. I didn't recognize this place. Somewhere on the strip but it just looked like any other buildings on the strip. "Where are we? What are we doing?"

"You'll see." Jasper grabbed my hand and pulled me into the building. We were greeted by a very nice middle-aged man who introduced himself as Mark. I still didn't know where the hell we were. I looked over at Jasper and he was pulling his wallet out of his pocket.

"Jasper, what's going on?" Realization set in and my heart completely stopped. Jasper grabbed both of my hands and dropped down on one knee right in the middle of the floor in what I finally realized was a wedding chapel.

"Liam, I know you love me. I know you know I love you. It wasn't until you came along that I was willing to make a choice and take a chance on love. I'm so thankful that I did. You are the absolute best thing that's ever happened to me. I want everyone to know that you're mine, Liam. I want them to know I'm yours. I want to know; do you love me enough?

Do you love me enough to take a chance and choose me? Will you marry me, Liam?"

My mind was racing in competition with my heart. I was getting the whole kit and caboodle; everything I've ever wanted! I loved Jasper with everything I was and he just asked me to marry him; and he wanted to do it right then and there.

31
JASPER

Liam and his parents didn't talk so I'd never have traditional in-laws. I'd seen the stress that Cammie put on both Sean and Simon and there was no fucking way that I was ever going to go through that. I took a chance and took Liam to a wedding chapel on the strip. I hoped like hell that he'd be willing to elope with me. I hadn't planned on asking him the first night we got to Vegas. We had three days there. I hoped to maybe slip away the second day. When I saw that stripper grab Liam's ass and smirk at me while doing it, my inner caveman came out and I became a possessive asshole. Liam was mine, and I was going to stake my claim. Of course, that all bordered on the hopes that he would say yes. I was still waiting. I had to remind myself that I needed to breathe. It was painful, and seconds felt like hours.

Liam probably didn't realize that it would destroy me if he turned me down. The waiting definitely wasn't helping any. After time slowed down even more, so seconds felt more like days than mere hours, I finally got the answer that'd change my life completely.

My Choice, My Chance   239

"What. The. Actual. Fuck. Jasper! Of course I'll marry you!" After those heartfelt and passionate words, I had one very happy imp wrapped around me. It felt, honestly, like quite the miraculous feat since I was down on one knee, but he managed. Liam's lips crashed onto mine and everything in my world righted itself again. Time sped up to regular speed, my heart and brain slowed to a regular pace, and I was able to breathe again. After sealing our engagement with a yes-worthy kiss, Liam detangled himself from me and we both got off of the floor.

"You're sure? You're ready to do this? Now?" I held him by the shoulders and looked him in the eye. "I can't go through what Sean's going through, Liam. I can't handle a large, crazy wedding. I want to marry you now. After all, we're in Vegas, so why not?"

"Yes! Green! Now! I'm all in, Jasper. I'll definitely marry you right now!"

After Liam said yes, once again to my surprise proposal, we took care of the required paperwork. Before I knew it, we were standing in front of the officiant with two witnesses, strangers whom I would never see again, as far as I could figure. Jesus, this was such a spur of the moment thing that, unfortunately, I didn't even have a ring for Liam. That was definitely something I'd remedy, fast. I was claiming Liam, and I wanted everyone to know he was taken. That meant I needed to put a ring on the man, and soon. But, first things first. I tried my best to focus on what the officiant was saying instead of looking into Liam's beautiful blue eyes. Liam squeezed my hands tightly, which cued me to what was being said.

"Promise to love and honor him in sickness and health, and to be loyal to only him for as long as you both shall live?" the officiant said to me and I knew this was it. This was the point where my life changed forever.

"I definitely do," I replied while smiling down at Liam and squeezing his hands back. Unfortunately, I zoned out again while staring into Liam's eyes while the officiant read the vows to Liam. I was coherent enough to hear Liam say "I do" and to repeat after the officiant when I needed to but, otherwise, I was pretty much on cloud nine. I was ecstatic to be marrying the man I loved, but at the same time the event was surreal. Before I knew it, the officiant said those magical words.

"By the power vested in me by the state of Nevada, I now pronounce you husband and husband. Gentlemen, you may now kiss your husband."

That was all it took, Liam was once again wrapped around me. I did the only thing a good husband would do; I grabbed his ass and claimed his mouth. We may not have decided on a traditional wedding, and I knew I was going to get a lot of shit for that once my family found out, but there was nothing traditional about Liam and me thus far, so why the hell would we change to say "I do?"

Trying to maintain a little respectability, I pulled back from the kiss and said something I knew I would never get tired of ever saying to the man in my arms. "I love you, husband of mine, so much."

When Liam smiled at me and gave me a quick peck on the lips, I knew I made the right choice. I knew we would make this work. We were probably going to hear a lot of shit from everyone, but they would just have to get over it.

We put our final signatures on the paperwork. As soon as I had our copy, we were off. There was a wedding night to get started and I was definitely going to take full advantage of that.

Part of the package I purchased when we arrived at the wedding chapel was a limo ride back to the hotel of our choice so we climbed into the back of a sleek, black limo when we exited the chapel. The driver asked which hotel as we were climbing in so there was no need to tell him after we settled in the back, which was a good thing because the partition was already closed, giving us privacy. I'm happy that it was because Liam immediately crawled into my lap and before the car was even moving, our lips were locked together and our hands were exploring each other's body. I already knew every inch of Liam's body, but now I got to re-explore it as my husband's. God, how long I'd been looking forward to that. The drive was too short to really allow much, but I didn't want to consummate our marriage in the back of a limo, anyway. We had a beautiful hotel room and we were going to make it there even if my dick was painfully hard and begging to be buried in what it knew as warm heaven.

We somehow managed to pull ourselves apart once I realized we were sitting in front of the hotel. I think we'd just pulled up because the driver opened the door at the same time that Liam crawled off my lap. He didn't stop moving until he'd crawled out the door. You would think that in Vegas seeing a limo wouldn't be a big deal, but we drew a crowd for some reason, and I just couldn't understand it. The driver congratulated us as we climbed out and we thanked him before we walked into the hotel hand in hand.

We made a bee-line for the elevators and once we were in the confines of the shiny box, I moved Liam in front of me and nibbled on his neck from behind. It seemed we were doomed to stop on every floor on our way up. I knew Liam was already turned on; he'd spent the entire limo ride in my lap grinding his dick against mine.

At one stop, the elevator filled half full. I knew it was time to be a little devious so I made my way to Liam's right side and nibbled on his neck right at the hot spot I knew. I discreetly wrapped my arms around his chest and pinched his nipples through his shirt at the same time I bit down and sucked on that magical spot. I knew I succeeded in getting the result that I wanted, Liam cumming in his pants, when he shuddered in my arms and I had to hold him up because his legs seemed to give out on him. It was probably wrong, and I knew I was going to pay for it, but I was also planning on making it up to him. He managed to remain mostly quiet through his orgasm, and I only heard him because I was so close to his mouth. The low, quiet moan he couldn't keep in had me almost cumming with him.

Thankfully, we finally made it to our floor. It took a second, but I managed to get Liam to exit by giving him a little push toward the open doors. Once we were in the hall, he gave me a dirty look telling me that I was in for it, but I didn't care. I already had a plan, and I was going to make it up to him just as soon as we got into our room.

When we reached our door I possessed just enough mental acuity to tell Liam to text Rhett, even though I knew he was with Logan. He needed to know we made it back and were going to be busy for a while.

By the time I got our key card in the slot and the little light turned green so I could open the door, Liam was putting his phone back into his pocket. Once we were inside it was no holds barred. We tore off our clothes before the latch clicked. As soon as the door was closed, Liam turned to me and my heart melted a little.

"I love you, Liam. I promise I'm about to make it up to

you. It's just so fucking hot knowing I can make you cum without even touching your dick." I was desperately trying to plead my case. I knew he wasn't really mad at me. At least, not too much. I had a plan and put it into action by grabbing his shirt and pulling it over his head.

"Kick off your shoes," I told him as I got on my knees. Once I was there, I undid his belt and popped the button on his jeans and unzipped his fly before I pulled them down his slim legs. I loved him in skinny jeans. He was very slender though his muscles were well defined. I saw the wet spot that covered the front of his lime green jock and looked up at him with an apologetic smile on my face. "I promise, I'm going to make it up to you. Starting. Right. Now." I peeled the wet underwear down and enjoyed watching his half-hard cock spring out when it was freed from its confines.

Most of the mess was in his jock, but the little bit that was left behind I quickly cleaned up with my tongue. Liam's moans told me that he forgave me and enjoyed what I was doing. Hopefully, he would continue to do so. After I got him cleaned up, I pulled away long enough to remove my own clothes. Liam only slightly protested until he realized why I stopped.

I pulled my shirt over my head at the same time I stood. I kicked my shoes off and bent over to remove my socks. While I was still leaning over, Liam fumbled with my belt. When I straightened, he got my belt open and my jeans unfastened in a hurry. He pushed my jeans and boxer briefs down in one go. My leaking cock rejoiced when finally freed from its prison.

"I need my wallet," I told Liam as I stepped out of my jeans. He retrieved it for me before he stood again. I quickly grabbed the condom and lube packet out of it and threw the wallet on the floor. While I was fumbling with the lube, I dropped the condom while I opened the lube. I looked at Liam and gave him his first command of the evening. "Turn around and put your hands on the door," I slicked my fingers with half of the lube. There was nothing romantic about the quick prep I did. I'd take just enough time to make sure I didn't hurt him. That was the very last thing I ever wanted to do.

"You ready?" I asked Liam as I slowly stood, kissing my way up his spine.

"Yes. Please, Jasper," he croaked, passion building so quickly I could feel his skin vibrating.

Liam's plea was all I needed to hear before I squeezed the rest of the lube into my hand and lubed up my cock. I was too far gone to remember the condom on the floor by my feet. I lined up my slick cock and within moments was pushing into Liam bare. It was the first time that I had ever gone bare with someone. The fact that Liam felt hotter than normal made me realize what I'd done. It wasn't until I was buried balls-deep in him that my brain caught up and I realized my mistake.

"Shit." I started to pull out of the best feeling I'd ever experienced.

"What?" Liam asked looking over his shoulder at me.

"I forgot the condom, give me a minute. I'm sorry, Liam. I didn't do it on purpose, I swear."

"Wait!" Liam said. He reached back and grabbed my hip. I was halfway out when he stopped me. He gently tugged me forward while blowing my mind with his next statement. "We've both tested negative twice since we've been together and we're married now. I don't want to use condoms anymore, Jasper. We're obviously committed and faithful, so why?"

I could only groan into his shoulder while I picked him up below the thighs and pushed the rest of the way back into him, bare. Forever bare, from our wedding night forward for all time.

"Yes, Liam. Fuck yes. Good. You feel so fuckin' good, sweetheart. Love you so much," I chanted while thrusting in and out from behind. Our height differences made it awkward since I had to pick Liam up but with him pinned between me and the door, it wasn't uncomfortable.

"Yes, Jasper. Harder. Please. Wanna feel you explode inside me."

I was already on edge since I didn't cum when Liam did in the elevator and I knew I wasn't going to last much longer. It felt too good, was too wonderful to be bare in someone for the first time ever.

"Gonna cum, Liam. I'm sorry. I can't last. You feel too good."

"Bite me, Jasper! I'm almost there too!"

I did as Liam asked. I latched on to the neck bruise I'd already gifted Liam and when I did, I couldn't help it, I exploded inside my husband. The feeling of his warm channel clamping down on my pulsing cock, combined from the scream that came out of his mouth was too much for me. My legs gave out and we fell to the floor. I sat with Liam in my lap, my cock still spurting inside. His cock left a trail of cum streaming across the door. I was still cumming. This was the biggest, most intense orgasm of my life. My God, my entire body was tingling from it!

I fell backwards, Liam falling with me. Now he was lying on top of me on the floor. I was panting, desperately trying to catch my breath and regain feeling in my legs. Liam seemed to be in a similar state if the dead weight above me was anything to go by.

"Fuck. So good. Don't know if I can move, Jasper." I heard Liam's quiet voice above me.

"I know what you mean," I panted. "Give me a minute and I'll get us to the bed. Maybe."

"I might be able to crawl, in a few minutes."

Thinking of Liam crawling across the floor interested my dick again and it twitched inside of Liam which caused him to moan. I gently kissed the side of his head and used what strength I possessed to gently lift him enough that I pulled out of him. He sat on top of me and I felt my mess start dripping out of him, pooling on my lower abdomen.

"That is so fucking hot."

"What is?" he asked.

"My cum dripping out of your ass and pooling on my stomach," I said.

"Mmm," was the only response I received.

Unsure, I was quick to give him an option to go back to using condoms. "If you don't like it, I can wear a condom, it's alright."

"No, that's not it. I'm just trying to get my legs to work enough so I can get up. I don't want the condoms. I haven't for a while but didn't know if you'd be willing to go bareback. It's what I want for us. I want there to be nothing between us, in any way, including condoms."

Oh, how I love this man! "Then that's what we'll do. No more condoms. Now, let's see if we can make it to the bed for round two. My legs aren't numb anymore, so I should be able to get us there," I said as I stood up and slung Liam up into my arms and carried him into the bedroom to continue our wedding night.

32

LIAM

I couldn't believe it. I was married to Jasper. I was content being his boyfriend and living with him in the house we bought together, but now we were married. That meant he was mine and I can keep him, forever. He chose *me*! If I didn't feel his cum leaking out of me, I'd have thought that I was dreaming, but nope, it was very much real. I was very much married.

Jasper carried me into the bedroom of our suite and threw me into the center of the bed. I couldn't help but giggle about the whole situation and he was almost immediately on top of me. Instinctively, I opened my legs to make room for him.

"You need to do that more often." Jasper kissed me on the tip of my nose. "It's an absolutely beautiful sound." Jasper looked down at me and brushed the hair off of my forehead.

"Do what?"

"Giggle. I love that sound. You laugh frequently, but when you giggle, it's completely different and I love to hear it."

"Well, I'll make sure I giggle for you more often then," I replied. "Now, where were we?" I pulled Jasper's head down to mine and kissed him.

We didn't go to sleep until almost five the next morning. Unfortunately when Jasper woke me up after only a few hours of sleep, I begged him to give me a little more time. The man had been, and obviously was still, insatiable. He completely wore me out. My ass was sore and my balls ached. I swear, they were completely empty and I honestly didn't know if I could get another erection again, and that's saying something. I never experienced anything like that around Jasper, ever.

Thankfully, he let me go back to sleep. I woke up a couple hours later wrapped in his arms. It was insanely bright in the room so I knew it was no longer early morning. Looking at the clock on the bedside table, I noticed it was almost ten and knew we were going to be busy with the rest of our group. I tried to untangle myself from Jasper without waking him but as soon as I got one arm free, he woke up.

"Hey, where do you think you're going?"

"To the bathroom unless you want me to empty my bladder on you." Jasper let me go and I was able to get up and make my way to the bathroom to relieve myself. I wasn't entirely surprised when Jasper followed me into the bathroom and wrapped his arms around me while I peed. When I was finished, it was Jasper's turn at the toilet while I started the shower. When I climbed out of the bed I realized one of the downsides to forgoing condoms was the sticky, and in places, crusty mess left behind if you pass out before showering. So a shower this morning was a must.

Jasper spoke up and caught my attention as he climbed into the shower with me. "How are you this morning? I know I was probably overly exuberant last night, but I couldn't help myself," he apologized. "I only ever plan on getting married just the once and that means I'm only ever going to get the one wedding night so I wanted to make sure it was memorable."

"Trust me, Jasper, it *was* memorable. I'm a little sore, but not any more than I've been before. I'm glad you only ever plan on getting married once, because you've already said 'I do' to me and that means you're stuck with me." I dove under the water to wet my hair and blindly reached for the shampoo we had placed on the shelf. Luckily, Jasper pulled me to him and started massaging the shampoo he had in his hands into my hair.

"That was the plan, you know?" Jasper said while massaging my scalp and neck.

I was surprised at what Jasper told me. "Really? You're saying you planned it now?"

Jasper chuckled and shook his head. "Naw, I absolutely did not plan on getting married last night. I was honestly planning on asking you today and then dragging you to get married tonight but things changed when I needed to stake my claim after a certain stripper decided to move in on what wasn't his. Rinse and I'll wash your body." He swallowed and looked at me with that occasional serious expression. After I rinsed my hair and stepped out of the stream, he continued. "That's not the point. The point is, if I'd planned better, you'd have a ring on your finger. Liam, I'm sorry, sweetheart. I didn't plan at all." Jasper picked up my left hand and rubbed my ring finger while looking at me. The look of sadness that he had on his face broke my heart and I had to fix it. I didn't know how, I just knew I needed to. I grabbed the shampoo and switched places with Jasper.

I rubbed my hand up and down Jasper's arm before pouring shampoo into his hand so he could wash his hair.

Our height difference made it difficult for me to wash his hair unless we were in the tub. Once he started lathering up his hair, I washed his body with the soapy washcloth and continued. "Hey, don't worry about it, Jasper. Just because we don't have rings doesn't mean we aren't married. A piece of jewelry doesn't make us married. We're not wearing rings and we're still married. If we get rings and start wearing them, that won't make us any more married than we are now."

After rinsing his hair, he pouted and lowered his forehead down to mine. "I know but I want you to have a ring. I want everyone to know that you're unavailable."

"Alright, Jasper. We'll get rings. I've got nothing against wearing your ring. When do you want to get them?"

"I don't know. We can go out to a jewelry store today and look if you want. Otherwise, we might have to wait until we're in California in a few weeks for Sean's wedding. I don't know if Crooked Bend has any nice jewelry stores or not. I've never needed to look."

"Why don't we just wait until we're in California? We can take an extra day after the wedding and go ring shopping in Monterey. Sound good?"

Jasper looked like he felt a little better. "Sounds great. Now, what would you like to do today, husband of mine?" Jasper asked me while giving me a little kiss. I love all of the different sides to him. Playful and attentive Jasper was one of my favorites.

I playfully pushed Jasper out from under the shower spray so I could rinse the body wash off of me while I answered him. "Well, you wore me out last night and this morning, so could we maybe start with brunch and then go from there?"

"Brunch sounds great. Then I was thinking maybe some

time in the spa? How about a massage and a mani/pedi? Sound good?" Jasper asked while rubbing my body, helping to rinse the soap.

I just about fainted. It'd been months since I had a mani/pedi. There were certain things you gave up to live in cowboy country with your sexy architect. Regular manicures and pedicures were two of them. "Don't tease. Do you mean it?"

"I'm not teasing, Liam. I mean it. I scheduled it this morning when I first woke up. We have an appointment at noon." I couldn't get out of the shower fast enough. When I realized we were both clean and rinsed, I turned off the faucet and opened the door. Grabbing two fluffy towels off the rack, I handed one to Jasper then started drying myself with the other.

"Jasper, you are my heaven!" I could feel my excitement level rising. "If the appointment is at noon, we have plenty of time to enjoy a relaxed brunch before we go. We should let everyone know that we're going to the spa."

"I'll send a group text when we get finished drying off and get dressed, before we head down to brunch."

We finished drying off, and got ready for our day. I was excited about spending some time in the spa. It'd been awhile since I was pampered like that and honestly, I missed it. If Jasper was offering a trip to the spa, ooh yeah, I was definitely on board with that!

We got dressed and made our way to the restaurant for brunch. I was starving and was looking forward to many breakfast foods; especially since I didn't have to cook them. I didn't mind cooking with Jasper, but since we were in the land of all-you-can-eat, I was definitely going to take advantage.

After we got our food, we found a table and joined the other buffet participants.

"Shit!" I said after I sat down and realized I wasn't sitting on my phone.

"What?"

"I forgot my phone in our room. I was going to text Rhett and let him know we were up and going to be out and about all day."

"I've got mine. I'll send him a text."

"Thanks. I just want him to know where we are."

"Hey, it's no big deal. I get it. There, text is sent. Now, let's enjoy our brunch and walk around for a bit before we head to the spa."

"Sounds perfect."

We didn't realize that our message failed to send and Rhett never got the message. With my phone upstairs in yesterday's pants, the battery dead, it wasn't receiving any messages or calls. For whatever reason, Jasper's phone chose that moment to spaz out and stop working so nobody knew where we were or how to reach us.

Of course, we didn't know that until hours later. We experienced a wonderfully relaxing day. After brunch, we walked around. We checked out the fountain in front of the hotel, and then headed to the spa for our massages, manicures, and pedicures. Afterward, we decided we wanted to check out the pool. We returned to our room only long enough to change into our trunks then spent an hour pool side until I had enough of Jasper growling at anyone who even looked our way.

"Alright, Cupcake. Let's go." I grabbed Jasper's hand and pulled him out of the pool area. He clearly needed to be reassured that he was it for me so that's what I intended to do—right after we showered. We made it back to our room in record time and I was naked before I crossed the bathroom threshold. I got the shower going and was stepping in just as Jasper made his way into the bathroom.

"Are you in a hurry or something?" Jasper asked as he entered the bathroom.

"Yes, so get your ass in here so I can wash you and get my mouth around your cock." His face lit up like a Christmas tree! He wasted no time in dropping his trunks where he stood, joining me in the shower. I had him washed and rinsed in no time, and was on my knees with his cock pressing against the back of my throat before he knew what was going on. It didn't take long before he was shooting down my throat. He pulled me up, pressing his lips passionately against mine.

"Not that I'm complaining, but what was that for?" Jasper asked, panting lightly.

I figured a little white lie was appropriate. I didn't want him thinking I didn't like how jealous he got. "All the growling you did at the pool. It was sexy and turned me on. I felt I should do something about that."

"Well, now that you accomplished your goal, let me return the favor," Jasper offered while reaching down for me. That was the moment that we heard a loud banging on our suite room door. The only reason we were able to hear it was because Jasper didn't close the bathroom door when he came in.

"You go find out who's banging on our door before we get in trouble and I'll hurry up and shower," I said after giving Jasper another quick peck on the lips. He was out of the shower and did a quick wipe-down with a towel before walking out of the bathroom and closing the door behind him. I hurried through my shower. I wanted to see what was going on, but didn't rush too much because technically, I shouldn't be in Jasper's room. I was incredibly thankful I thought to wrap a towel around my waist before exiting the bathroom, because I never expected absolutely everyone to be in the room with Jasper.

I stuck around long enough to know that Sean was extremely upset, then became a coward and ran back into the bedroom to hide. Of course my mind was running scenario after scenario thinking that I was causing a problem between Jasper and Sean because he found out about us. Thankfully, Jasper came into the room a few minutes later and let me know not to worry and that no matter what, he still loved me and that he chose to be with me because he wanted to. We quickly got dressed and left the room.

It wasn't until after we left the bedroom of our suite that we discovered Jasper's phone never sent the text to Rhett this morning and that everyone had been looking for us all day. I felt bad about that, and I knew Jasper did as well. We did our best to calm everyone and they finally relaxed a little once we showed them my dead cell phone and Jasper's non-working one.

It seemed to take Sean a moment to really put two and two together. Sean wanted to know if we were seeing each other. He was a little slow on the uptake, I thought. We did our best to explain that yes, we were seeing each other and that we had been for a while.

Sean seemed to finally catch up. "Wait! Liam was the one you've been seeing all these months?"

"Yes, he is," Jasper replied.

Thankfully, Sean seemed to accept that as is and let it go. I knew if he hadn't been so stressed and preoccupied by his wedding lately, he probably would've dug a little bit deeper about everything that had been going on with Jasper and me. As it was, I knew our days of keeping our marriage a secret were short. It was definitely not the time to spill that particular secret. The last thing I wanted to do was take anything away from Sean after the hell he went through trying to plan his wedding.

33

JASPER

*A*fter the whole *where the hell have you been* moment, we decided to spend the rest of the evening in the casino at our hotel. It wasn't like they didn't go out and enjoy their day. They went to the aquarium for shit's sake!

Liam chatted with Rhett briefly. My brother assured him everything was okay between the two of them. Rhett did say they needed to talk about what happened after Logan took him back to the room after the strip club. I didn't know if I wanted to know about that or not.

We all lingered around the casino and did the normal touristy things like watch the fountain, play the slots, and just kill time before we needed to get up in the morning to catch our flight back home.

It was a relief that Liam now had every reason to be at our house. I hated that we hadn't let everyone know that Liam was the one that I was seeing. Now they knew, so we could move forward with our lives together. I only hoped they were as understanding once they found out that we eloped before Sean was able to walk down the aisle. I didn't see that conversation going well.

Liam and I enjoyed our second night in Vegas and turned in early. We needed to be up early and, honestly, we were still recovering from lack of sleep the night before. I made sure I made it up to Liam that he didn't get to finish when we were interrupted that afternoon. He went to sleep with a smile on his face. That was how I always wanted him to fall asleep. Of course, in my arms. If I had those two things every night, I'd be the happiest man alive.

All too soon, we were back in Crooked Bend and our daily grind. Liam spent his days at home with Hemingway, writing about whoever his current characters were. Collin and I went to either the office or whichever ranch or site we were scheduled for. Nothing was really different except that Liam was now legally my husband and everyone knew that we were dating, though, not that we were married.

We called my dads and let them know who I'd been seeing. They weren't overly surprised, they seemed to already know. Then again, they were my dads and they always seemed to know what was going on in our lives. I just really hoped they would be forgiving when we told them we eloped so they wouldn't be getting a wedding out of us.

Both Liam and I were no strangers to paperwork. When people got married, there was an almost endless supply of new paperwork to fill out. We talked about it and Liam really wanted to take my last name. I figured we would either hyphenate our names and both use both last names or we would both keep our respective last names. Liam didn't want to keep his. I suppose I could understand. After all, his parents didn't want him, so why should he want to be affiliated with them? I was happy to have him choose to take mine. Of course, that added more paperwork.

I made it my mission to make Liam happy, but that was nothing new. For months I'd been doing whatever I could to make sure he knew I wanted him, that he was special, and that he was happy. I wanted my husband to be happy. There was nothing wrong with that. He'd gone through so much negativity and unhappiness before I met him and I wanted to make it up to him as much as I possibly could.

The secret was out at home when Collin saw our paperwork on the table. We didn't necessarily want to tell him first, but we were left with no choice when he saw the last names on the forms.

"Hey, I think you made a typo here, Liam. You put Liam Welsh instead of Campbell," Collin pointed out on one of the many forms lying on the table. Liam and I looked at each other and when he just shrugged, I decided that we would just tell him. After all, someone should know, right? That was the whole point of getting married. I wanted everyone to know that Liam was mine.

"No, it's not a typo, Collin. Liam filed a change of name with the proper administrations after we got married."

Collin coughed, choking on *my* words. "What? You're married? Since when? I thought you two were just dating."

Listening to Liam laugh beside me while looking at Collin's face had me quickly joining Liam before I could reply. "We eloped in Vegas. You're the only one that knows so please don't tell Sean."

"Why doesn't Sean know? Why would you keep *this* from *him*?"

"It's not malicious, Collin. We just don't want to steal any of the attention away from him and Simon. We've already agreed to tell everyone as soon as the newly married couple is away on their honeymoon or just as soon as they get back."

"Speaking of honeymoons, if you two are married, when are you going on yours?"

"We had a wonderful wedding night, and, for now, that'll work. I'll take Liam away after Sean gets back from his and things calm down."

"Wow, I can't believe you two got hitched." Collin winked at us. "Well, congratulations. I'm really happy for you two. You've seemed really happy and perfect together so I really mean it."

We both thanked him before he walked off and we went back to filling out paperwork. The end of the stack was in sight and I was ready for it to be over. Who knew that getting married required so much additional paperwork after you said *I do*? I never would've.

Collin wasn't gone long; he quickly came back in and picked right back up where he'd left off. "Oh yeah, I almost forgot, I'll finally get to move in on the fifteenth. I know it's two weeks later than I originally told you but the owner of the condo I was going to take decided he wanted more rent. That stuck me with finding somewhere else to stay with almost no notice. I'm really sorry, you two. I promise I'll be out of here just as soon as I can."

"Hey, don't worry about it. Unless you're uncomfortable here, we've got no problem with you staying here with us. We wanted to ask you if you would check in on Hemingway while we're at the wedding, anyway. I know you're going up for the wedding, but we have to be there the entire three days and I just don't want to leave him here by himself that long. He should be fine overnight but not for three days," Liam said, reassuring Collin.

"Hey, it's no problem. Your cat is pretty cool. I don't mind staying here with him as long as you two don't mind."

"Didn't I just say we didn't mind you being here?" Liam said while busting out his finger.

I couldn't help it, I again laughed. It was so wonderful to have that man as mine. Life was never going to be dull or boring with him around.

"Yes, you did, but I still feel bad about crashing here. Especially since I know you two are newlyweds!"

"Seriously, it's okay. You aren't bothering us and as long as we don't bother you, it's all good. Hey, have you given any more thought to giving Rhett a call? After everything that happened in Vegas, I think he's probably not going to be talking to Logan anytime in the near future," Liam said with what I knew was his I'm up to something smile on his face.

I looked between the two of them, confusion written in flashing neon across my face. "What about Collin calling Rhett? Why would Collin call Rhett? What happened with Logan?"

"Calm down, Jasper. I promise, I'm not going to call your brother. I already told Liam that I thought it was a bad idea for me to get involved with him. He's your brother. Dating my boss' brother is never a good idea."

I felt a little better after Collin's reassurance. "Alright, so you're not interested in Rhett, got it. Now, what happened with Logan and Rhett? I specifically told Logan to either grow a pair or leave him alone. Didn't he listen?"

I couldn't believe it but Liam started laughing. Not just a little chuckle either, a full-on belly laugh.

"Calm down. I was just giving Collin a hard time is all. From what I got from Rhett, Logan seems to have decided to 'grow a pair' as you put it. I'm really happy for him.

Although, I have a feeling that Logan's going to move at a snail's pace and it's going to drive Rhett insane. Otherwise, I think they're heading in the right direction."

"I should've known you were up to something when I saw the look on your face. Now, explain this conversation about getting Collin to give Rhett a call?"

"Nothing. I just thought that Collin might be a good fit for Rhett is all. He said no and made some very valid points so it's all good."

"Yeah, the biggest two being that one: he's my boss' brother, and two: he's hung up on Logan. I'm not looking to be anybody's rebound guy. Been there, done that, no thanks, not again."

Liam waved his hands up and down to stop Collin's unnecessary explanation. "Okay, okay. Still, we need to find you a guy or something. This place is full of sexy cowboys. That's what you need! We need to find you a sexy cowboy!"

Collin looked more than a little annoyed at Liam's insistence that he needed help getting a date. "No, you don't. You really don't. I told you, Liam. I'm perfectly happy with being single right now. Seriously. No, I don't need a cowboy."

Liam didn't seem to want to take a hint, or even a direct point. "Why the hell not? It worked for Sean and its most likely going to work for Rhett. Don't you want someone, Collin?"

Collin tried to keep his voice even and calm. He sighed and tried again. "That's not it, Liam. I *do* want someone. Eventually. I just moved here and am waiting to get my own place. I really want to get settled before I jump into a relationship. Really, I'm okay."

Liam finally seemed to realize he might have been over enthusiastic. He probably just wanted Collin to be as happy as he was. "Yeah, I get that. I'm sorry. The last thing I wanted to do was make you feel uncomfortable."

"You didn't. I promise. I'm trying to get settled and everything. I've spent the last few years in a location in Alabama where, if you were gay, you automatically went into the closet. So, being in such an open environment is an adjustment. I really appreciate the thought, Liam."

"Yeah, no problem." Liam seemed like he was a little ashamed of himself.

"Anyway, I'll let you two get back to your paperwork. Have fun with all of it. I'm glad it's you and not me. I think I'd go crazy if I had to do it." Collin grabbed a bottle of water from the fridge before he walked off.

Liam's face brightened up again for a moment. "Hey, what about introducing Collin to Tyler? They would be hot together."

I groaned before I answered. "Leave it alone, Liam. Just let him get settled before you start throwing men at him, alright?"

My man's posture sunk a little. He was dejected once again. "Yeah, I can do that I guess." He shrugged before continuing. "Think about it, Jasper. You have to admit, Collin and Tyler would be so sexy together."

"If I do, will you finish this paperwork?" Liam nodded, his grin bright and his blond hair flopping down over his eyes. I mentally sighed and then spoke again. "Yes, they would be hot together. Collin's not looking and I honestly don't think Tyler is either. Now, paperwork. Please. I have plans and we need to finish this first." Looking down at the pile of papers in front of us, I reminded Liam that we were so close to being finished and that I had plans for the two of us that included us, our bed, and a bottle of lube and nothing else.

Imagine that, he quickly got to work on finishing the papers that needed to be filled out before we could move on to more enjoyable pastimes. Sometimes all you really needed was a good incentive to look forward to in order to motivate yourself to do a mundane task.

34

LIAM

I was still getting used to being a married man. I was happy to have been living with Jasper for a while now and that was more than enough for me. If we just remained committed to each other as boyfriends, I'd have been content with that. The man had to do something awesome and propose. There was no way I wasn't going to say yes. I never felt so much love and passion for anyone before and I knew I never would again. That's why I had no reservations about marrying him even in the spur of the moment.

What was even better was that everyone now knew that we have been a couple. I could hold his hand if I wanted to. I could be seen at our house and nobody would think anything of it. It was quite freeing. I hadn't realized just how much added stress I was under because we felt that we needed to keep our relationship from Jasper's family. He had so many reservations because of what happened to him in college. Because of one horrible man, he was afraid to take a chance again and that had an impact on his relationship with his brothers and fathers. Hopefully, now that he was in a steady relationship, he'd be more open toward the rest of his family.

We finally finished our paperwork and it was official. I was going to become Liam Welsh. Actually, I already was. It was definitely different. Luckily for me, I wrote under a pen name and I wouldn't have to change anything with regards to that other than the paperwork with my publisher. Being Liam Welsh was something I would have to work on getting used to. I spent the last twenty-five years as Liam Campbell. I guess I had learned how women felt when they got married and all of a sudden they had a new name.

We were packing for our trip to California for Sean's wedding and I was really glad that Jasper was more the let's-elope kind of guy rather than the let's-have-a-huge-wedding kind of guy. I'm sure the wedding was going to be beautiful but there had been so much stress, even with the wedding planner they hired helping out.

Collin moved out last weekend and although it's been great having the entire house back to just us, in a way, I miss him. He really was a great houseguest. Hopefully, we were good hosts, too.

I had missed the frotting sessions on the couch, the blow jobs in the kitchen, and the fucking on the stairs. Pretty much whenever the mood struck Jasper, he was on me and I had no complaints about that. We hadn't been able to do that with Collin in the house.

Sean and Simon were leaving tomorrow for California and as soon as Collin arrived to house sit, we would be leaving ahead of them. It seemed odd to help him move out last weekend only to have him come back this weekend to stay for a couple of days, but Hemingway was already comfortable with him and it just seemed like the most logical thing to do. We trusted him. With both the house and our fur baby.

"Liam! Have you seen my dress shoes?"

Ah, the joys of married life. I didn't have any real complaints though. Jasper was just stressed because of the wedding. I knew exactly where his shoes were, so instead of yelling back down the hall, I put Hemingway in his kitty tower and headed toward our bedroom.

"Yes, I've seen your dress shoes. They're exactly where you left them; they're in their box on the shelf," I told him as I walked into our room. All I saw was Jasper's back as he walked into the closet.

"Ah-ha! I must have looked right at them at least a dozen times. Seriously, what would I do without you?"

"Let's not find out, okay?" I was pulled away by my phone ringing in the office. I must have left it on the desk. It was Rhett's ringtone and that meant something was up because he was going to see me in just a few hours.

"Better see what Rhett wants. I have to finish packing."

Ding-dong

Jasper seemed in a right state, he jumped when the doorbell rang. "Shit, that's probably Collin. Why is he ringing the doorbell? He lived here until last weekend. He still has a key!"

"How would I know? Either answer the door or text him and tell him to just come in," I said as I ran out of the room trying to reach my phone before it stopped ringing.

"Hey, Rhett. You there?"

"Yeah, I'm here. Everything okay? You sound winded. Please tell me I didn't interrupt you and Jasper. Is that all you two ever do?"

"Shut it. No, you didn't interrupt. I was in the bedroom helping your brother find his dress shoes and I left my phone in the office. I'm going to see you in just a few hours, so what's up?"

"Nothing, I just needed to vent. Logan called. He said he's not coming today and that he's waiting until Saturday night now. Basically, I'm not going to get to spend any time with him at all. Seriously, Liam, do you think he's worth it? I get such hot and cold feelings from him and I just don't know anymore."

"Do *you*?"

"Do I what?"

"Do you think he's worth it? I can't really answer that question for you, Rhett. I don't know him all that well. I do know he's insanely busy. Right now they're doing fall cuts with their cattle so maybe that's why he's not coming today. Hey, at least he told you. He could've just not shown. Do you remember back in February what you told me about Jasper? How if I had the chance to take it? If he's willing, Rhett, I think you have a chance and I think you'd kick yourself later if you didn't take it. Did you ask him why he's not coming until Saturday?"

"He said he was busy. That's it. He didn't give much of an explanation, just that he's busy and can't get away until then."

"Well, then I'd guess that he's busy and just trust that. Hell, Rhett, they have something like fifteen hundred cattle, don't they?"

"I think it's more. That's not the point. The point is I want to see him and I am being a whiny bitch and you're supposed to be my best friend right now and just let me vent, okay?"

I smiled to myself and changed my tone. "Got it. Please continue." Before I knew it, we were both laughing into the phone.

"Okay, that's what I needed, really. Back to the reason I called, I'm just, I don't know. I'm confused. I mean, I like him. A lot. He doesn't seem to like me as much. What would you do?"

"Honestly, I'd just give it a try and see. Think about it, Rhett. You're living in Northern California. That's a long-ass way from Wyoming. He can't just pick up and come and see you every weekend. He has a lot of responsibilities here. Kind of like the situation with me and Jasper. I was more mobile than he was. I still am. He has a job here and lots of people depend on him. He can't just up and leave. Seriously, this would be so much easier if you lived here, Rhett." One of those cartoon light bulbs lit up above my head. "Hey! Maybe that's what you need to do. Did you ever think about that? Maybe that's why he's hot and cold. Maybe he doesn't feel that there is really any chance because you're so far away."

I heard a groan through my earpiece. "Well shit, Liam. Why didn't you say that months ago? Alright, I'm coming back with you guys. You don't mind if I bunk with you for a while, do you? I don't want to ask Sean because he'll be a newlywed and all."

I tried to hint to Rhett that Jasper and I were newlyweds, too. "What? I'm not?" He didn't seem to pick up on the hint.

"Dude, you're not getting married this weekend. *They* are."

"Yeah, I'm not getting married *this* weekend. I'm more of a newlywed than they are. They've been together since last year, Rhett. I've only been with Jasper since this year. My relationship is definitely newer, but moving much faster than theirs."

"Seriously, are you going to let me stay there or not? Because if you're not..."

Exasperated that my best friend couldn't get my obscure hints, I interrupted him. "Of course I am. You know that. You get to be the one that tells your brother you plan on crashing here. We just got rid of our houseguest. He's rather enjoyed not having one again."

"Shit, I didn't think of that. Well, you two will just have to go back to fucking in a bed. Like normal people."

"Do either of us strike you as normal?"

Rhett chuckled. "Now that you mention it, no."

"Okay, anyway. I've gotta get off of here. Collin is here to house sit for us and I need to get to the airport. I'll see you in a few hours and we can talk about this more."

"Good. I think I need all the help I can get."

"You'll be fine, trust me. Just be you."

"Yeah, well, since Mike..."

"Stop. Rhett, Logan knows you. He knows what happened. He knows and he still seems interested so let it go. What Mike did was not your fault in any way. If any man has a problem with your scars, either the physical or mental ones, then he isn't worth your time. Got it?"

"Yeah, I got it."

"Good. Now, I'll see you in a few hours, alright?"

"Yeah. See you. Have a fun flight."

"I'll try."

I hung up and went in search of Jasper and Collin. I found Collin with Hemingway on his shoulder.

"He missed you this week. What did you do to steal my cat away from me?"

"Nothing. You realize cats love to be in high places, right?"

"No. What does that have to do with anything?"

"Liam, I'm almost a foot taller than you. Hemingway just

likes to be on my shoulder because I'm so tall. You're still his favorite, I'm sure. Are you ready for the big day?"

"I've already had my big day. What are you talking about?"

"Okay, are you ready for Sean's big day?"

"No. I don't think Sean is either. The last time I saw him he was so stressed. I swear the man is only thirty but he's headed for a stroke if he doesn't relax."

"Yeah, I know what you mean. You should've seen him at the office this week. Jasper and I finally convinced him to just go home."

"Well, hopefully he's in a more relaxed mood once he gets to California. I'm looking forward to seeing Rhett again before everyone else arrives. We have a few last-minute details to take care of but otherwise, everything is set."

"Are you going to tell your fathers-in-law that you two are married?"

"Not until after the wedding. They've already started hinting that I was going to be next. Let me tell you, I'm going to take great pleasure in telling my dads that I'm already married and that there's nothing they can do to get me to go through the hell that Sean's gone through," Jasper said when he finally joined us in the office.

"You ready, Liam? We really need to get to the airport."

"Yeah, my bags are by the front door. Thanks so much, Collin. I'll feel better knowing he's only going to be alone for the day you're at the wedding."

"Don't worry about it, Liam. Hemingway and I are just going to chill and watch TV."

"Seriously, thanks for watching him," Jasper said while patting Collin on the shoulder as he walked out of the office with his bags.

"Okay, see you Saturday night," I said while following Jasper.

"Yep. Have fun, you two."

We made it to the airport in almost no time. Since we were flying on Stealth Securities' company jet, we didn't have to check our bags. Which was a blessing. I didn't know James and Taylor had a jet. It wasn't until we were already airborne that I realized that we were the only ones on the plane besides the pilot and copilot. When I asked Jasper where the attendant was he said he told his papa that we didn't need one for such a short flight. I found out exactly why shortly afterward when Jasper grabbed my hand and pulled me toward the back of the plane.

"You ever join the mile high club?"

"No," I replied.

"Well good, you're about to."

35

JASPER

There were so many times I wondered if I'd ever get to join the mile high club. It only took thirty years for me to finally be inducted. I loved that it was with Liam. It was a great way to kill the couple hours we had on the flight to California. By the time we landed, Liam was once again well fucked and I was a very happy and satisfied husband.

We were headed to my dads' place first to finish up some last-minute details for the wedding and honeymoon. We'd be traveling to the vineyard by car as it was only a short drive. It was unusual for me to go so long without seeing my dads or Rhett but life had been especially hectic since Christmas and the timing just never worked. Sure, there was all the work we'd done. There had not been that much time off, but I'd be the first to admit that I'd been equally busy with Liam.

We decided to give a relationship a try and then we were almost immediately living together. Our arrangement probably wouldn't work for most people but it worked for us. I had no regrets except that we were married and hadn't told anyone. I wanted everyone to know. I talked to Liam and he agreed, it was definitely time to tell my dads. They needed to know.

The closer we got to the house, the more nervous Liam got.

I reached over and patted his knee. I could feel the tension in his muscles. "Don't worry about it. Everything is going to be fine, sweetheart. You know my dads and they already love you so what are you so worried about?"

"I don't know. Maybe because we're already married and didn't tell anyone? Are you sure you want to tell them? Wouldn't it be better to wait?"

"Liam, we've been over this. We need to tell them this weekend. It's better to tell them in person rather than wait until after we leave and then we have to tell them over the phone. It's also better to tell them sooner, rather than later."

"Yeah, but if we tell them over the phone, then Taylor can't hurt me."

I felt so bad for doing so, but I laughed at that. I got it. I really did. To someone as small and petite as Liam, Papa could seem quite intimidating. He was tall and had broad shoulders and very defined muscles. I could definitely see Liam being intimidated by him, but Papa was a marshmallow and Liam knew it. I looked over at my husband and saw he didn't think it was funny, at all. "Do you honestly think Papa would hurt you?"

"No, but couldn't you have a less intimidating Papa or something? Why did James have to go and marry a giant?"

"I don't know. Why don't you ask Rhett the same thing? He's got a thing for Logan and he's just as big as Papa. We don't all choose who to love."

"Okay, let's just get this over with. When exactly are we going to tell them?"

"I'm not sure. How about we just play it by ear and see?"

"Yeah, that sounds like a good plan."

We were pulling up to the gate so we decided to end the conversation for the time being. I was positive that the correct time for our conversation would present itself, I just didn't know exactly when that would be.

We were greeted by Rhett running out the door and flinging himself at us. I really missed my little brother and it was so wonderful to see him back to his old self.

"Well, I'd ask how your flight was, but you've got a quite relaxed look on your face so I don't need to, huh?"

"Well hello to you too. Do I seriously have a *just fucked* look?" Liam looked a little concerned. "I don't want to see your dads looking like that."

"Liam, it's you and Jasper. When don't you?"

"He's got a point, Liam. Anyway, we can't change the way we look. Here they come now so let's go say hello." We headed toward our dad and papa. "By the way, hello little brother. How are you?"

"I'm good. I really need to talk to you two so can we talk later?"

"Sure. Everything alright?"

"Yes and no. Later."

"Jasper, Liam. I hope your flight was good?" Dad said while wrapping me in a tight hug. Liam had wrapped his arm through Rhett's and didn't appear willing to let go anytime soon. I didn't get why he was so nervous.

"Hello, Liam. How have you been?"

"Hi, James. I've been good. Busy, but good. Hi, Taylor." He sounded so polite and cordial. That made me worry a little. Finally, Liam gave both of my dads a wave that I found comical. It appeared that they did as well because Papa just smiled at Liam like he knew what was going on.

"Alright, grab your bags and let's get inside. We have a lot to talk about," Dad told us after he released me from his hug.

"We do? I thought there were only a few things left to take care of for the wedding?" Liam responded.

"Do you really think that with the wedding being in a few days that we wouldn't have everything taken care of yet, Liam? We wanted you two to come a day early because we needed to talk to you two." He pointed from Liam to me.

Liam fidgeted in place. My baby was so uncomfortable. I walked up and put my arms around him and kissed his temple. I whispered that it would be okay before I pulled away. I knew he was nervous and Dad wasn't helping. I also knew that Dad was probably doing it on purpose to make Liam squirm.

I took Liam's hand, and walked to the back of the SUV to get our bags.

"Hey, look at me." I looked down at my husband. "It's going to be okay. I promise. Do you know why it's going to be okay?" I asked while forcing Liam's eyes up to mine with a finger under his chin.

"Because you love me."

"Yes. That's all that matters. Trust me, it really will be alright."

"Okay." He didn't sound particularly assured. "Let's go before your dads decide we need to sleep in separate rooms or something."

"Not going to happen."

"I sure hope not. I don't know how well I'd sleep without you beside me at this point. I'm quite spoiled."

"Well, it's not going to happen so don't worry about it."

When we walked through the door, I led Liam upstairs to my old room. It was more a guest room now as there was nothing personal left but it still had the same furniture I used growing up and it was drastically different from what Liam and I had at home.

After we dropped off our bags, we made our way back downstairs but stopped short when we heard arguing. It took me a minute to figure out that it was Rhett and Papa. I was shocked because I couldn't ever remember Papa ever yelling at us like that before. Tugging Liam behind me, I quickly made my way into the kitchen to see what was going on.

"I've already told you, you're not going," Papa yelled at Rhett.

"I've already told you that you can't stop me. Papa, I love you, but I'm an adult. If I want to move, I'm going to move. You can't keep me here for the rest of my life. I need to leave."

"No. Absolutely not. You aren't moving to Wyoming. Period."

"Are you two at it again?" Dad asked coming in the room. "Jasper, Liam, maybe you two could talk some sense into your brother. For whatever reason, he's got it in his head that he's going back to Wyoming with you two after the wedding."

"That was the plan," I told Dad and Papa and they both just looked at me like I had a third eye.

"What do you mean that was the plan? Whose plan? Rhett's not moving to Wyoming. Period. He needs to stay here where we can keep an eye on him," Papa said while glaring at Rhett.

"You two can't keep him here. He's an adult. He's already moved once. Liam, you said you wanted to talk to Rhett when we got here, why don't you two go out back and talk?"

I needed to get Rhett away from Papa who looked like he was about to explode.

"Alright, let's go, Rhett." Liam gave me a small peck on the cheek as he walked by on his way outside with Rhett.

"You want to explain to us why it is that your brother seems to think he can just up and move to Wyoming?" Dad asked.

"Rhett told you and I told you, Dad. Because he's an adult. He's not a child. He's a grown man and you can't keep him here."

"Jasper, I thought you'd be on our side," Papa replied.

"Why would you think that? Like I said, he's an adult. He gets to move if he wants to."

"He needs to be watched," Papa stated.

"Why? Why does he need to be watched? You said that the guys caught up with Mike. You said he's not alive anymore. What's the problem then?"

"What if something happens to him? Huh? What then?"

"I'd imagine the same thing if something happened to either me or Sean. He's twenty-two. You can't keep him here. You guys know that. You can't protect him for the rest of his life. He has to be able to live, and from what I've heard, he's not doing that here."

"What do you mean?" Papa asked.

"Just think about it. Rhett wants to come to Crooked Bend. He's going to make his own decisions and that's it. I know you two worry about him, but he already left once, and maybe it's time for him to leave again. He needs to live his life. He *wants* to be in Crooked Bend. Look, Sean, Liam, and I are all there. As are Simon and his family. I'm sure Rhett will be just fine. You've got to let him go or you'll just piss him off. If you don't let him, you risk losing him."

Dad crossed his arms over his chest and looked at me, impressed. "When did you become so smart?"

"I don't know that I am. It's just the way it is. Seriously. You two might want to look for a house in Wyoming if you want to be closer to us because I don't see any of us leaving there."

"Rhett's just *talking* about moving. Do you think he might stay?" Papa asked. He seemed extremely distressed over the idea of Rhett moving away again.

I hated to disagree with Papa, but Rhett was determined and had good reason. "Yeah, I do, Papa. He wants to open his own bakery there. I'm sure there are other reasons as well."

"I don't like it. Look what happened before."

I hated where this conversation was going. Bad shit happened to good people all the time. The best way to get over something like what Rhett had been through was to go on with his life. I decided to try to change the subject. "Anyway, so you really didn't need us to come a day early for anything?"

"No, everything is taken care of. Why?"

"No real reason." I looked from one paternal figure to the other. "I'm going to take Liam out shopping later on. There are some things we need to look at and maybe pick up before we head back to Wyoming."

"Okay, so you going to tell us what's going on with you and Liam?" Dad asked.

I looked at Dad and shrugged. "Sure, what do you want to know?"

"Is it serious?"

"Hang on." I knew this was the moment. It was definitely the right time to tell them. Hopefully Liam agreed. I went to the patio door and called for him to come inside. He and Rhett were on one of the loungers by the pool talking. Once he joined me at the door, I threaded my fingers through his before I rejoined my fathers with my husband by my side.

"Yes, it's serious. It's very serious. Liam's the one for me," I told them but I was looking only at my husband.

We were interrupted by Papa's phone ringing. It was Sean. He silenced the ringer, sending it to voicemail.

"You were saying?" Papa asked when the distraction was eliminated.

"As I was saying, yes, it's serious. We..." I hesitated and looked back down at Liam. I was searching for something, but I didn't know exactly what. He shocked me when he finished my answer for me.

"To answer your question, Taylor, yes, it's serious. It has been serious since I left in February to visit Jasper in Wyoming. While we were in Vegas for the bachelor party, we eloped. We're married and not just dating. It's that serious."

Rhett jumped up and down, laughing. He pointed at his dads and back at us. "Yes! Told ya! I *so* saw that coming! That's why you two went missing that second day, isn't it?"

"Wait, what do you mean you *told* them? Told them what?" Liam asked my brother.

"After our talk, I knew Jasper would end up being it for you, Liam. Then when things went the way they did in Vegas with you two going missing that second day, I was so sure you two got hitched while we were there."

"Is it true? Did you elope?" Dad asked, though he wasn't as surprised as I thought he'd be.

"Yeah, Liam isn't just my boyfriend. He's my husband."

36

LIAM

Oh shit. Oh shit. Oh shit. This was definitely not how I wanted to let my new fathers-in-law know that they were my fathers-in-law. Up until that point, we'd gotten along pretty well. Hopefully, they were still going to feel somewhat favorably toward me now that they knew I married their oldest in secret. Hopefully they wouldn't hold it against me.

"Let me get this straight. You two decided it was a great idea to jump into a wedding, elope, while you were at your *brother's* bachelor party?" James asked while pinching the bridge of his nose with his fingers.

"Well, we were in Vegas and I figured why not? I didn't want to go through all of the stress that Sean's been going through just to have a big wedding. I knew Liam was who I wanted to spend the rest of my life with. I've been in love with him for months, Dad. From the minute I laid eyes on him, I think. I don't see what the problem is."

James was completely in denial, and I knew it for sure when he replied to Jasper. "Your brother isn't stressed, so you can try again."

Jasper sighed and shook his head. "You're not with him on a daily basis, Dad. I am. Trust me, Sean's stressed. So much so that Collin and I had to send him home several times over the past few weeks because he just couldn't function. He's stressed, Dad. He may not tell you, but he is. I refused to put myself through that much stress. Nor did I want to put Liam through it. You always told us growing up that when you knew, you knew. Well, I knew back at Christmas, the first time I saw Liam, that I was going to marry him. I wish you were happy for us instead of upset."

James' demeanor changed like a switch. "Jasper, no! I'm not unhappy. It's just that I wish you would've told us. Hell, we didn't even know you were dating and then all of a sudden you're married? It's just a bit overwhelming. I didn't get to see you get married. That's something I've looked forward to doing with all three of you. I wanted to watch each of you get married to wonderful partners."

"We talked about it, a lot. We didn't want to take away from Sean's spotlight. He's going through hell and Cammie didn't help anyone. She added so much stress for both Simon and Sean about the wedding plans. First it was because they weren't planning it fast enough for her, then it was because of the location for the ceremony. She put herself in the center of *their* wedding planning. Even after Sean secured a professional planner, she didn't stop interjecting her own opinion. All of it really affected him. I sure as hell didn't want anything like that. I was happy with just a small ceremony."

"Yeah, but what about what Liam wanted? Did you think to ask him what he wanted?" Papa scolded before looking over at Liam.

I spoke up in defense of my husband. "Yeah, he did. I was there. I didn't have to say yes. I didn't have to say I do, but I did because I love him and have for a long time. I even talked to Rhett about it before I went back to Crooked Bend. I don't see Sean as often as Jasper and Collin do, but living with the two of them the past month, I saw how much stress they were under because they both were not only doing their jobs but picking up Sean's as well. I'm not saying anything about Sean not doing his job, just that it's been obvious that he's stressed. I've met Cammie several times. She can be quite forceful when she wants something and isn't getting her way."

James looked from me to Jasper. He looked a little tired. After a moment, his face lit up. "Well, are you two willing to have a reception at least? Give me something here."

I felt bad for Jasper's dads. They really were good guys and were really just thinking of their sons' happiness. "Yes, we can have a reception. After Sean and Simon get back from their honeymoon, though, because we agreed to not tell them until then. Again, we don't want to steal Sean's thunder at all." It wouldn't be bad to have a small reception. At least, I didn't think so.

Jasper looked a little less stressed, himself. He added a caveat to the request. "A *small* one. Emphasis on the word *small*. Okay, Dad?"

James nodded and agreed with Jasper's request. "Alright. I'll work on putting together a small reception for the two of you. I assume you'll want to have it in Crooked Bend?"

"Yes, please," we said in unison.

"Okay, now that that's out of the way. Where are your rings?" Dad asked us.

"It was kinda spur of the moment, to tell the truth. We don't have any yet. We didn't get any in Vegas and there isn't a really good jeweler in Crooked Bend. We were planning on looking for something here. We won't be wearing them until after the wedding. Again, I don't want to take any attention away from Sean's moment at all. He's more than earned it and I don't want to step on that in any way."

"There are several good stores around for you to choose from so I'm sure you won't have any issues finding what you're looking for," Papa let us know.

Jasper seemed to think the conversation was finalized. "Good. If we're finished here, I'll just take Liam and go ring shopping. That okay with you?" His tone was a little abrupt. He was clearly still a little annoyed by his dads' insistence on being so involved in his life.

"Yeah, sounds good," James said.

I tried my best to give both of Jasper's dads a smile but I just couldn't. I knew they were upset and it wasn't something I wanted. The last thing I wanted was for them to be upset with us or about our marriage.

When we got outside, and back into the SUV, I couldn't take it anymore and broke down as Jasper pulled out of the driveway. I was a man, but I had no problems with crying. It happened. There was absolutely nothing wrong with that. That conversation went better than I hoped but not as well as I wished. The way I saw it, all I could do was suck it up, avoid Jasper's dads at all costs, and wish for the weekend to fly by quickly.

Jasper looked at me with concern written across his face. "Hey, don't worry, love. They're just shocked. We knew they would be. They'll get over it and it won't be an issue. I promise. Trust me, I know my dads." He patted me on the arm. "Now, completely changing the subject, have you thought about what type of ring you want?"

I choked back a sob. "Something plain and simple. Like us."

Jasper feigned offense and put his left hand over his heart. "Ouch. I don't know exactly how to take that."

"I didn't mean anything *bad* by it. You know we're pretty easy going and simple. We don't really like a lot of frills so I thought a no-frills ring would work for us. Did you want something frillier?"

"Frillier? Really? This is the man who asked you to elope at a moment's notice in Vegas. You think I want frillier?"

I loved my husband and he knew exactly what I needed and right then. Jasper found a way to make me laugh. I *so* needed that!

Jasper gave me the sweetest smile I'd ever seen. "That's better. Seriously, do you know what you want?"

"Something fairly simple. Sean's ring is gorgeous but I want something that is just a band. No stones."

"Alright. Let's see what they've got."

We got out of the SUV and walked into the small jewelry store. Well, it *looked* small from the outside. It wasn't wide, but we could see it was a long shop. An eager sales clerk greeted us. He was only too happy to help us. In the end, after spending almost an hour looking at more styles of wedding bands than I knew existed, we decided on a combination of platinum and yellow-gold rings, simple yet elegant. Both of our sizes were in stock but we were told it would take two days to complete any engraving we wanted. We told the clerk that was fine and that we would be back in a couple of days to pick them up.

I was both anxious and nervous as we rode back to Jasper's dads' house. Like always, Jasper reassured me that things would be okay. I just wished I shared his positivity. It didn't take any time at all for us to be back in his dads' driveway and were headed inside. Too soon if you asked me. We found everyone on the back patio. I was incredibly surprised when James and Taylor both jumped up from their seats and walked over to us and enveloped us in a group hug. If the hug surprised me, I was even more shocked by what came next.

James pulled back from us and looked from me to Jasper. "We're really sorry, you two. We've been talking about it and we want you to know that we're happy for you. We really are. We're sorry if we came across as upset or disapproving or anything like that. We really are happy for the two of you and we understand the reason why you went about it the way you did. Yes, we would've preferred to have been at your wedding but we're more than happy that you've agreed to have a small reception."

"Wow. I don't know what to say except thanks," Jasper said while looking at his dads. I didn't know how he did it but then again, like he said, he knew his dads and he knew things would be okay.

"Did you two pick out rings then? You're not wearing them so I'm assuming they're being sized?" Taylor asked while looking at our hands. We all moved to the loungers to sit down and talk.

"Not sized, engraved. We were lucky that they carried a variety of sizes in stock. Liam picked out beautifully simple bands for us. We wanted them engraved and they said they would be ready in two days so we'll pick them up after the wedding."

"If you think you'll have issues with Sean finding out about you two getting married before him, just let us know. We can be there for you, if you want, when you tell him," James told us.

"Thanks, Dad. I think it'll be okay. Sean seemed really happy when he found out that Liam had been the one I was dating for so long. I really think it'll be okay. I'm hoping that he'll be relaxed after he gets back from his honeymoon and will take the news better."

"Sounds good. Alright, who's ready for supper?" Taylor stood from the chair he was in. We all agreed that it was time to eat so we headed into the kitchen. I'd gotten used to cooking dinner with Jasper over the past several months but it was a different story when you put the five of us in the kitchen making dinner. That took the term "family dinner" to a whole new level. I knew that Taylor was an amazing cook and that Rhett was wickedly good at anything that went into an oven so I just did my best to stay out of the way. I was happy to slice vegetables for the salad.

We ate a wonderful dinner and the conversation flowed almost as freely as the wine. Before I knew it, we were headed up to bed. Things seemed to be looking up for us. That was, until I realized that the next day we were going to be going to the vineyard and would start the crazy, hectic chaos that'd be Sean's wedding. I was *so* happy that we had eloped.

The trip to the vineyard didn't take long and there were so many different things to do and activities planned that before I knew it, we were getting ready for Sean's big day.

I loved Jasper no matter what. He looked great in anything he wore, but I had never seen him in a tuxedo until that moment. Jasper in a classic black tuxedo made me want to strip off my clothes and let him have his way with me.

"What?" Jasper asked me when he realized I was staring at him.

"You look hot. Like really hot. Like, I-want-you-to-fuck-me-right-now hot."

"We don't have time for that. Trust me, I'd love nothing more than to fuck you right now. I promise I'll do just that just as soon as possible, okay?"

Groaning, I knew he was right so I adjusted myself and turned to leave the room before I did something irresponsible, like rip the tuxedo off of him. Would I ever get enough of him? I met Rhett in the hallway and gave him a hug and then went on my way. I knew Rhett was meeting up with Jasper and then they were going to go get Sean and then the wedding would begin. I set about finding either of the fathers and taking my seat with them so I could watch Sean and Simon get married.

The wedding was more beautiful than I imagined. The setting was gorgeous and the added flowers made for stunning scenery. Jasper walked down the aisle beside Graham and then Rhett beside Isaac. Then the grooms came down the aisle with both of their parents. After James and Taylor both walked Sean down the aisle they joined me to watch the ceremony. It was truly beautiful. When the grooms both finished reciting their vows, I don't think there wasn't a person who wasn't crying. The love they felt for each other permeated the room. We could tell how much of a pair they were just by looking at them.

Once they were pronounced husbands and they shared their first kiss as a married couple, I clapped and cheered along with everyone else. My heart skipped a beat when my husband winked at me as he walked back up the aisle beside Graham.

After what seemed like a million pictures, we were finally able to join the reception. It was a loud and joyous event and I was so glad that I didn't have to hide my relationship with Jasper because I was looking forward to getting out on the dance floor with him. He had some incredible moves and I wanted nothing more than to plaster myself to him and never let go.

When The Calling's *Where You Will Go* came on, my heart started beating double time because I had joked with Jasper before that I thought of it as our song.

"Dance with me?" Jasper asked, reaching for me.

"Always."

37

JASPER

I'll be one of the first to admit that Sean and Simon's wedding was beautiful. It definitely wasn't for me though. I didn't mind getting dressed up to celebrate with my twin. Hell, I wouldn't have it any other way. He liked these things more than I did. Always had. I always thought that was odd because he was so much more shy and quiet. For the most part, he was the shyer of the two of us; a lot like Liam was around a bunch of people he didn't know. Once he got to know you, he opened up and was quite friendly.

I was happy for Sean and was looking forward to dancing with my own husband just as soon as the two grooms had their moment in the spotlight. I made a request and was looking forward to dancing with Liam in my arms in front of everyone. We were quiet about our relationship for so long, too long to tell the truth. I was more than ready to let everyone know that Liam was mine and that I was his.

After what seemed like forever, the grooms decided to finally fling their garters over their shoulders. Logan caught Simon's and Liam caught Sean's. Technically he wasn't single, but Sean didn't know that, not yet. He would soon enough. Shortly after that ceremony, the grooms were both hugging us and were running off to start their lives together as husbands. I knew what that was like and I was so happy for Sean and Simon. I was more than ready to take my own husband back to our room for the night. I finally got my opportunity an hour later when we were arm in arm on the dancefloor.

"Wanna sneak off to our room? The grooms have been gone for about an hour and I think that's an acceptable amount of time to wait before sneaking off," I whispered near Liam's ear.

"I thought you'd never ask. Let's go."

We made it back to our room in record time. Liam was naked before I even had my shirt off. In all fairness though, I was cursed with more difficult buttons than he was and I was distracted several times as his delectable body was revealed to me with each bit of clothing removed.

"What was it that you were saying this morning? You wanted me to fuck you or something like that?"

"Yes. That. That's exactly what I want. I've been hard most of the day, Jasper. Please."

"Alright, let's give you a head start and then we'll play. How does that sound?"

"Play, as in?"

"As in, I'll make sure you're still *green* before I continue."

"Yes, I'm so green right now."

"Good. Go lie on the bed."

I sent Liam to the bed and grabbed the lube that I knew we were going to need. I loved that we agreed to no longer used condoms. It brought a level of intimacy that I didn't want with anyone other than Liam. I needed to make sure he experienced at least one orgasm before we got started. If I didn't, things were going to be over before I even got inside him. After finding the lube, I went to the bed. After removing the rest of my clothing, I went about giving Liam some relief before we got started. If he had indeed been hard on and off since this morning, I knew it wouldn't take long.

I started by crawling up in between his legs and giving him little kisses and licks along his legs. When I got to his groin, I didn't hesitate to flatten my tongue and lick from his balls up to the tip of his leaking cock and then swallow it down completely in one motion. I was expecting his hips to thrust up like they often did, so I had my hands ready to keep his hips down on the bed while I worked on giving him his first of several orgasms of the night.

It didn't take long because I knew Liam's body so well and as he said, he'd been hard and ready for a while. When he shot down my throat, I quickly swallowed all that he gave me and massaged his balls, hoping to get every drop. I never got tired of the taste of Liam; it was something I didn't think I ever would get tired of.

Looking up at my husband's face, I saw that he had a satisfied, sated expression. It didn't take much to please him, but he was always willing to keep going for me.

"Now that we've got number one out of the way, are you ready to play?"

"Green."

"Good, husband. I love you, Liam, don't ever forget that. If you ever don't want to do this, you know all you have to do is say no, right?" I asked him as I crawled up Liam's body and gently lay down on top of him. I nibbled and kissed his neck and chin before getting to his mouth. "Are you ready for round two or do you need a minute or two?" I asked.

Liam answered by thrusting his hips up into mine and

giving me a quiet yes. I chuckled at him before asking, "Yes you're ready? Or yes, you need a minute?"

"Both?" Liam replied and started laughing right along with me. "I can't help it, Jasper, you still blow my mind."

"I'll take that as a compliment." I moved up until I was beside Liam and wrapped my arms around him.

"If you cuddle up with me, I'm going to get sleepy. Especially after that huge orgasm you just gave me," Liam warned, pushing me away. He wasn't overly convincing in letting me know that he didn't want me to cuddle him.

"A nap sounds perfect. Why don't we take a nap and when we wake up we can start round two?" I noticed Liam tried his best to cover a large yawn.

"No, I want to keep going."

"Later. I promise. For now, sleep and I'll wake you up in just a bit."

It didn't take Liam long to doze off. When he did, I grabbed the blanket and covered us both up after turning off the bedside lamp. After I crawled back into bed, I wrapped my arms around my love and kissed his temple before I also fell asleep. We never did get around to playing that night because neither of us woke up until the next morning. We just barely had enough time to shower and get dressed before checkout time.

We returned to Monterey with my dads only long enough to stop off at the jewelers and pick up our rings. I knew exactly where I wanted to put Liam's ring on him so I asked him if it was okay if we waited until we got back to Wyoming to put them on. He didn't seem to understand but willingly went along with my request.

I had a plan, and that plan included doing my best to recreate our first night together in our home. Later that evening, when we got home and said hello to Hemingway, Liam went off to unpack and I set about getting my ring on my husband's finger.

There was a nice, plush rug in the living room but a blanket was definitely much easier to clean so I went upstairs and grabbed a blanket out of the guest room since Liam was in ours. I returned to the rug and spread the blanket. I picked up the battery-powered candles, something we realized we needed after we got Hemingway, and set them up around the blanket. I then removed lube from where it was stashed in the coffee table. I also retrieved the rings before calling my husband. I needed for him to come to me, just like that first night.

"Liam, can you come here for a minute please?" I shouted up the stairs before retreating to the living room. I decided to wait in the middle of the blanket and hoped like hell he approved of my idea. It didn't take long before I heard him coming down the stairs. Just like the first time, he stopped once he reached the living room doorway.

"Oh my. You didn't. How can you get any better?" Liam asked me while walking my way.

I noticed that his eyes were full of unshed tears. Like before, I knew that if I didn't get through this soon, I wouldn't make it through without tearing up myself. I opened the box with our rings and dropped down onto one knee.

"Liam, I know I've made so many mistakes along the way, and I know that I'll make more in the future. You're it for me and that's never going to change. I love you. Everything about you, I love. I'm looking forward to spending the rest of our lives together. I'm thankful each and every day that I get to wake up next to you and that you're my husband. I was wondering, even though you already married me, if you would wear my ring? If you'd show the world that you belong to me and that I belong to you?"

I was expecting to be knocked over so when Liam gently sunk to his knees in front of me, I was a little surprised.

Liam gave me a sweet smile, one that the angels would honor, and answered my heartfelt request. "Yes, of course I'll wear your ring. Proudly." He reached up and wrapped a hand behind my neck before pulling me toward him for a kiss. When we parted, I took his ring from the box and placed it on his finger, where I hoped it would never leave.

"You're *my choice*, Liam. Just like the inscription says. Thank you for saying yes."

Liam accepted the ring, and added his own comment. "You're going to wear mine too, aren't you? That way all those cowboys you work with know you're taken?" Liam asked with a mischievous glint in his eyes.

I laughed at what he asked. Cowboys were more Sean's taste than mine. Liam knew that. I was keenly aware that he was really worried about me running into a past hook up in Jackson but I wouldn't bring that up. I was taken, completely, and no longer had any desire to look elsewhere other than at the man that was currently on his knees with me in our living room.

"Yes, Liam, I'm going to love wearing your ring. Now put it on my finger, husband of mine, so we can get to the rest of the evening. By the way, what did you decide for the inscription in mine?" I asked as he slipped the matching ring on my finger.

I couldn't help but look down at my ring as he pushed it past my knuckle. I loved seeing it resting there. Not nearly as much as I loved that Liam wore a matching ring on his finger.

"Well, with everything that had happened before I met you I didn't know if I would ever be able to take a chance with someone again. Until you. So, that's it. You're *my chance*, just as your ring says."

I pulled Liam into my lap and kissed him as I gently lay back on the blanket. Yes, there was a perfectly good bed upstairs as well as a very comfortable couch right beside us but the point was to make love on the blanket in the living room like we did when we bought the house.

We somehow managed to get our clothes off with minimal breaks in kissing. This time, Liam wrapped his lips around my cock. I loved it when he played with me and he drove me nuts when he used his lips to gently tug on my foreskin before taking me deep into his throat and swallowing around me. He was so good at that but I didn't want to finish in his mouth. I wanted to finish buried deep inside him so I pulled him off of me after a few minutes.

"Later, I'll finish in your mouth if you want me to, but right now, I want you to ride me just like you did that first night here."

Liam's eyes darkened to a dark, stormy blue, almost black and then he nodded before grabbing the lube and pouring a generous amount into his hand. He slicked up both my cock and then his. He added some more lube and reached behind himself and prepared himself for my entry. He was done quicker than I'd have liked but he knew what he wanted and I wasn't going to stop him. When he sunk down onto my cock, we both moaned. It was the most beautiful sound I'd ever heard. He always felt so wonderful wrapped around me and that moment was no different. Liam set a slow, lazy pace but made sure to alternate so I couldn't get close enough to cumming before he was ready for me to.

It wasn't until both of us were covered in a sheen of sweat that he started rocking his hips in a back and forth rhythm that I knew would have us both cumming in just moments. I wrapped my hand around Liam's leaking cock and jacked him to the rhythm of his hips. After the fifth stroke, his channel clamped down on me and he let out a hoarse cry just as his cock sputtered all over my chest and hand. That tipped me over the edge and I joined him, shooting deep into him.

Exhausted, Liam collapsed down on top of me and snuggled, mess be damned.

"I love you, Jasper."

"I love you too, Liam. Thank you so much for wearing my ring."

"Thank you for asking."

38

LIAM

We both seemed to enjoy married life. It was freeing and wonderful to be out. I never wanted to hide, and neither did Jasper, but he didn't want to overshadow his twin either. I often wondered if he felt that way growing up but when I asked him, he said he didn't. Growing up, they were as close as twins normally were but in university, after the whole Rupert incident, they started to grow apart.

We had plans to have dinner together at our place when Simon and Sean got back so I was surprised when Sean called Jasper several days early to let him know they were back and wanted to know if we wanted to have dinner with them. Of course, Jasper agreed and texted me to give me a heads-up. I was both happy they were back, and curious about why they were back early.

Over the past couple of weeks, we'd made sure we were out together more in Crooked Bend. We were no longer limiting our dates to Jackson. The fact that we were seen together wearing our wedding rings in Crooked Bend didn't go unnoticed. We needed to tell Sean that we were married before we made any type of announcement to anyone else. So, we planned on doing that at dinner.

When Jasper got home, I was a nervous wreck. Jasper kept reassuring me where his family was concerned but this was his twin we were talking about. The man who we had deceived for the past several months. The man who seemed happy that Jasper had found someone he wanted to be with, but would he still be happy once he realized we got married behind his back? While attending his bachelor party?

No matter how many times Jasper told me how wonderful and amazing I was and did his best to reassure me, I still had doubts. I had always gotten along well with his family but I was definitely nervous about telling Sean just how much we hadn't told him. It was time to come clean though. After we did, I would definitely feel more comfortable around Sean's family.

I was in the kitchen when Jasper arrived home. That wasn't unusual, I was often in the kitchen prepping what we were going to cook for dinner. Normally I was happy when Jasper arrived, but that night, I was obviously stressed about the dinner that we were about to have. I did my best to calm down when I realized just how much stress I was putting on my husband.

"Hey, look at me," Jasper said while walking up to me and gently tugging my arm to turn me toward him. "It's going to be okay. We've been over this before. We've been through this with my dads. Why are you more nervous now than you were before?"

"Because. He's your *twin*, Jasper. And we've been keeping this huge secret from him. I just *know* that it's going to come back and bite us somehow. I thought twins were supposed to be like super close or something."

"Yeah, I think most of them are. And we were until we

went to college. But after the whole thing with Rupert, we just grew apart. Most of that was my fault, and I know that. Hopefully we can become closer than we have been over the past decade or so. I know it's going to take time and it won't happen overnight." He kissed me on the nose. "So, subject change. What are you making for supper and can I help with anything?"

"I'm just making lasagna and breadsticks with a salad. You can get us some wine or beer or whatever. Does Simon drink wine? I don't know." I know I was jabbering, but I was so nervous!

"Calm down. I'll get some beer. I know that Simon will probably prefer that to wine but I know that you prefer wine so why don't I get you a glass of that? Sound good?"

"Sounds great."

Jasper went to the fridge to get the wine. I definitely needed it. While he was removing the cork, the doorbell rang. The festivities including Sean and Simon were about to begin. Jasper left me in the kitchen to answer the door. He took the bottle with him, so I didn't get my wine as soon as I would've liked.

When Jasper answered the door, he was still holding the bottle in his left hand, unfortunately, that put his wedding ring prominently on display when he opened the door. That, of course, would be the first thing that Sean noticed.

"Hello, but what is this? You're engaged?" I'd never heard Sean's voice go quite that high before. "You got engaged and didn't tell me?"

Jasper seemed to choose to not address the question directly. "Hey to you too. Hey, Simon. How was your honeymoon? Come on in you two. Liam's in the kitchen throwing together dinner," he said while walking back toward me in the kitchen. When they reached the kitchen, I saw that Sean was glaring at Jasper. Jasper finished removing the cork and poured a glass and handed it to me before wrapping his arms around me and pulling me to his chest. We stood there in front of his brother and brother-in-law and spilled everything.

"Actually, no, we didn't get engaged without telling you."

"Okay, so what's with the wedding band then?" Sean asked again.

It was Simon who seemed to put two and two together first. "I think you hit it there, baby, when you said *wedding* band. Emphasis on the word wedding. Am I right?"

"Yeah, you're right. Jasper and I aren't engaged. We're married."

"You're *married*? As in like married, I do and all that?" Sean questioned.

"Yep. Sure are," I answered.

Sean was clearly stunned, and stuck on Jasper keeping a secret from him. "When did you get married? And what the hell? You're married and didn't tell me?"

Simon was really on a roll because he was figuring things out before Sean, left and right. "Vegas. You two got married in Vegas, didn't you?"

"Yeah, we did. We didn't want to deal with the stress you two went through and we figured, it's Vegas so why not?" Jasper told them.

"Seriously? You're married? Wait. So you got married before us?" Sean was finally starting to pick up on things.

"Yeah, I did. About a month before you, actually," Jasper replied.

"Why didn't you say anything?"

"I already told you. Because you were going through so much stress and we could see that. And that's not what we wanted. The biggest reason was that we didn't want to steal any of the spotlight from you. We were both very happy and content to quietly get married in Vegas."

Like all the other things that could cause a confrontation, I took this personally, as though I was responsible for the reactions of Jasper's family. "Yeah, I'm sorry, Sean. Please don't be mad. And please don't hate me. I just couldn't handle the stress of everything that you did," I pleaded to him.

Sean seemed truly surprised by my request. "Hate you? Why would I hate you, Liam?"

"Because. We kept our dating from you and then getting married from you. We just didn't know when to tell you."

"Wow. I'm sorry I made you feel that way, Liam. It's a shock, but are you two happy?"

"Yeah," we answered together.

"Then that's all that matters. That and congratulations," Sean said while walking toward us and wrapping his arms around the two of us to give us a group hug. It wasn't difficult because I was still within Jasper's arms as he was standing behind me.

"Yes, congratulations, you two," Simon said while joining us in the kitchen as well as in the hug.

"So, what brought you two back from your honeymoon early?" I asked the other pair of newlyweds.

"Long story, and we'll tell you over dinner. At least the parts we can over dinner," Simon told us.

"Sounds good. Dinner's almost ready. If you guys want to go to the den and sit, I'll let you know when it's ready." I hoped they would leave me in peace in the kitchen so I could gather my thoughts and guzzle my glass of wine.

No such luck. They chose to keep me *company* and sat at the barstools we had near the counter. I thought, *What the hell*, and guzzled the wine anyway. Of course, astute and observant Simon noticed.

"You okay there, Liam?"

I know I snapped at him. "Yep, just peachy. Why do you ask?"

"Because you just drank that wine like it was water?"

"Give us a sec; we'll be right back, you two," Jasper told our guests while taking my hand and leading me out of the kitchen. We stopped in the den and Jasper pulled me onto his lap after he sat on the couch. He placed his hands on my cheeks and forced me to stare into his beautiful brown eyes.

"Liam, look at me. Calm down. I know you're upset and nervous but it's going to be okay."

I did my best to calm down but I couldn't help it. I didn't want anything to jeopardize Jasper and Sean's relationship. It already wasn't what you would expect of identical twins. But hopefully they were on their way to repairing their relationship.

I took a couple of deep breaths and replied. "Okay, Jasper. I'm trying. Let's get back to our guests, shall we?"

"Yes." Jasper gave me a reassuring smile before he gave me a peck on the lips. I wanted nothing more than to turn that peck into so much more, but we had dinner guests so I would have to wait.

When dinner was finally ready, we sat down at the table and surprisingly, the atmosphere was relaxed and friendly. Sean seemed genuinely happy for Jasper and me. It was such a relief that he finally knew everything and Jasper no longer had secrets between them.

After an enjoyable dinner, we went to the den to finish our conversation. We hadn't gotten to the reason why they were home early and I was so anxious to find out. What could cause them to come home early?

"Okay, spill. Why would you return from your honeymoon early? You were in Tahiti! Nobody leaves Tahiti before they have to," Jasper said after we all had gotten comfortable in the den. Simon and Sean had cuddled up on the loveseat while Jasper and I were on the couch.

Just then, Hemingway decided to make his appearance. I guess I didn't realize that Jasper had never told Sean we had rescued a kitten. He found out when Hemingway decided he needed to investigate the newcomers by jumping up onto their laps and demanding attention like my spoiled cat normally did.

"Oh. My. God. You two have a kitten?" Sean took Hemingway off of Simon's lap.

"Hey, I was petting him," Simon weakly protested.

"Yeah, well, I'm stealing him. He's so adorable, you two."

"You wouldn't think that at three in the morning when he decides to spaz out on you and run circles on your bed," Jasper told his twin.

Sean laughed. "You're probably right, but I won't be around him at three in the morning. Right now, he's adorable. What's his name?"

"Hemingway. I found him for Liam's birthday a couple months ago. We adopted him from a rescue in Montana."

"That's great, you two," Simon told us while reaching over toward his husband to pet Hemingway. My cat was such a mooch when it came to attention.

"So, are you two going to tell us why you came back early or not?"

"Yeah, I can tell you some of what's going on, but not all. Not yet. But the summarized version is that Isaac needed me. Remember that girl he was seeing? Well turns out she was pregnant and didn't tell him when they broke up. She went home to her parents and had the baby. I guess she died about a week after childbirth from complications. Her parents found Isaac and are trying to *sell* his son to him. He desperately needed my legal advice as well as support so here we are," Simon told us.

"Holy shit!" Jasper and I said in unison.

EPILOGUE

Jasper
October

I couldn't believe what Isaac was going through. Simon was able to recommend some friends from a law firm he worked with on occasion and it only took a couple of weeks for Sheriff McCoy's team of law-enforcement to get what they needed. In the end, it was really no issue whatsoever. They were able to get Jessica's parents on tape and video asking for an exorbitant amount of money in exchange for his son. And though I didn't want children of my own, I would be one of the first to admit that little Mack was quite a cutie. Of course, I saw him more than I would have expected, because of Rhett and Sean. We'd started spending more time out at Wild Creek with Simon's family.

Liam and I welcomed Rhett while he was getting things taken care of and situated with his new bakery. It seemed as if we were back to having a houseguest just as soon as one left. Though I would never complain too much about Rhett being near us. He was nine years younger than Sean and me; a big difference. We missed so much of him growing up that I was only too happy that he decided to take our advice and move to Crooked Bend. It was a win for all because we were eventually going to get a bakery back in town, Sean and I got to spend more time with our little brother, and Liam got to see his good friend every day.

The previous owners of the bakery were only too happy to sell their abandoned bakery to Rhett. He got it for a steal and was able to make several updates to it as well. Of course, Sean and I offered our services to help Rhett's dreams come true. In his short life, he'd been through so much and we wanted to do whatever we could to help him move on from the past.

Just because Rhett was now living in Crooked Bend, didn't mean things with Logan were going well for him. If anything, I would say they were nonexistent. After dinner one evening, I found out why.

"I realize you're busy trying to get everything ready on your bakery and the apartment above it, but what else is going on in your life lately? You haven't mentioned Logan for a while and I was wondering if something was wrong," I asked Rhett while lounging on the couch with Liam's head in my lap.

We were so much more comfortable around Rhett than we ever were with Collin. I think it's because he's my brother and was already good friends with Liam even before we met. Collin, although a great guy and amazing architect, was one of my coworkers. He seemed to want to keep our friendship more distant than the one I had with my brother.

"Well, there isn't much to tell. Logan still texts and calls me but he seems to have pulled away. He's friendly enough but I don't think he's really interested in a relationship with me. Well, other than friendship."

"Why would you say that?"

"I don't know. Probably because he really just seems disinterested for lack of a better word."

"Huh. Well what did he say when you told him you'd moved to Crooked Bend?" Liam asked.

"He didn't say anything because I haven't told him. He doesn't know I'm here. I spend all of my free time at the bakery trying to get it ready. I figured if he really wanted something with me, it wouldn't matter if I was in Crooked Bend or in Monterey. So he doesn't know."

"How could you not tell him? Seriously, I've said it before and I'll say it again. He's incredibly busy and responsible for so much out at Wild Creek that maybe he seems so disinterested because you are so far away in Monterey. Seriously, Rhett. Did you not think about that?"

"Yeah, but why should my location really matter?"

"Not everyone is willing to try a long distance relationship, Rhett. I'm almost positive that Logan is one of them. You have to remember he had a fiancé but his fiancé cheated on him. He caught him in bed with other men, as in plural. That really has to have had a negative impact on his ego as well as his take on relationships. Think about it. That was someone who was supposed to love him. That was someone he was going to spend the rest of his life with and it was thrown away for an easy fuck. How do you think that makes him feel? I know if Liam ever did that to me, it would really mess me up emotionally. It sure would make it incredibly difficult for me to trust any man ever again."

"Well shit, I didn't think about that. I've been so focused on getting Son of a Biscuit up and open that I haven't really given it to much thought. Maybe it's for the best. I don't really have a whole lot of free time and neither does he so really, where does that leave us?"

"Well, Rhett, it leaves you wherever you want it to. If you want a relationship, you have to be willing to work for it. It wasn't easy when Liam and I first got together. Things were crazy at work. I worked such long hours that there were nights that I came home just in time to shower and pass out," I told my brother.

"Yeah, but luckily for you Liam works here at the house. You saw him on a daily basis. Tell me, how often does Logan leave the ranch? I'm going to have such insane hours at the bakery that there's not much I can offer in a relationship to anyone really."

"Sure there is, you can offer yourself. You're an amazing man, Rhett. You're loving and so giving. You'd do just about anything for those you love. Why would you say you have nothing to give?" Liam included.

"Again, if you want it bad enough, you'll make sure you find a way to have it. If Logan is the man you truly want, you'll find a way to have a relationship with him. Period. I did with Liam, and look at us now. Can you honestly say you ever thought I would end up in a relationship, let alone married?"

Liam nodded. "The *first* step is to let him know that you're *here*. He has a whole bunch of cowboys who work for him; it's not like he can't come into town every so often to see you. It's not like the bakery is going to be open twenty-four hours a day. You'll be able to go see him, or even spend time with him when he comes to see you. You'll find that the stolen moments will be what you look forward to most. You'll treasure spending even ten minutes with him if that's all you get. I know I did when Jasper was working so many long hours before Collin joined their firm."

"All right. Next time he calls or texts I'll let him know that I'm here. And then I guess I'll see what happens."

"That's all you can do, little brother. You never know unless you try. And like Liam said, if you really want Logan you need to let him know and so far you haven't."

"So, do you think I fucked up by not letting him know that I was in town?"

"No, I don't. But I know you'd better have a good reason why you haven't let him know that you were here. He might be upset, but if you explain to him how busy you've been, trying to get the bakery and your apartment ready, then I think he'll be more understanding," Jasper told him.

"I guess," he conceded. "Well, I'm beat so I'm going to go upstairs and wait for him to call before I turn in."

"All right. Just remember, if things are meant to be, they'll work out," Jasper said again.

"Thanks, Jasper. You too, Liam. Good night, you two."

Rhett left the den and walked upstairs towards his room. He was young, but he was running himself ragged trying to open the bakery as soon as possible. The new name, Son of a Biscuit, definitely reflected his personality. I only hoped he made sure to have a life outside of his bakery, too. Maybe I needed to have another chat with Logan. It'd been a few months since the bachelor party. I justified my idea by telling myself I was only watching out for my little brother. Perhaps I could get Sean to help, too.

Liam and I didn't stay up after Rhett turned in. We were back to behaving everywhere except our bedroom and although Rhett did limit where I could make love to my husband, Liam and I both were happy he was here with us.

After shower sex, because it's wonderful to get dirty where you can clean up afterward, Liam and I crawled into bed. As usual, he immediately snuggled up to me. I would never get tired of Liam falling asleep on my shoulder. It was so comforting to have him there beside me.

"You falling asleep?" I asked.

"No, not yet. What's up?"

"I was just thinking. I'm worried about Rhett. I'm afraid he's going to overdo it where the bakery is concerned. I don't want him to put everything he has into it. He needs to make sure he saves some energy for something other than just work."

"Think back, Jasper. Did you devote everything to your and Sean's architectural firm?"

"No, I didn't. But I didn't have to. I had Sean to help. We went into it equally and never had to do it all on our own."

"Yeah, but Rhett doesn't have anyone to help. It's just him. Sure, he's found some part-time employees, but he doesn't have a business partner like you do. It's all on him."

"What exactly are you getting at?"

"Just that he doesn't have any choice but to put everything into the bakery. It's just him. That's all."

"I guess you're right. I wish he'd accept more help from us though. Sean and I have both offered him any help he could need but he keeps turning us down."

"I imagine he wants to do it on his own. Maybe if Logan finds out he's here, he'll decide to accept a little more help or something. I don't know. If you think about it, Logan will probably complicate things for him," Liam told me.

"How do you figure?"

"I would imagine that Logan would be a distraction. Remember when we first got together? You didn't want to be at work all the time anymore. You wanted to be here with me. I would think that Rhett would feel the same way about Logan. That he would want to be with him. He's lucky that he can set his own hours, but think about it. Bakeries are usually open really early. Logan's day starts equally early from what I understand."

"How is that a problem? If they end up together, then they can get up early together. Rhett can feed Logan some sort of fresh-baked pastry and coffee before he sends him on his way to the ranch. How is that a distraction?"

"Do you honestly think it'll work out that way, Jasper?"

"Truthfully, I think it'll work out exactly how it's supposed to. If they are meant to be together, then I believe that they will be."

"I hope you're right. I really do. Rhett needs Logan more than I think he realizes."

Want to stay up to date with Taylor's new releases and sales? Join her newsletter here.

You can find the complete Men of Crooked Bend Series on Amazon.

ABOUT THE AUTHOR

Thank you so much for reading My Choice, My Chance. I hope you enjoyed Jasper and Liam's story.
 Hugs,
 Taylor

Printed in Great Britain
by Amazon